THE LAVENDER MENACE

TALES OF *QUEER VILLAINY!*

**EDITED BY
TOM CARDAMONE**

**COVER BY
JOE PHILLIPS**

The Lavender Menace: Tales of Queer Villainy!
Edited by Tom Cardamone

Book design by Charles "Zan" Christensen

"The Ice King," by Tom Cardamone, was previously published as "The Ice King Cometh" in *Unmasked II*" by Starbooks Press, 2010.

"The Origin of the Fiend," by Hal Duncan, was previously published in *Icarus, The Magazine of Gay Speculative Fiction*, issue #14, 2012.

The Lavender Menace: Tales of Queer Villainy!
ISBN: 978-1-9387202-2-2
First Northwest Press edition, July 2013.
Printed in Canada

To Leo,
my heroic villain,
my villainous hero.
—Tom

ROGUES GALLERY

-this thing of darkness I
Acknowledge mine.
— Shakespeare,
The Tempest

INTRODUCTION
Tom Cardamone

Our bikes dropped on the front yard, more dirt than grass, as we bolted onto the sagging porch to rifle through my best friend's comic book collection. We were in elementary school but old enough to have some freedoms and bold enough to taste and test their boundaries: one was riding our bikes to the limit (the limit being major highways), the other getting our hands on any comics we could find. This trip was special because it was my first sampling of another's accumulated knowledge. We were building personal libraries, developing truths and secrets and my friend was about to share one of his: a dog-eared issue of *The Uncanny X-Men*, issue 120. Their plane crashes in Canada. Aliens in a hostile land, their complexities share the same genesis: they were born this way.

He was proud to introduce me to this new title to which I was eminently addicted. The attraction was primal—I was a neophyte at the dawn of a post-nuclear mythology, new, wet and full of fission. Comic books were maps with which I ran the cosmos and rushed the future and the only family tree I ever bothered to climb was my own imagined lineage of mutants. Call it escapism and I'd wholeheartedly agree. I escaped with *relish*. What were my alternatives? This was the early 80's: the era of Reagan and caviler Cold War rhetoric. I was obsessed with Nostradamus, the coming nuclear winter and studied any and all *Mad Max* VHS cinematic scenarios I could get my hands on for survival tips. All I was able to discern about being gay was categorized as either a "phase" or a "disease." As a comic book fan, I also read the morning newspaper (and get this, the soon-to-cease evening edition, which was worthwhile as it had a whole set of different comic strips), trying to pull as much mystery and adventure from "The Phantom" as I could while I equally coveted the science fiction and horror movie ads (the "R" rated films were especially alluring forbidden fruit). It was at the breakfast table, sharing the paper with my family that I first read about "gay cancer." AIDS darkened the back pages only, with a supple subtext of sin. Fast forward to now: *why gay super villains?*

Because my closeted-self didn't see what the big deal was with the effeminate serial killer in *The Silence of the Lambs*. Even hiding in the corner of my soul, I possessed enough awareness to know that demanding only positive portrayals of gays was ludicrous. Sure, after decades of negative cinematic stereotypes, enough is enough. But not with this film. Here, the villain just happened to be gay. There was no pigeonholing –his sexuality was an accoutrement and not the cause of malevolence –and irony of ironies, Hannibal

Lecter proved to be the intellectual dandy of the decade. Queer kids identify with the monsters in the movies, empowered outcasts, bogeymen bursting out of the closet; villains are cool. They wear their shadows well and if you're going to be expelled into the darkness, you might as well flaunt it.

🜨

Now, how did I go about decorating this Hall of Doom? I stayed close to home and queried authors I knew (Lee Thomas and Rod Santos, and Rod introduced me to Damon Shaw), and then I asked Lethe publisher, Steve Berman, if he had come across any likely lads while editing his magazine, *Icarus* (Jeffrey Ricker, Stellen Thorne and 'Nathan Burgoine), and he'd recently published a novel, *Queeroes*, by Steven Bereznai, so naturally I reached out to him. I also contacted writers I'd read (Hal Duncan and Marshall Moore). I've published a few stories featuring gay villains and heroes, and in reviewing the table of contents of one such publication, *Unmasked II* (featuring a version of my own story here, *The Ice King*), thought fellow contributor Jamie Freeman would fit right in. Other formidable foes were found online. Charles "Zan" Christensen, and Matt Fagan had profiles on prismcomics.org, a fantastic resource for queer comics and proof that putting yourself out there can catch an editor's eye.

That all of the contributors to this book are gay men is no coincidence. The forum of comic books (and Dungeons and Dragons and certain video games and films, those shared imaginative universes kids *live* and adults fetishize) among pre- and early-adolescent boys was probably the last time we were on completely equal footing with our straight friends while maintaining an enthused discourse. The emerging erotic energy that would propel us in opposing directions had yet to surface, and for some it would deepen our commitment to the cult of outcasts, that colorful and dangerous mutant menagerie. The boys in the majority grew into to a world that was made for them, reflected them, greeted them with opportunities mostly available to all, just that for them it was reflexive (cue the Bowie song, *Boys Keeping Swinging*, with the insurmountable lyric, *boys always work it out*). Thus our shared mythologies developed starkly different meanings.

We can't *just be* heroes and victims—that would create a fictitious reality, one where we are more vigilant in our denials than in our quest for equality.

Gays can be just as bad as the bad guys, and denying that weakens our ability to deal with the real world. I was lucky enough as a kid to find something to hold onto, but there wasn't any way to share it. So in a small way, this book corrects that. And it also recognizes that what we sometimes share, we do so masked, in the dark, at the tip of a knife, and though the characters here are queer, caped or clawed—their actions are undeniably human.

LIGHT AND DARK
Damon Shaw

Damon Shaw lives in the Canary Isles, fifty miles off the African Coast. He has sold stories to *Daily Science Fiction, Flash Fiction Online, AE*, and *Bull Spec*. He also has stories in several Lethe Press anthologies. Follow him at *damonshaw.livejournal.com*. He wrote "Light and Dark" in Autumn 2010 when his partner, Angel was gravely ill with cancer. Angel passed away in January 2011. Damon would like to dedicate this story to him.

"Who is the fairest?" Armeggon tucked in his bat-wings and dropped into a cumulus cloud.

Somewhere high above the suburbs of London, Mirror clutched his master's broad back and wrapped his legs tighter around Armeggon's waist. He closed his eyes. It didn't help. "While admiring your agility," he said, "your superior musculature, stamina and cunning, I have to say Lightnore is still the ladies' favourite."

Armeggon grunted. He spread his wings and jerked to a stop within the grey cloud. "And the gents'?"

"Um, them too, sir."

"What, even with his black eye?"

"I cannot lie," said Mirror. "It makes him more butch, more battered, less—"

"Bugger," said Armeggon. "Won't I ever be fairer before the end?"

He sounded so wistful. Mirror relaxed his grip and patted him on the shoulder.

"It might not end tonight, sir."

"Everything has led up to this," said Armeggon. "Only he and I remain."

"I'm here, sir."

"Yes, Mirror mine." The Dark One laid a metal clawed hand on Mirror's own. "But you are witness, not participant. Tool, not user."

Mirror nodded. Part of him wished he was witnessing from further away, from a bunker say, deep underground. He could always communicate his super-knowledge by mobile. But his gift brought pleasures, too. Clutching the Dark One's muscular back, his cheek pressed against Armeggon's neck, while Lightnore's eyes sent silver beams through the clouds around them, there was nowhere he would rather be.

The cloud lit up for a moment, sprays of droplets glistening like diamond dust. Mirror held his breath, hoping the beam would pass on, but instead it brightened.

"Curses, he has found me. Hold on, my Mirror." The Dark One wrapped his bat-wings about them as a shield, and they plummeted.

Mirror inhaled the smoky musk of his master as the darkness brightened and Lightnore approached. He gripped tighter, praying the Lord of Light's impact would fall on Armeggon and not himself. Out of all the henchmen, only Mirror survived. He had not dared ask himself why. Lightnore smashed into them at the speed of a flying bullet. Perhaps only the smallest fingertip grazed his leg, but Mirror heard bones snap, felt a sudden deadness—an aching, hissing rush that promised agony to come. He heard Armeggon grunt, and lost his grip as they spun away from the blow. He hit the elastic steel of the bat-wing pod, his leg doubled under him, and the pain roared up from his shattered shin-bone like a red train—crushing him into a dark place, where someone screamed a lot, and blows rained against the Dark Lord's shield-wings like thunder. There came an impact greater than any other, perhaps they hit the ground, and Mirror shattered into unconsciousness.

He woke alone, on a ledge of a ruined skyscraper in the centre of London's Docklands. He was healed, of course. These days Armeggon could do that kind of trick with a twitch of one immaculate eyebrow. Mirror stretched his limbs, feeling a low ache that faded even as he stood. Armeggon had written, "Trafalgar Square - Keep Him There - * 3 2 1 *", in neat letters on the ledge, probably in Mirror's own blood. The second asterisk had extra lines radiating outwards and was much bigger than the first. What Armeggon meant by it, Mirror had no idea. He peered downwards, but the sheer face of the building offered no handholds. The brown scrawl of the Thames river bed steamed far below. Even up here, the stink was awful. Flaize, one of the last heroes, had boiled the river dry to stop Mr. Ice using it as a frozen runway for Armeggon's flying death-ray machine. Instead, the machine smashed into Tower Bridge at supersonic speed, crushing both Flaize and Mr. Ice in a twisted mass of steel and ancient stone. Those were the days. Mirror sighed. The snag-toothed skyline and empty streets showed how far they had come since then. Most Londoners had been recruited and had fallen with their super-commanders. He doubted three thousand still scrabbled for survival in the ruins. Everything had to end.

The building trembled under his feet. Somewhere Armeggon and Lightnore fought on. With a spray of bricks and broken glass, Lightnore burst out of the face of the skyscraper, some twelve floors below. Mirror smiled. The Dark One could still pack a punch. The building shook in earnest, and Mirror felt a repeated, shuddering crash through the soles of his feet. He looked up to check the top storeys were not falling on him, then realised Armeggon had smashed his way up through the centre of the skyscraper. With a shout of power, the Dark One burst into the sunshine. A pale, daytime crescent moon hung, framed between his outstretched wings.

Mirror's heart melted. He was glorious.

Shards of glass and office furniture fell all around. The building swayed. Mirror leapt for something, anything solid, as the ledge fell away under his feet.

"Help," he screamed. He knew Armeggon heard, but not whether he would decide to save him yet again.

It seemed not. Mirror tumbled. Air shrieked and tore at his clothes. A chunk of plaster the size of a car was falling only a foot away. Mirror lunged, grabbed and pulled himself above it to give Armeggon a clear line of rescue. But Armeggon did not come. The ground roared up towards him. Mirror leaped from the lump of rubble, hoping to slow his fall by some minuscule amount. The chunk dwindled away. He saw it shatter—just as strong arms swept him from the air. Lightnore. His blond hair whipped in the wind. The black eye made him older, more dangerous. His jaw was clenched, his mouth bleak. Lightnore had not smiled easy since the first innocent bystander had been killed.

Mirror hung in his arms, like a barmaid rescued from a pub fire. He didn't mind. He hardly dared breathe as the super-hero spoke his famous lines.

"You're safe now." His voice buzzed, warm in Mirror's chest. He smelled of peppermint. "Where would you like to go?"

He remembered the message on the ledge. "Um… Trafalgar Square? I, ah, fancy seeing the lion statues."

Lightnore stared at him with a look of deep, understanding pity. "As you wish."

Mirror felt dirty, but guessed that Lightnore did that to everyone. Unlike Armeggon's juddering wing beats, the Lord of Light soared smoothly between the pillars of black smoke rising from the ruins. They swept along the course of the Thames, the sun glinting off the scattered puddles of green water below. Mirror counted off the stumps of ruined bridges; Tower, London, Southwark… The Millennium Bridge still swung, absurdly slender over the cracked, orange river bed, but Blackfriars and Waterloo Bridge had both disappeared. Mirror couldn't remember how, but felt guilty all the same.

All too soon, Lightnore set them down between two scarred, bronze lions, near the broken off stump of Nelson's Column. Mirror staggered out of the hero's arms. Well, he was here. What did Armeggon want him to do next? He turned to see Lightnore tense, ready to leap into the sky.

"Wait!"

Lightnore paused. He stood out against the background ruins like a vintage special effect. His beauty left Mirror breathless.

"Could I... Would you–"

"I'm sorry." Lightnore's mouth curled up but his eyes were sad. "I'm not that way inclined."

"What? No!" Mirror's cheeks burned. Lightnore had a tradition of kissing every woman he rescued, full on the lips. In the old days it had rained secretaries. "I meant—Could I have your autograph?"

"Do you have a pen?" asked Lightnore.

Mirror sighed. "No."

He thought Lightnore would fly away then, but instead his broad hands fumbled at his silver power-belt.

"Here." He unbuckled his sword and held it out. "Take this, son."

Mirror blinked. He worked his jaw but no words emerged. His finger floated up and touched the carved hilt. A spark leaped from the white metal. Forged from meteorites, able to slice through any armour, priceless to a collector. . . Hell—priceless to anyone.

"Wow." He took the heavy sword while the Lord of Light re-clipped his belt around his abs. "Thanks. Um, won't you need it?"

Lightnore's steady eyes shone, ice-blue. "I should have passed her on a long time ago," he said. "You'll know what to–"

A flash of light cast sudden shadows on the paving slabs around them.

Shit, thought Mirror. Three. Two. One. He dropped the sword and ducked.

Light roared soundless from the sky. Mirror clapped his arm over his eyes. His hair crisped. The back of his neck sizzled like bacon. He saw the bones of his forearm through his flesh. Then darkness. Around him, stonework cracked and boomed. Rubble spattered his back and the air filled with dust. Above the thunder of falling brickwork, a howl lifted, filling Mirror's chest, spearing him with grief.

"My eyes!" Lightnore cried. "My eyes!"

Mirror straightened. His skin crinkled like a crisp bag. He lowered his hands, hissing at the pain. Through a haze of dust, the sun shone in a midnight blue sky. Where the daytime moon had hung, a smear of white slowly faded. Lightnore stood, powdered with cement, but sturdy and solid. Pain stretched his face into an enduring grimace. His blue eyes had turned milky and opaque. "I'm blind."

The laughter began far away but dopplered closer, building in volume and manic glee until Armeggon landed in a thump of dust, screaming his joy to the sky. More buildings crumpled under its onslaught.

"Well done, my Mirror." Armeggon wiped his forehead and cleared his throat. He healed Mirror's burns with a wave of one hand. "The focus of the explosion was very tight. It would have been wasteful to miss."

Mirror picked up Lightnore's sword, fighting the urge to hide it behind his back. "You blew up the moon?" he asked.

"I had help of course." Armeggon waved a hand in the air. "All those stock-piled weapons just lying around. Someone needed to use them up."

"But how…?"

"Details, details." Armeggon chuckled. "Tell me, Mirror mine. Who is the fairest now?"

Mirror looked from one to the other. His super-calm shivered through him like smoke, and the answer came. Lightnore may be blind but he wasn't beaten. He vibrated with steady conviction. His white eyes gave him a tragic grandeur. This was his lowest point, but watching him, Mirror was still somehow con-vinced he would climb back up to a glorious victory. But Armeggon was equally charismatic. He crackled with power. He left purple after-images on Mirror's retina. His powers had grown in recent months. He filled the taut fabric of his costume with dark purpose and his certainty thrilled Mirror to a Machiavellian future of pain and pleasure.

"It's closer," he said, "but he has the awww factor now."

Armeggon's mouth twisted. "He's still fairest?"

"I'm afraid so."

"Ahh, everything I do makes him more perfect…" Armeggon cleared his throat and shook his wings. "Well, I think some plastic surgery is in order." He leapt to the fallen length of Nelson's column and grasped it in both hands. His muscles bunched and swelled. Slowly at first, then faster and faster, the pillar of stone lifted and swung into the sky. Lightnore tensed, his head cocked, but he braced himself in the wrong direction. Nelson's Column smacked into his side, sending him high over the ruins north-west, in the direction of Buckingham Palace.

"Fore!" shouted Armeggon, one hand shading his eyes, the other holding the enormous pillar of stone over his shoulder at a jaunty angle.

"Good shot, sir."

"Yes," Armeggon said, watching the Lord of Light dwindle into the distance. "It hasn't escaped my notice that you hold the sword of my arch enemy in your hands. Would you care to explain?"

Mirror gulped. "He ah, didn't have a pen."

"Reeeeeeaally." Armeggon slipped out from under Nelson's Column, letting it shatter on the rubble-strewn plaza. He turned his gaze on Mirror. His pupils swelled until his eyes were completely black. Mirror clenched his thighs together to stop himself peeing in terror.

"I know," said Armeggon softly, "that you have never really been on my side."

"I have—I am, always! You're awesome. I couldn't–" Before he could say anything really pathetic, Armeggon lifted one clawed finger. Mirror's mouth closed with a snap.

"Why did you join me, Mirror?"

"Because I hate the hypocrisy of the other side, sir." If he hadn't been holding the sword, he would have saluted.

"Go on."

"They say they value honesty but–"

"But they can't bear to hear your truths. Yes, yes."

Armeggon nodded and Mirror began to breathe again. Perhaps he would survive this.

"Whom do you want to win, this day?" Armeggon asked.

"Me? You, of course."

"Mere factions aside, look at yourself with that super power of yours. Whom do you want to win?"

Mirror blinked. He did not know. He never used his power on himself. He didn't dare. "I can't," he said. "I have to be impartial for it to work."

"So, impartially tell me the answer." Armeggon grinned. His many silver teeth glinted in the sunlight.

"I… I…" Mirror tried. He really did. He found the calm and aimed it inward. Something inside him bowed and stretched under the pressure of his gaze, but did not break. He knew with a sick certainty that if it snapped, he would never see clearly again. "I can't."

"I pity you," said Armeggon. "How empty you must be with no desires of your own."

Mirror looked at his feet. He had plenty of desires, just no... preferences. "Yes sir."

Armeggon's crackling presence approached, and Mirror tensed for the final blow. How sad not to see the end after all, he thought. But instead of swiping off his head, Armeggon hooked one claw under his chin and lifted him until his heels left the ground. Through the pain, Mirror met Armeggon's gentle, brutal gaze. His eyes filled with tears. He did not know why.

"So, should I too give you a gift?" Armeggon's voice was silken. "To keep things balanced and impartial?"

"There's no need," Mirror said, trying not to squeak. "I'm fine."

Armeggon pulled him closer with his hooked finger. Mirror felt the Dark One's other hand cup the back of his head. Hairs all over his body lifted in the electric aura of power. And then they kissed. Waves of pleasure swept through Mirror's body, bouncing off his ribs, shaking his pelvis, ricocheting down his hollow legs and bouncing back upwards leaving his toes curled and aching. His knees collapsed. The Dark One held him upright, drinking from him, spilling his own dark desire back into Mirror's open mouth. Mirror felt one of his teeth break. Armeggon hooked the tooth from his mouth with his tongue and swallowed it without breaking the kiss.

When Armeggon pulled back, Mirror felt as if his soul slipped out too, trapped between those silver teeth. He opened his eyes to find the emptiness inside reflected by a gulf of open air all around. He straddled Armeggon's knee, Lightnore's sword dangling from his hand. Five hundred feet below, a perfect circle of blackened concrete showed the precision of his master's lunar explosion.

Drop me, he thought. Nothing can top that kiss.

"Think of it as a first instalment," said Armeggon. The wind whipped his cloak out behind him like smoke. "Tell me, Mirror mine," he said. "Are we equal now?"

Mirror sighed. "You sure are."

Armeggon tutted. "Are we equally matched," he said. "Now that he is blind and has no sword. Will I win?"

"Oh." Mirror took a breath and felt super-clarity fall over his blushes like cool rain. Victory was always uncertain—as both Lightnore and Armeggon accrued the powers of their fallen enemies, it was inevitable one of them would draw momentarily ahead. Lightnore had been more powerful for months, using his sword to double his own super-strike power. But Armeggon was faster by say, fifteen per cent, had recently gained Mr. Bendor's super-stretch power, was far more ruthless, and cleverer too, and now Lightnore was blind…

For the second time that day, Mirror could not answer. "Too close to call," he said.

"Those are my kind of odds." Armeggon spun Mirror round, clasped one arm around his chest, and they dropped from the sky.

Lightnore waited in the centre of the Women's Bathing Pond on Hampstead Heath. He stood on the rippling, green surface, his knees flexed. His face tracked them unerringly down through the sky.

"He's using the water as a sound board," whispered Mirror. "He can hear us through the soles of his feet."

"So stop whispering," hissed Armeggon.

He dropped Mirror into a rhododendron bush and landed near the water's edge. Mirror spat out twigs, grabbed the sword from above his head, and pushed through the foliage into late afternoon sunshine. The broken tooth had cut his tongue, and he had a long scratch down one shin.

Armeggon faced Lightnore over the shifting water. Mirror forgot his pains at the sight of them. What a privilege, he thought, to be here for the end. He wondered if they would have an at-last-old-foe-the-time-has-come type conversation, but they both just nodded and raised their right arms, palms outstretched. A straight power duel then. He smiled. Nothing like a classic.

At no signal Mirror could see, bolts of energy tore the air with a staccato roar. Lightnore's beam flared white with streaks of electric blue; Armeggon's flashed a colour the other side of black, shot with unearthly purple. The bolts met and exploded above the water, sending up clouds of steam exactly at the midpoint between them.

The skin on Mirror's face tightened and he shielded his eyes against the heat. Lightnore slid backwards across the surface of the water until his white boots lodged in the far bank. He crouched and the glare from his open palm brightened until Mirror had to look away. Steam boiled into the air, hiding the combatants. Gusts of wind, hot and cold, tousled Mirror's hair. A bolt of lightning struck a tree somewhere to his left, and the earth shivered under his feet. He craned through the smoke and steam, but could see nothing for long minutes. The steam dispersed when the pond boiled dry. The duellists had dropped to one knee but their beams blazed even stronger. Mirror asked which would win, but his super-power showed no advantage, nothing that would turn the fight one way or the other.

In the centre of the dry pond, beneath the conflagration where the beams met, the earth glowed orange and crumbled away. Mirror swore and jumped to one side, as a crack snaked across the pond bed towards him. Still the two increased their power. Lightnore's body shook, but he raised his free hand, and a twin white beam joined the first. A writhing vein in Armeggon's temple popped and one eye turned red. Crimson lava dripped from between his teeth. He screamed, and from his gaping mouth a bolt of fire speared to join battle against the good.

It was the most glorious, mind-blowing, utterly awesome thing Mirror had ever seen. Better than fireworks. Better than sex. Better than being kissed by the Dark One himself. He jumped up and down and shouted. He stabbed the air with Lightnore's sword. He turned and saw Armeggon's eyes and his exhilaration slipped away like a body under ice. Mirror saw fear there, desperation, and an unspoken entreaty. He turned and saw Lightnore had also lifted his face to him, and he too seemed to plead. Both fighters shrank, weakened as he watched.

"What?" asked Mirror. "What do you want?"

But he knew.

Nobody would win this fight. Both would drain themselves. Both would die in a final futile blaze. They wanted him to decide.

"Oh no," He shook his head. "Not me. I'm witness, not participant. No way."

In response, the two jerked and shuddered and increased the fury of their beams. Gusts of howling wind buffeted Mirror, shoving him to his knees. In his hands, Lightnore's sword burned in resonance. He turned to crawl away, but stopped. If he did not intervene, both would die. The Earth would never see such men again. The loss burned deep. Mirror would be alone in a world of suspicious and vengeful survivors. He couldn't let that happen. He had to look inside himself.

"Oh no," he said. "Oh shit. Oh no."

Mirror tried to find his inner super-calm, but the howl of air drowned out his thoughts. How could he choose between them? It was impossible.

Armeggon's eyes closed. Across the fire pit, Lightnore nodded, or perhaps he just trembled. Mirror took a deep breath. The sound of the battle faded. Again he felt the surface within him bow under his questioning pressure. A sick dread churned in his stomach. He gulped and swallowed. Sweat poured from his forehead. Who did he want to win?

Two futures blossomed in his mind. In one, Armeggon ruled, inventing ever new ways to enjoy pain, offering free will to terrified survivors, only to crush them with the futility of their hope, time after time. And people always hoped, so he always had dreams to crush.

In the other, Lightnore helped rebuild. He single-handedly carried super-tankers loaded with supplies to starving cities, set up refugee camps, unsealed the source of the Thames, and let the river flow. With time, he became a city vigilante, catching drug lords and child traffickers, after he had established a society that could support such things, of course. And in the end, he sat in a rocking chair, recounting his adventures to his disciples until one day they buried him under an enormous bronze statue… and forgot him.

It became icily clear to Mirror, while clashing fires raged, light and dark combining to form a rainbow spray of colour across the sky. If he killed Armeggon, then Lightnore died in that same instant. Armeggon could survive his adversary's death, but Lightnore would become a has-been. An ex-superhero, with his charity projects and official biographies. He would never be this glorious again. And by all that was great, all that was more than mundane, Mirror wanted another kiss.

Something broke in him then. A flare of energy blasted the calm away and he flinched in a storm of leaves and smoke and screaming power. He knew what he had to do. He fought to stand against the wind, drew back the sword, and threw it as hard as he could—

Time slowed.

Black fire boiled in slow motion against white. The sword swung end over end. It sliced the air with a whoosh, whoosh, whoosh above the low, crackling roar of the battle. Mirror held his breath. Lightnore's blind eyes glowed blue. He smiled.

"Terrifying to find out what you really want, eh son?" The voice echoed in Mirror's head like a choir.

"What? Lightnore?" Mirror glanced towards Armeggon. His master's mighty wings had shrivelled to nubs. His eyes rolled back in his head.

"If you get off that fence, you'll find it only comes up to your waist," Lightnore said, while sprays of silver fire fizzed in a slow torrent from his palms.

"What are you talking about?" Mirror had an absurd desire to shout— Watch out! But he gritted his teeth. He could not back out now.

"Here. Remember."

Mirror gasped. A map appeared in his head. Deep underground vaults glowed green. "What's this?"

"Arcs," said Lightnore. "Survivors. They're your job now."

"What? Lightnore, the sword—"

If anything, the hero lifted his chest to meet the blade. It pierced his sternum without a sound, only stopping when the hilt thumped against his silver breastplate. The blow shoved Lightnore back. His hands flew apart. The white beams of power died. Time returned in a rush. Armeggon's deadly bolts converged on the falling figure. For an instant, Mirror saw an inverse silhouette, a white skeleton impaled on a black background and then the darkness swarmed and Lightnore was consumed.

Armeggon's beams blinked out. Mirror's ears popped in the sudden silence. Leaves and dust fluttered down around him. At first he did not understand why the world glowed red, then he saw the setting sun caged behind a row of skeletal trees. Night was coming. A chunk of glowing mud slipped into the crumbling chasm where excess superpowers boiled like lava. Sparks rose into the twilit sky. On the far side, the sword stood upright in a pile of silver ash. As Mirror watched, the sword tipped and fell.

He walked away.

The Dark One stirred as he passed. "Mirror... Help me."

Mirror ignored him and walked on around the pond bed. An itch grew between his shoulder blades until he had to look back. His heart lurched to see Armeggon drag himself towards the glowing, heat-wraithed hole.

"No—"

But his master rolled over the edge and disappeared with hardly a sound.

Mirror asked himself if he cared, and found that he did. A lot. But what could he do? He would fall in, too, and be just as dead. He continued around the circumference of cracked mud until he reached the pile of ash. Gingerly, he took the hilt of the sword and shook dust from its blade. Was it his now? Could he keep it? He had no one to ask. The sound of earth shifting made him turn. The sides of the pit slumped and fell inwards. The ground trembled.

Bat-wings arched high above his head, Armeggon rose renewed and glittering from the depths. Twisters of energy spun off him. His cloak lifted and hung in the shimmering heat waves, and his eyes shone, utterly black. Poised and perfect, he floated to the shore. Mirror could not read his expression. He stepped aside as Armeggon glided inexorably past. The Dark One knelt by the pile of ash. He slid his fingers deep, and lifted twin palmfuls to his face. With horror, Mirror thought he was going to eat Lightnore's ashes, but Armeggon just stared at the silver grains trickling between his fingers until his hands were empty.

"Are you… happy?" Mirror asked. "With me, sir?"

"I loved him," said Armeggon. "And he is gone."

Mirror blinked in shock. Of course, he realised. Who else was worthy of Armeggon than the Lord of Light?

"I will never forgive you, of course."

"Sir?" Mirror's breath caught. He would never get that kiss. "What… what are you going to do?"

Armeggon lifted his head. His pupils shrank to black pinpoints. "You are marginally more interesting to me now, Mirror," he said, "but infinitely less useful." He turned back and began piling Lightnore's ash onto his cloak. "How could I trust anything you said? How could I know you weren't just trying to please me?"

"I can have an opinion and still use my power, sir," Mirror said. "It's the truth." But was it? Had he not felt something snap?

Armeggon did not look at him. "Who is the fairest?"

"Sir?"

Armeggon continued to scoop and pile silver ash. "Who is the fairest? Tell me, Mirror."

He didn't need his power for that. "You, of course. There's no one left."

"Look inside." Armeggon's voice was a low rumble.

Mirror dared not disobey. To his surprise, clarity fell over him like a veil. He saw himself holding a gifted sword, his shoulders smudged with ash. His back was not bowed. He looked solid, competent, weary. His exterior did not reflect the joy that danced within him. He still had his gift. He could still see!

"No, it's still you," he said. "I couldn't compete."

"You see?" said Armeggon. He gathered the cloak into a bundle, and stood. "You have no idea. I am full of worms."

"I don't understand, sir."

But Armeggon did not explain. "If you are still here when I return, I will kill you."

It was a dizzying, unexpected blow. Tears sprang into Mirror's eyes. "Sir... I just wanted to be with you."

"A glory has passed from the Earth," said Armeggon. "Prepare for the Time of Darkness." He lifted into the air, spinning slowly. The last rays of the setting sun painted him red and gold. He spread his wings to blot out the sky and in a thunderous pulse of wind, beat once—and was gone.

Mirror sat down on a fallen tree. A crushed stem of yellow flowers glowed in the last light where the ashes had lain. He pointed the sword at it.

"Zap," he said.

Softly, with no fuss, the stem straightened, petals unfolded, and a faint scent of peppermint reached Mirror's nose. He looked at the sword, and the flower, and then the sword again. "Zap," he whispered. "Zap."

Leaving a trail of exotic flowers blooming from the charred branches, Mirror climbed away from the devastation. He didn't know where to go. He had half a mind to return to Armeggon's cave and try to join forces with the Dark One once again. But then there were the arcs full of survivors under the Cairngorms and the Welsh valleys. Something needed done about them, too.

First, he decided to scrounge the ruins, hopefully find a coffee and some strong cigarettes. As he walked, dusk fell on Hampstead Heath. Fragments of the shattered moon streaked across the sky in a silver rain. Or perhaps it was Armeggon scattering ashes, screaming his triumph and his grief, far above the atmosphere. Mirror did not ask and so he did not know.

THE WEB
Steven Bereznai

Steven Bereznai is the author of the gay teen super hero book *Queeroes*, the gay dating bible *Gay and Single… Forever? 10 Things Every Gay Guy Looking for Love (and Not Finding It) Needs to Know*, and the children's picture book *The Adventures of Philippe*. He can be reached online at *stevenbereznai.com*.

Daytripper stood outside the mesh fence, trying to grapple his fear. Daytripper was not the name on the young man's birth certificate, but he insisted it was his real name. His curly reddish-blond hair was clipped short, ready for action. White sporty sunglasses hid his blue eyes, pale as pastel. He wore a white shirt, but barely. It was cut off at the sleeves, exposing his impressive delts and arms. A deep V exposed the cleft of his chest, and he'd snipped off the shirt's midriff, revealing his washboard abs coiling in and out with every breath, and leaving his nipples poking out every time he moved.

A bright orange sunburst was stitched onto what was left of the fabric. It was his crest—also not his by birth. The symbol was as made up as his name, but he would earn both, no matter what it took. Orange racing stripes descended on either side of his white shorts, wrapping around his firm bubble butt. The fabric stretched tight around his impressive thighs. Tear drop calves descended into a pair of sneakers as sleek as his hairless skin, each with a tangerine Puma crouching at the outer toe.

Daytripper had grown up with the burden of banality. He was Richard to Mom, Dick to Dad. As the pawn in their bitter marriage and corrosive divorce, he had failed to live up to both the short and long version of his name. Even now, standing alone on the precipice of changing his life forever, he could feel them trying to pull him apart in an endless tug of war.

"I have a new home now," he whispered to himself, trying to distance himself from the sound of his father's belches and farts, the stink of his wife beater shirts, and his mom's shrill voice, burnt Thanksgiving dinners, and the continual clatter of ice in her martini shaker. Daytripper exhaled slowly, trying to detach from the memories that were seeped into every fiber of his muscular form, no matter how far he might trip to. No matter what his parents called him, he was neither a Richard, nor a Dick.

"Not a boy," he murmured, "Not yet a man."

Like the infamous chanteuse whose words he'd taken for his own, he'd rise like a phoenix, downing a double shot of fierceness, with a chaser of can't touch this. Daytripper may have been a baby the year that iconic song hit the charts, but he knew a motto when he heard one.

He stared at the polished sign attached to the fence one last time, and then at a piece of paper just below it.

"All right Daytripper," he said to himself, "Let's do this thing."

A flare of swirling orange light and he was gone. The fence remained, and the sign, which read, "Academy of Super Heroic Excellence." On the piece of paper were the words, "Tryouts begin at 8:00am in the Arena. No latecomers admitted."

Five hours later there was a flare of swirling orange light in a little visited storage room off the Arena of the Academy of Super Heroic Excellence. The room was cluttered with an array of training equipment. A broken swivel machine was shoved into a corner, it's once flailing tentacles hung limply, covered in patched padding that was frayed and in need of stuffing to keep from killing newbie speedsters and flyers as they practiced whizzing around it. Damsels and dudes in distress mannequins were lined up along the wall, as if for a firing squad. Many of their faces were melted beneath singed wigs, arms ripped off, torsos slashed by claws. At their feet lazed old issues of *Superhero Weekly*in, bundled and ready for recycling.

The orange light died down, and in its wake stood Daytripper—barely. He swayed on his feet, and flopped onto a wrestling mat. His panting echoed off the warehouse ceiling.

He'd survived tryouts, but barely.

His clothes, what was left of them, were torn and shredded, practically falling off his muscular frame. He was drenched in sweat, covered in scratches and bruises, and streaked with dried blood, some of it his own.

Curling into a ball, he held his stomach. Now that he was alone, it was Okay to puke. That's why he'd teleported into the storage area, safe from prying eyes. He was not going to be known as Vomit Guy. Of course the telepaths might rat him out, but they were probably so frazzled by their own tryouts they wouldn't even notice he was gone. He doubted they had enough psychic energy to pinpoint what was left of their own egos. He took several more ragged breaths. His lungs burned, but the nausea eased off, if only a bit.

"Come on Daytripper," he said to himself, forcing himself to his shaking feet, "You can do this."

Leaning on his knees, he reached within, pulling forth his power as he prepared to teleport back into the Arena. Time to see if he'd made the cut, and if this grueling day had been worth it. His signature orange swirl of light started up, heralding both his departures and his arrivals, when someone called to him from above.

"Going so soon, handsome?"

The swirl of light disappeared and Daytripper stayed put. He peered up into the cavernous darkness of the warehouse space. Silent as creeping death, a figure dropped from seemingly nowhere to land with an acrobat's grace.

"Hey blondie," he said, pulling out a glowing green sphere from inside his leather vest. He let it go, and the glowing ball bobbed in the air like a tied off balloon.

"Snagged it after my duel with Firefly. Man is she a bitch," the stranger explained.

Daytripper recognized him now.

"Arachnid," he said.

In the dim glow of the floating sphere, Daytripper examined the other youth. He was the taller of the two, with jet black hair, matching black irises, and eerie white pupils.

Daytripper couldn't help but stare.

Arachnid blushed, and despite his bravado, glanced away.

"They freak some people out," he said, shielding his eyes as if he stood in the noonday sun.

"I like them," Daytripper said, though he wasn't altogether sure if he did. Still, it was the nice thing to say, and he felt bad for making the other newbie feel self-conscious. Tryouts were hard enough as it was.

"Yeah?" Arachnid asked. "Well let's see your Betty Davis'."

He reached forward and gently removed Daytripper's sunglasses. They stood arm distance apart now, neither of them saying anything, just looking at each other quietly. Freak eyes or not, Arachnid was undeniably handsome, with defined cheekbones, a Romanesque nose, and a strong chin. He was broader than the blond teen, with more muscle, clearly built by many hours in the gym. He wore a black leather vest, with a white spider on the front and back. It stretched tight across his body. A matching spider was tattooed onto one of his knuckles. The two young men were the same age, but from the neck down, Arachnid looked very much a man.

The smaller boy found his breath quickening. He turned, not even trying to get his sunglasses back. One of the lenses was cracked anyway.

"I should go, the announcements…"

"Are at least half-an-hour away," Arachnid countered, "Plenty of time."

Daytripper didn't dare ask for what, and the dark-haired super entity, with leather gear and defined arms, didn't wait before giving clarity. He slid one hand under the blond's torn shirt, stroking the firm chest. From each digit spread a warm ripple. Daytripper smiled with wonder at the mild yet firm suctioning sensation.

He wasn't called Arachnid for nothing.

He lips played with one of the arms of Daytripper's sunglasses, smirking oh-so slightly. Arachnid's arm drew back, bunching his biceps into a ball, and pulled Daytripper into the taller teen's hunky body. The leather vest radiated heat against the blond's exposed abdomen.

"You were pretty awesome against Armadillo Boy," Arachnid said. "Who knew he could be so fast with that shell."

"Right?" Daytripper agreed. "And that tail!"

Arachnid stroked the blond's tanned face. The suctioning of his spider fingers turned on and off in controlled pulses, sending soothing waves into Daytripper's scalp. It was like being immersed in a gentle pool of water. Daytripper forced himself to exhale. Arachnid pulled back, and Daytripper's chest went cold as the taller youth's hand unsuctioned from above his heart.

"Let's chill for a bit," the spider powered young man said.

He pointed his wrist towards the rafters and squeezed his fingers to his palms. The spider tattoo on his knuckle undulated , and translucent gobs shot out of his forearm, casting a web that shimmered like crystal in the soothing light of Firefly's globe.

"See you up there stud," Arachnid said, leaping to the wall, crawling up it, somersaulting onto a stack of crates, then leaping off the silent swivel machine and into the net. In a flash of orange light, Daytripper was already there, waiting for him.

The young blond tried to recline in the web and look cool and seductive without seeming trampy. But what a red-headed actress, a green screen, and a team of CGI experts pulled off for the big screen, was tougher to fake in real life. It was like trying to be sexy in a hammock. Daytripper went to lean on his hand and it went right through a gap in the web. His arm shot through right up to his arm pit. His cheek was smushed against the webbing and he could feel a bit of drool coming out his lip. This was not the soft-porn look he'd been going for. He tried to get up but his other hand was stuck to the gooey strands. From the corner of one eye, Daytripper looked up at Arachnid.

"You look adorable," he said, stripping off his leather vest and tossing it onto the defunct swivel machine. His muscular chest glistened in the light of Firefly's globe. The fingertips of one hand suctioned onto Daytripper's delt. With a strength that more than matched his physique, Arachnid deftly pulled Daytripper into the air. An exhilarating moment, a fraction of a second where his flight stopped but gravity had not yet had a chance to pull him down, and then Arachnid gently lowered Daytripper on top of him.

His fingers unsuctioned, and then just as quickly stuck like glue to Daytripper's measly shirt, pulling it over his head. It fluttered through the air and landed atop Arachnid's vest, just as Daytripper lay atop Arachnid, bare chest to bare chest, abdomen to abdomen, crotch to crotch.

Daytripper was instantly aroused, and his erection pressed against his shorts into the impressive mound hidden inside Arachnid's tight jeans.

Arachnid cupped Daytripper's firm ass.

He stared into the blond's blue eyes, and Daytripper stared back. Arachnid's groin slowly ground into him, and Daytripper matched the pelvic rhythm.

"You're really cool, you know that?" Arachnid said.

Daytripper had waited so long to hear those words, from someone like this that he'd almost given up on it ever happening. Hearing it now made his chest swell—it was like a peach pit had caught in his throat.

Please don't make fun of me, was what Daytripper wanted to say, but he swallowed the words, terrified of ruining this stolen moment. His inner voice whispered with wonder, *he thinks you're cool*. Arachnid arched his neck, bringing his lips a breath away from Daytripper's own. The blond's heart pounded, and their dry humping slowed to a barely perceptible pulse. The crackle of a loudspeaker made them both freeze.

"All applicants are called to the Arena for final grades. You have five minutes."

"I... I have to go," Daytripper murmured, though the words barely came out, gripping his heart like a cold fist.

"Well so do I," Arachnid playfully whispered back.

Their gaze never broke, and Arachnid kissed Daytripper gently. The suction of his lips was unlike anything the young man had ever experienced. And his tongue. It seemed to stop time. He stroked the blond's cheek, and before Daytripper even knew what was happening he was tossed over a muscular shoulder and Arachnid was bounding nimbly out of the web, grabbing his vest and Daytripper's shirt, then crawling down the wall, before flipping onto the floor. He set Daytripper safely onto his feet. His muscular legs trembled.

"I guess it's time to see if you made the cut," Arachnid winked, sliding back into his leather vest and strutting out into the Arena.

Daytripper breathed heavily, his erection aching inside his shorts.

That night it was easy to see who had been accepted into the Academy, and who had not. Music blared at the Caped Crusader, an all night dance club frequented by those with enhanced abilities. The rustic haven was made from rough hewn stones salvaged from the Aztec-style volcano lair of Doctor Centipede, whose evil conglomerate had gone into receivership after the housing market collapsed. During an interview with *Take Over the World Times*, he'd claimed that contributing to the destruction of the free market was a success in and of itself for any evil genius, but he lost credibility when a gossip site posted cell phone video of him bawling into his cape as his yacht was repossessed.

The title gamely read, *Centless Centipede*.

There were many this night who could share his pain.

The rejects from this year's tryouts were slouched over at the bar. Among those drowning their sorrows at the Caped Crusader was the voluptuous Lard Ass, who overflowed three bar stools shoved together. Next to her sat Manorexic, who pushed away a bowl of peanuts with his paper thin hand. He turned in profile and thinking the seat was free, the jockish One Eyed Serpent nearly sat right on top of him.

"What up, what up!" he flirted with the purple barmaid, his gold visor glinting in the torchlight.

"Watch it!" Manorexic growled, his body rippling like a vibrating saw, the sound making the Serpent cover his tiny ears.

"Peace man, peace," the hero offered, downing a shot, his forked tongue darting in and out. He was known for being a happy drunk.

Manorexic slammed his shot glass onto the bar and gave the muscular jock one translucent finger.

"Well excuse me for lacking depth perception," the One Eyed Serpent slurred.

And then there was Daytripper.

His face was downcast as he watched the handsome youth with a giant eye in the middle of his head swagger away to hit on the "triplet" blond bombshells known as Multeepla. She never had to worry about showing up alone, and guaranteed there'd be even more of her duplicates once the night got going. The "triplets" each took a Tequila shot. They rubbed lemon chasers on one another's breasts and licked, pouty lips sour and seductive all at once. Suddenly three became six. Girl could not hold her liquor. The bouncers were pissed. Multeepla invariably threw off the head count. But she sure as shit put on a show. A Lady GouGou song came on and Multeepla's duplicates began grinding against each other and making out. The twincest vibe was off the charts, to the delight of ogling hormonal heroes.

Daytripper took it all in shyly, waiting nervously for the multi-tentacled barmaid to notice him. Torches were rammed into the walls, firelight flickering off her purple scales. Her three red eyes moved right over him as she started serving The Towering Toledo. He dwarfed the stocky blond, and made him want to shrink inward.

Daytripper was not, however, invisible. Nor did he go completely unnoticed.

A skeletal man with a wide brimmed hat and fluttering cloak stared at him, and the youngster quickly averted his gaze. Daytripper focused on his feet, occasionally glancing up to see the shadowy figure move amongst the rejects, putting a comforting hand on Discus Debbie as she tapped a cigarette into her weapon of choice and used it as an ashtray.

The barmaid rapped one tentacle in front of her and pointed at the sign of a red circle with a slash through the silhouette of a figure shooting laser beams from its eyes.

"What?" D.D. asked.

The barmaid realized her mistake and tapped on the no smoking sign next to the "no shooting death rays" warning.

"Seriously?" D.D. demanded. "This is a bar."

A bouncer with the head of a rhino and armor to match glared at her.

"Fine, fine," she muttered, stabbing the butt into her discus. "You know, I could kick Captain Freedom's butt," she seethed to anyone who would listen, wiping the tears rising in her eyes, "I just need a fair chance!"

"Of course you do," the skeletal man with the wide brimmed hat agreed, leaving a measly tip as he took a pitcher and poured a round of beer for the outcasts. He was a known recruiter for the Institute of Evil World Domination, which was not to be confused with the smaller, boutique Ecole de L'Alliance Cauchemar.

It was a Parisian export, and thought very highly of itself.

"Ok Twinkie," the barmaid said to Daytripper, noticing him at last. "Let me guess. A dirty eyeball to drown your sorrows and herald your first step onto the spiraling staircase of villainy. I'm going to need some I.D."

He pulled his license out of his tight jeans.

"I was thinking a Velvet Vault or Ruby Slipper," Daytripper said.

The barmaid shrugged.

"You're never going to be more than a lisping henchman with girlie drinks, but suit yourself."

"Oh, I'm not going to be a villain," Daytripper said quickly, "I'm going to be a hero."

She looked up from his driver's license with surprise.

"No shit. You passed tryouts?"

"Yeah," he blushed proudly, stuffing his hands into his pockets.

"Right on junior. But I gotta tell ya, no one would know it by looking at ya. You're all hunched up and defeated like. You should be celebrating."

"I am," he defended himself, "It's just, I don't really know anyone in my class, and the one person I do know hasn't shown up."

"Ah," she nodded sympathetically. "Well, I don't know this or that about saving the world and all. I'll leave that to you do-gooders. But I do know a thing or two about swimming with the in-crowd. So here's what you do." She leaned forward, and as she whispered into Daytripper's ear he actually forgot about Arachnid, and started to smile.

The latest hit from genetically enhanced teen pop sensation Bedazzled blared from the speaker, fulfilling her mad scientist mother's pageant daughter dreams with a mutant voice that was so over-synthesized technicians had to bring her levels back into the normal auditory range. Her dance remix of the chart topper, 'Unmask Me' had the new recruits, and most of the free world, shaking their butts, bumping and grinding, and in the case of Slyborg, quite literally throwing his hands in the air. The irony of course was that it was this crew that would probably face off with Bedazzled after the diva's inevitable decent into her mother's madness, signaled by an impromptu head shaving at a Rodeo Drive salon, a back to back Las Vegas wedding/divorce, and an ill-informed attack on the local nuclear power plant. The Paparazzi couldn't wait.

As Bedazzled crooned about the Commissioner shining Captain Freedom's eagle emblem in the night sky, a swirl of orange light heralded Daytripper's arrival in the middle of the dance floor. He held up a metal tray holding a dozen test tubes filled with glowing, swirling liquid.

"Who wants a Silver Shower?" he cried.

His classmates cheered loudly all around as he passed around the shots. He held his own aloft and everyone followed his lead. They clinked their glasses together, before downing them as one.

He "yee-hawed" liked the Cowboy Kid (and got a dirty look from same) ripped off his tank top, and twirled it in the air.

"Trip! Trip! Trip!" they shouted his name, scooping him off his feet and flying him around the dance floor.

"Amateur," the Pigeon cooed bitterly. He stuck a note he was supposed to be delivering between his beak and gnawed on it angrily. He'd had it up to his craw with being a low-level paper pusher between big wig Legal Eagles and their gangster Faux Hawks. They could choke on scrambled eggs for all he cared.

Daytripper had no time for ruffled feathers. He'd left the nest and reached the aerie.

A laser light show flared above.

"I could do better," Firefly sneered at the display, her sinewy body rubbing up against Crimson Clare in her glittering red Lycra outfit.

The booze swirled in Daytripper's head as he was finally put back on his feet. He panted, dizzy, accepting a Cosmic Ray Martini as it was shoved into his manicured hand.

"Well someone's having a good time," a deep voice said.

He turned, and stared into Arachnid's handsome face. His beautifully muscled torso bare except for a white spider pendant hanging from his neck, matching the tattoo on his knuckle. He wore tight black jeans rolled up to his knees, and a pair of red high tops with white laces.

"Hey," Daytripper said a little breathlessly.

"Hey yourself," Arachnid replied, gently suctioning his fingertips onto Daytripper's bare pec. It made the little hero bite his lower lip, and his eyelids fluttered every so lightly as Arachnid pulled him close. As if the villainous Purple Puppeteer were in control, Daytripper's arms lifted on unseen strings, and wrapped themselves around Arachnid's neck.

The taller man's hand gripped the blond's bubble butt to lift him onto tip toes, and their lips met in wet wonder. The evening was now truly perfect.

I made it, Daytripper realized with wonder, *I really made it*.

They paused, staring into each other's eyes.

"Can you believe we get to see each other every day now? In class I mean," Daytripper added hastily, not wanting to appear too clingy, when in fact he never wanted his dark savior to ever let him go.

A stormy look crossed Arachnid's face, reminding Daytripper of his dad.

"About that," Arachnid said. "I'm not going to the Academy."

"That's crazy" Daytripper said, "You got in. I was there when they announced it."

"Doesn't mean I'm going to go," Arachnid replied.

"Of course it does!" Daytripper snapped, hating how high-pitched his voice had turned. "That's exactly what it means. You either go now, or you're out forever. They don't give second chances."

The Amazonian legend Gladiator Gal had been very clear about that, impressing upon them the seriousness of their commitment, and how they'd never be eligible for admittance into the Academy ever again if they failed to live up to it.

"This is not a place for the wishy-washy," she declared, her golden armor glinting under the glittering light of the Arena.

Arachnid pulled away from Daytripper, and the sudden distance was like a serrated spoon scooping out his heart.

"Listen, I can't stay that late."

"Well neither can I," Daytripper replied, "I've got to be at the Academy at eight AM sharp. No latecomers."

He still couldn't believe Arachnid wouldn't be there.

"Why are you doing this?" Daytripper demanded.

He wanted to play it cool, but it was like his brain was on fire.

"Come with me," Arachnid said, "And I'll explain."

He a shot a web up into a window, grabbed Daytripper around his tiny waist, and pulled them both up to the sill. They sat there, and Daytripper tried to quell the worried beating in his heart. Below, the party continued. Beyond, they stared into the quiet of the harbor. The moon glinted off a crane helping to repair the city's main dock after it was pulverized in a battle between the Forces of Freedom and the terrorist mermen, Agents Aquatic.

"You have to go," Daytripper said, as if by sheer force of repetition he could get his way. It worked for the bestselling self-help author, the Hypnotist, author of *Goulash for the Superhero Soul, Back From the Darkside: Vader Did It, So Can You*, and of course her fitness book, *Abs of Steel, For Real!*. Unfortunately for Daytripper, she was a mentalist with a direct line to the subconscious. He was a teleporter who could barely afford bus fare. Not that he ever needed to take the bus. Still, he couldn't give up.

"You can't *not* go to the Academy," he insisted.

Arachnid stroked the blond's hair.

"You sound like my aunt, and not just because of the double negative. Listen, there's a lot you don't know about me."

"So tell me. I want to know," Daytripper said, "I want to know everything there is to know about you."

Arachnid pondered this. He cast a web in the window frame, and pulled Daytripper into his arms. The larger youth leaned back into the web, and held him like a teddy bear.

"I feel like I can trust you."

"You can," Daytripper insisted, "With anything."

"You ever hear of an old school hero by the name of Captain Invincible?"

"Yeah, sounds familiar. I remember… something bad happened to him, didn't it?"

"The dude could take a tank shell at point blank range, but no one, and I mean no one, is invincible at the end of the day, not even my dad. He was facing off against Methtwisto. Can you imagine? He's not even an A-list nemesis. But we'd had a fight that day, over a video game if you can believe it. It was some stupid concept, where you go around shooting hookers and homeless people. My dad was furious, said that was villain's work, that heroes protected the weak, and helped them become strong. I called him a pansy and slammed the door in his face.

That was the night he cornered Methtwisto. He was going to poison the city's water supply. Lame, right?"

Arachnid laughed a mirthless laugh, and there were black tears in his eerie eyes. He shot webbing into the party below them and yanked a bottle of beer out of Manorexic's hand, who was passed out on the bar anyway. The bar maid was using his face as a towel after Discus Debbie, busy making out with the rhino bouncer, had knocked over a pitcher. Arachnid took a swig of the beer.

"So there was Dad, Captain-fucking-Invincible. He had Methtwisto's neck pinned under one knee. He'd already dropped the poison into the water supply, but Dad had the standard anti-toxin kit. It was a simple case of mixing compound red with compound green, and he had himself a broad spectrum neutralizer. Textbook stuff. But instead he mixed red with aqua. He poured it in and instead of stopping the poison, it turned into a toxic gas. Dad got a concentrated dose of hallucinogen right in his face. He went nuts. I'm talking cuckoo bananas crazy. He's been in an asylum ever since. It devastated Mom. She went on a manic frenzy of crime fighting, got arrested after killing the Terrible Twins at their cousin's wedding. She railed against the system for siding with villains, decried the press for calling her a vigilante, demanding more be done for her husband. The world owed him that much. But that's not how it works, is it?

"Heroes are only heroes until they need to be saved. Anyway, the lawyers got my mom off, but she was broken by then. I think she was on a suicide run when she hunted down Molten Lava. She had mad martial arts skills, but at the end of the day, all she could do was turn invisible. She was so beautiful, and that fucker turned her into a bed ridden shell of skin grafts and open sores. She couldn't even hide it from the world, or me. Her powers were in her epidermis, and that was damaged beyond repair. She was on life support for two years before she died."

"I… I'm sorry," Daytripper said.

He twisted around, and kissed away Arachnid's dark tears. They tasted like licorice. He gazed into Arachnid's gloomy eyes.

"I don't want to seem out of line, but… don't you want to take revenge? Or you know, right the world's wrongs?"

"That's what my aunt wants from me, to vindicate my folks, carry on their legacy. Methtwisto's got a nephew, and Molten Lava a daughter, both at the Institute of Evil. I mean I've got a classic super hero death and disaster back story, and built in arch enemies, so of course I should become a hero. But you know what, I'm not a graphic novel. Maybe the most heroic thing I can do is break the cycle, put all this shit behind me."

"You're running away," Daytripper said.

It wasn't a question or accusation, and there was no judgment in his tone.

"Yeah," Arachnid agreed. "I guess I am. And I want you to come with me."

Daytripper pulled away at that, Arachnid's words hanging in the air.

"Arachnid, I…"

"Call me Jim," the larger youth said. "Please, just call me Jim."

"No, I'm sorry, you're not a Jim. That's… that's boring and lame. I feel terrible for what you went through, I can't even imagine, but you *are* Arachnid. You're a hero. You don't get to run away from that."

Arachnid leaned forward and kissed Daytripper. With their lips entwined, the blond had never been so happy, or so sad.

"Just think about it," Arachnid said, keeping his lips close to Daytripper's. "And if you're in, and I hope you are, meet me here." He handed Daytripper a folded pieced of paper. "Tomorrow morning, eight AM."

He kissed the little hero-in-training again, their mouths feverishly swallowing each other with desperate intensity. Neither noticed the fight breaking out below. The lithe Colonel Copernicus shot solar flares at muscle bound Geocentric Gym as yet another of their philosophical debates spun out of control. Singed in the cross fire was the One Eyed Serpent who was helping Manorexic to the washroom as he began to throw up, making his entire body undulate. An oblivious Arachnid shot out a string of webbing, and swung away into the night.

☙

The next morning Daytripper stood in front of the mesh gate surrounding the Academy of Super Heroic Excellence. *Shouldn't they have a proper wall or something? Not some flimsy fence?* He wondered idly to himself. It was a futile attempt to distract himself from the sacrifice he was about to make. After all, the fence may appear flimsy, but could easily repel a tank. Winged youths were landing on the roof of the crystalline building within. A muscular dude covered in short fur and tiger stripes drove by in a convertible, three cheetah-esque cheerleaders purring to one another as they roared through the open front gate. There were a slew of other cars, a hybrid that left a slime trail in its wake, a pickup with what looked like a giant boulder in the back, but which was in fact one of Daytripper's classmates, and overhead, a sleek rocket ship belonging to the Genius family, flew by, to land softly in one of the upper hangar bays.

This is where I belong, Daytripper told himself.

And yet it seemed hollow without Arachnid.

Can I do this alone? Do I want to?

It was 7:56 in the morning. Time to decide.

He took a deep breath, and disappeared in a swirl of orange light.

An instant later he reappeared—on the other side of town from the Academy of Super Heroic Excellence, standing on a dilapidated dock at eight AM sharp, exactly where Arachnid had told him to be. It had been a hard decision, but he trusted his heart, and his heart told him that the tall, dark stranger was *the* one, and whenever he'd fantasized about going to the Academy, wasn't he really fantasizing about meeting Mr. Forever?

A huge smile crested Daytripper's face. He spun around, waiting to be enveloped in Arachnid's strong arms.

"Arachnid?" he shouted, taking off his sunglasses and shading his eyes.

A lone gull flapped its wings at him and screeched mockingly. He looked around. Something wasn't right. He didn't need to be a graduate of the Academy of Super Heroic Excellence to know that. He gazed up at the broken windows of the surrounding warehouses, and he caught a flash of sunlight, and a blur of shadowy movement. Someone was there, he was sure of it. In a flare of orange light he landed inside the abandoned warehouse. He soaked up the scene in an instant. Dust and old machinery were everywhere, rusted and stacked with birds nests, covered in droppings. By the window was a video camera on a tripod, pointed toward the dock where he'd been waiting. A note was taped to it. He read the note, the ache in his chest deepening with every word.

Hey Sucker,

As you've probably guessed, you've been had. I'm a Sophomore at the Institute of Evil World Domination. I was assigned to find the most gullible, innocent, pathetic dupe at the Academy of Loser Do Gooders, and get him to drop out. Mission accomplished. The hilarious thing is, it's not even for finals, just some lame ass mid-term homework worth a measly 2%. But hey, whatever it takes to be top of the class. Thanks for the A+ dork.

Your Nemesis,

Arachnid

PS: I set up the video camera to send a live feed, with a time stamp, direct to some key Herobook profiles, so all your would be classmates and teachers could see you make a complete ass of yourself. I don't even get extra credit for that. Welcome to my web :)

Daytripper expected to cry, to sob in fact, to feel the full weight of his gullibility bitch slapping him from here to the Academy and back. What stupid romantic notions filled him to the point of throwing away his dream for this, a super villain in training? And that's when he knew what he was feeling: anger, pure, blind anger. In a crackle of furious light that shot out like lighting all about the room, he was gone.

An instant later he rematerialized in a rustic toilet stall. He opened the creaking door slowly. The dormitory washroom was scrawled with graffiti. Someone was in the shower. From beneath the shower curtain he spotted scaled feet. The toe nails had been sharpened into talons. He slipped from the washroom and into the hall. There were long scratches from a set of claws in the wall. The paint was flaking off in places. Scorch marks splattered the ceiling. Daytripper stepped forward, drawn by the sound of laughter from a half open door.

"The look on his face! Wait, rewind, let's see it again. Aw, puppy dog looks like he's going to cry!"

It was Arachnid. Daytripper would never forget what he sounded like. For a moment he felt angry tears, but he wiped them impatiently away. Taking a deep breath he lost himself in a flare of burning light. When it cleared he crouched on Arachnid's bed, towering over the villain-to-be.

"What the fuck!" Arachnid shouted, tumbling off the mattress. Daytripper jumped after him, and grabbed him by his vest.

Three of Arachnid's dorm mates were crowded around a computer screen, all of them laughing at the video of Daytripper on the dock. To his dismay it already had several hundred hits, and the number was growing exponentially, going viral before his eyes.

"Fuck my life," he murmured.

The would-be villains turned around to see Daytripper standing over their friend.

A feline female looked ready to pounce. A granite giant lifted it's rocky fist. A lithe young man of Middle Eastern decent placed his hands together in a prayer gesture, and the crimson ruby set into the choker about his neck glowed ominously.

"You are going to regret this you psycho little stalker," the young man with the choker swore.

Arachnid laughed.

"Show 'em what you got Mesmerito! Make him think his eyeballs are melting."

Mesmerito was dressed in a form fitting silk robe. The ruby around his neck flared brighter. Daytripper didn't even flinch.

"Nice try," Daytripper said coldly, "But someone's already fucked with my head once today, and no one else is getting in."

Arachnid's smile faded, and in a dazzle of angry orange, the pair disappeared.

A bright light flared in the storage room off of the Arena in the Academy of Superheroic Excellence, the very place where Arachnid and Daytripper first met. Daytripper rematerialized with his kidnapped villain high in the air, and threw him into the net Arachnid had cast less than twenty four hours ago. Arachnid's frame slammed into the netting and ripped it free of the wall, tangling his limbs so that his normally agile form fell and landed with an echoing thud against the ground.

A moment later he ripped himself free and flipped onto his feet, gazing about angrily. Daytripper was nowhere to be seen.

"That all you got you pansy-assed little punk?" Arachnid shouted angrily.

His face was flushed with anger. He took long deep breaths, searching for the blond. Only now did the villain realize where he'd been brought.

He laughed. "Back to the scene of the crime I see, very original. Gotta say, I'm surprised this place doesn't have an EM field or something to keep teleporters from jumping in and out whenever they want."

"They do," Daytripper said, smashing Arachnid's knee with a crowbar.

"Mother fucker," Arachnid shouted in pain, taking a swing at Daytripper, but he was already gone in a swirl of orange.

"The EM field's good," Daytripper shouted, hidden behind the broken swinging machine with its padded tentacles, "I'm better."

A tool bench was pressed against the wall. Daytripper took a mallet from on top of it.

"You know it's not too late," Arachnid said, "For you to suck my dick."

He flexed his fingers, making the spider tattoo on his knuckle dance.

Orange light flared behind the villain, and Daytripper swung the mallet at the back of Arachnid's skull. He turned nimbly and caught the weapon in one hand, and with his super human strength easily ripped it from Daytripper's grasp. Arachnid tossed the mallet aside, and punched empty air: Daytripper was gone.

He reappeared right next to Arachnid. The villain's foot flew at Daytripper's abdomen but the blond was gone.

"Spiders can lift thirty times their own mass," he shouted. "All I need is a glancing blow and you're a dead man. And I can do this all day."

Daytripper hid behind the dudes and damsels in distress mannequins, panting. Arachnid wasn't bluffing. He wasn't even breathing hard. Daytripper was exhausted and covered in sweat. He had to end this, and fast.

He teleported, ready to head butt Arachnid in the groin and the villain literally swept him off his feet with one leg. Daytripper teleported away and landed on his backside behind some massive girders that boys of steel would use for their weight workouts, and then hide behind to make out with each other.

"Don't you ever read comic books, dick-wad?" Arachnid taunted. "Spider sense, remember? You caught me by surprise in my room 'cause I smoked a joint. A villain's gotta have some bad habits you know. But the head's clear now. I can feel you coming from a mile away"

Orange light flared, and Arachnid swung at Daytripper's head. He ducked just in time, and aimed his fist at Arachnid's abdomen. The villain was a blur of motion, somersaulting over Daytripper and landing on his feet, kicking the teleporter in the back, slamming him to the ground and knocking the wind from him. Arachnid was playing with him, like a cat with a mouse.

"This is fun," the dark haired youth taunted, getting a good look at Daytripper's butt in his tight little short shorts.

Daytripper turned over, and Arachnid waited for the teleporter to once again disappear. Instead he pushed himself to his feet and got ready to charge. Arachnid fired a glob of webbing that caught Daytripper's wrist with such force he flew backwards. The webbing pinned Daytripper's arm to the floor. He tried jerking himself free when another glob of webbing trapped his other wrist. Then two more shots of webbing pinned his ankles.

"Stay down," Arachnid ordered, lowering himself to his knees on either side of the trapped youth, and sitting on his stomach. The villain's fingertips suctioned onto Daytripper's white shirt and ripped it away, baring his sweaty muscular chest.

"It's kind of cute how you tried to take me on. But from the moment we met, I spun my little plan, and you were only too eager to be trapped in my web, not the other way around." Arachnid suctioned his finger onto Daytripper's nipple and pulled. The boy hissed

"I'm the spider, remember? You're just a stupid little blond with muscles. No family. No friends. No future. What happens to the little wannabe-hero now?"

"You're right," Daytripper agreed, gritting his teeth as Arachnid worked the other nipple, the spider on his knuckle wriggling. "I am stupid. And since I can't outfight you, I let you beat me. Sometimes you have to lose before you can win."

Arachnid scoffed, but looked worried.

"You're bluffing."

"Not so much. I'm a teleporter, moron. All I needed was for you to touch me."

Orange light swirled from Daytripper's deviant cells, coiling out from his nipple and around Arachnid's finger. The villain tried to pull away, but it was too late. The orange light enveloped them both, and with a pop of imploding air they disappeared from the Academy of Super Heroic Excellence.

✄

Daytripper rematerialized with his usual pyrotechnic display. He panted, staring down at three super villains in training. Their jaws gaped. He'd come back to Arachnid's dorm and stood on the villain's bed. Soot covered Daytripper's white shoes, and fanned out on the bed sheet in a circle around him. Daytripper clutched Arachnid's vest. It was smoking, and smelled of rotten eggs.

The villain was nowhere to be seen, until one looked closely. The three evil students did, and gaped at what was stuck to Daytripper's nipple. It was Arachnid's finger, cut off at the base of the knuckle. The skin was riddled with burns, making the spider tattoo look as if it had been squashed under a heel.

"What have you done with him?" Mesmerito demanded, tears of rage and anguish building in his eyes.

"Dropped him in a volcano," Daytripper replied calmly. "Most of him."

On cue, Arachnid's finger finally unsuctioned from Daytripper's nipple and dropped onto the bed.

"I'm going to kill you," Mesmerito cried.

But the feline femme fatal held him back. She gazed at Daytripper with new admiration, a deep purr rising up from her throat.

"All's fair," she meowed.

"Are you crazy?" Mesmerito demanded, tears streaming from his eyes.

"You want to be next?" Daytripper asked coldly.

"Are you threatening us?" the football- player sized youth covered in granite asked in a rumbling voice.

"I'm not here to fight you," Daytripper said, settling Arachnid's steaming vest about his shoulders. He wrinkled his nose at the smell, wondering if it could be dry-cleaned.

They stared at him.

"So if you're not here to fight us, why are you here?" the cheetah woman asked, her cat eyes glinting excitedly.

He zipped up the vest. It was too big for him, but that was ok. He knew he'd grow into it.

"Isn't it obvious?" Daytripper asked, knowing he was going to have to change his name yet again, "I'm here to join you."

THE MEEK SHALL INHERIT
Jamie Freeman

Jamie Freeman (*jamiefreeman.net*) went to college in D.C. but now resides in a blue county amid the predominantly red counties of North Florida. His short stories have appeared in a variety of anthologies including *Blood Fruit*, *Unmasked II*, *I Do Too!*, and *Best Gay Erotica* (2009, 2010 & 2012). His novellas and ebooks have been published by Dreamspinner Press, Forbidden Fiction and Untreed Reads.

Washington, D.C.
Christian States of America

The first time it happened I thought I was being Raptured.

I'd grown up in a world in which the Rapture was a real and exciting possibility. We believed there would come a day when the bodies of righteous believers would literally ascend from this earth into the Kingdom of Heaven. On the playground we practiced and prepared, standing in the hot Georgia sun looking up into the sky and waiting; we made lists of classmates who would be left behind to confront the Tribulations; we knew we would be among the chosen. And although I had renounced this particular set of beliefs long ago, the first thought that raced through my mind as my body ascended into the light and heat and noise was that I was being Raptured. I was being lifted from this earth by the hand of God Almighty.

And then I woke up half an hour later curled in a fetal position behind a dumpster on L Street. The sun was starting to set and the gritty, powdery residue of incinerated bricks and mortar and concrete made everything look pale and surreal. It took me a while to realize the silence all around me was the result of hearing loss. My clothes were singed and torn; my hands and face were blood-smeared and blistered.

I staggered out of the alley into complete chaos. Dozens of ambulances, District Police cars, Cee Bee vans, military vehicles, and fire trucks clustered around an enormous, perfectly round crater that stretched across the intersection of Connecticut and L Street. Inside the crater, through gaps in the concrete and asphalt I could see the Farragut North Metro station where a Metro train was engulfed in flames and billowing noxious black smoke. There was movement everywhere. Bodies—some badly burned or waving amputated limbs—were embedded in glassy patches inside the crater or jutting from piles of rubble. Rescue workers and people in business suits clambered around the edges of the crater like insects, calling out to each other in distant, indistinct voices.

A hand grabbed my arm roughly, turning me around.

I stared dumbly into the blue eyes of a lantern-jawed Cee Bee, his crimson uniform smudged with dirt and blood and white ash. His lips moved, stopped, and then moved again.

"I think I lost my hearing," I said, touching my ear.

His eyebrows knitted for a second and then he pointed to me and pointed down the street away from the crater. Then he disappeared, scrabbling down the inside of the crater. I stumbled south toward Farragut Square and sat on the warm concrete in front of a darkened office building.

I held my head in my hands, looking down at nothing, trying to regain my equilibrium. My eyes strayed to my shoes, following the dusty contours and lighting upon a single drop of baked red blood. And then it all came back to me in a flash: pale afternoon light, heat shimmering on the pavement and me hurrying north on Connecticut, hearing the horrible screams, and then running around the corner into a pack of them. Cee Bees standing in a ring, bloodied boots and two women—one clearly dead, draped across the other woman's lap like the Pieta—and the wailing, the unearthly, tragic voice that made the hair on the back of my neck stand on end.

"Move along, faggot. Just a couple of Levitican offenders. Nothing to see here."

"What's going on?"

He looked at me in surprise and then he was right on top of me, grabbing my shoulder with one hand and slamming his fist into my midsection. I stumbled and there was a gunshot. The mournful wailing stopped and I saw the woman's body flop backward, heard the dull impact of her head against asphalt, and then I felt something inside me burst. The Cee Bees started to surround me, moving in predatory circles. I felt nauseated, started to retch, but then, instead of throwing up, I felt heat and light exploding out of me. My body rose off the ground, spinning slowly, and then exploding like a supernova. Everything went white and the world switched off.

And then I woke up next to the crater in deafened silence.

Starbucks is crowded for a Thursday afternoon. The plate glass windows are vibrating from the sound of shelling north of the city where U.S. troops are pounding the suburbs around Friendship Heights and Chevy Chase with long-range, laser-guided British-built Bluebird warheads. It's been a couple of days since the birds fell here in the District, but we can hear the constant rumbling thunder of Chinese-built J-10s flying low over the city, the red cross and white stars on a field of blue clearly visible from street level. We've grown so accustomed to the noise we rarely look up as our protectors shoot down Bluebirds or chase straying F-22 Raptors back into U.S. airspace.

Despite the intermittent bombing and our proximity to the front, the city seems unhurried, unruffled. The streets are crowded but not chaotic, and the first cold snap after a summer of record high temperatures has left me smiling and rejuvenated.

I know there are refugees fleeing the relentless advance of the U.S. Infantry, clogging the northern arteries in and out of the city, but they are being diverted to staging camps in Anacostia Park and for the moment we can forget the horror of their flight. The newscasters are upbeat and optimistic, assuring us that our good Christian brothers and sisters will be whisked south for new lives in Richmond or Norfolk. There's one particular video that gets a lot of play featuring orderly processions of wealthy, well-dressed Christian Americans laughing and joking as they board luxury touring coaches.

On a day like today, I almost want to believe them.

But it's hard to know what to believe. While the media paint pretty, reassuring pictures, the stories passed clandestinely lips to ears are horrific tales of butchery and barbarism. People can't process it anymore. Or they look away, the conflicting narratives so muddied that nobody can successfully parse the twisted convergence of reality and propaganda.

The one truth we have all come to understand is that most of us are no safer here in the city of wolves than we would be at the front.

My teaching partner Sarah has a sister, Rebekah, who used to live in Somerset, Maryland. A couple of weeks ago, a squad of Cee Bees—members of the President's elite Christian Brotherhood, charged with enforcing the Executive Orders known as the Levitican Code—arrived at her door in the middle of the night, dragging her and her girlfriend into the street in their nightgowns and lining them up with some of their neighbors. They stood in the street while a pair of crimson-uniformed Cee Bees patrolled the line, berating them for their sins against the Lord and then yanking people out of formation, seemingly at random, and beating them until they were bloody or unconscious. One of them grabbed Rebekah by the hair, calling her a "filthy dyke" and throwing her to the ground. He and his buddy stomped on her ribs and kicked her repeatedly in the face, neck and legs. She screamed and tried to crawl away, but eventually she let her instincts tuck her into a tight ball of blood and bruises and fear. Rebekah's girlfriend, who had been restrained by a couple of her neighbors, finally broke free and launched herself at one of the Cee Bees, clawing at his eyes with her fingers. He grappled with her, wheeling in circles, his gruff laughter transforming into an angry snarl as her fingernails dug into the vitreous fluid of his eye. He finally shook her loose, throwing her to the ground and standing over her sobbing form. Tracks of blood slid down his face like demonic tears as he pulled his sidearm and slowly, methodically put four bullets through her head. Rebekah only survived because the other Cee Bee dragged his buddy away, telling him he needed to get to a hospital and they could come back and finish off the gender traitors later. Rebekah fled. Sarah's been hiding her, sharing her rations and praying nobody thinks to come looking for her.

I order a coffee—black and bitter because I don't have enough points on my ration card for sugar or cream—and find a seat near the window.

I glance up at the flat screen TV over the counter and watch a story that's been unfolding over the past few hours. The terrorist insurgent known as "the Inheritor" caused an enormous explosion near the 19th Street entrance to the DuPont Metro station late yesterday afternoon. The explosion, which killed two dozen Cee Bee cadets conducting an anti-terrorism training operation in an adjacent office complex, left an enormous semi-spherical hole in the sidewalk, street, and surrounding buildings. Video footage of the scene shows rescue workers excavating the edges of the perfectly round crater, searching for survivors.

I can't hear the voiceover, but the relentless crawl of words along the bottom of the screen tells the story: *$10M reward for capture of the Inheritor. Yesterday's death toll rises to 113. President Bush saddened by Wednesday's losses, prays for families of the dead, vows swift vengeance. Eyewitnesses describe a booming voice shouting "The meek shall inherit." This is the ninth bombing attributed to the Inheritor in the past year. The Inheritor's official death toll reaches 1,206.*

The scenes at the crater are replaced by footage of a slab of angry muscle in Cee Bee dress reds speaking from the sandbagged steps of the Capitol. Behind him a dozen Cee Bee foot soldiers stand at attention. He's wearing the three gold crosses of a deacon—the equivalent of a colonel in the army—and he's angry, fists pounding the podium, straight, blond hair flopping in his red face.

There's a quick jump cut, the volume ramps up, and the story wraps with a clip of Vigilance Roberts, the President's Chief of Staff, also pounding on a podium—this time in the White House Press Room—and shouting. "The Bible tells us, 'He will avenge the blood of his servants, and will render vengeance to his adversaries!' And let me tell you something, gentlemen: His will shall be done!" His face is purple with rage; his eyes are wide, black, and glistening with lupine intensity. And then he is gone, replaced by a pair of vacuous studio anchors who banter about Metro Transit delays as a lead-in to an Old Navy commercial featuring boys in khakis and girls in cheery summer print dresses dancing to an old Carpenters song.

I sip coffee and open the binder in my lap. The title, printed neatly across the top of each page reads, *Jericho and the Conquest of Canaan: Lessons for Twenty-First Century Statecraft*. The text beneath the ludicrous title is a recent biography of Pier Paolo Pasolini e-published by Princeton University press and downloaded by a friend on a free-chip Blackberry. It's on the proscribed list, of course, and grounds for immediate arrest, but it reminds me of my past and Pasolini's angry politics suit my mood.

Long before the Wars I studied film at American University, earning a degree in Literature and Film Studies. My father liked to tell his cronies I'd earned my degree in Lies and Flim-flam Studies. There was only room in his life for one book, one set of stories. I went to A.U. to spite him, walking away from his money, and only managing to enroll and stay alive through the generosity of my indulgent, wealthy grandmother, Margeaux. She always loved me, rescuing me from my father's house at least once a month after my mother died, whisking me away to the theater or to dinner or, more often, to the movies. She took an unseemly pleasure in thwarting my father's wishes by taking me to movies my father warned his flock were the work of the devil's own hands. She introduced me to Hitchcock, Bertolucci, Pasolini, Fellini, Cassavettes, Lynch—the more subversive the better. And when the time came, she rescued me from four years of puritanical religious indoctrination at my father's alma mater, Liberty University, where I would have earned a degree in Biblical Studies, Church Ministries, or Apocalyptic Pre-History.

My film degree and my undistinguished career as a newspaper film critic have been crushed to dust beneath the jackboots of the current occupant of the White House and his battalions of faithful Christian Brothers. The newspaper

I used to write for was closed by the government; the films I reviewed have been banned; and my heroes, Pasolini among them, have been declared Enemies of the Lord. So, all legitimate employment prospects having disappeared, and despite my initial reluctance, I've managed to parley paternal influence into a teaching appointment at Wildmon High School where I lecture quasi-illiterate teenagers about Biblical History, Intelligent Design, and the Prophetic Sciences. Pasolini would spit in my face.

My grandmother would have chosen a more lady-like way to express her contempt, but she would be no less appalled by my life in hiding, the mindless curriculum I peddle, the civil war that's ripped her beloved country apart. If she were still alive, she would urge me to take to the streets and fight. She would say I bear particular responsibility because of my intelligence, my sexual orientation, and my father's princely position among the ravenous wolves.

And she would be right.

But she's not here. And I'm facing the wolves alone.

On the morning of her death Margeaux lay in her hospital bed, entangled in tubes and monitors like a butterfly captured in a spider's web. I stood beside her looking down into her sad, distant eyes and wondering when it would be over.

She took my hand, bringing my fingers to her dry, papery lips. She kissed me and, as if her vision had already telescoped beyond the crisp September morning to the events that would unfold over the next few years, she said, "For I know this, that after my departing shall grievous wolves enter in among you, not sparing the flock."

She held my hand tightly for a long time, her eyes suddenly as clear and blue as the sky outside the hospital window. "The wolf will tear you apart unless you fight it. You must fight the wolf, Joshua," she said. And then she died.

Margeaux was a woman who knew how to deliver an exit line.

When the bedside alarms sounded, the nurses who should have responded instead stood immobile in front of the television, eyes tearful, ears deaf to everything but Charlie Gibson's matter-of-fact description of a second plane striking the South Tower of the World Trade Center.

I heard bits and pieces of the commentary and thought someone was watching a movie. *Die Hard*, maybe, or *Airport '77*.

I stood at the window for a long time looking out over the slow-moving Potomac, numbed by my own grief.

I picked up the bedside phone and called my father.

"She's dead," I whispered.

"Who's dead?" he demanded.

"Margeaux, she just—"

My father roared into the phone. "The whole world is going to hell and you're worried about that stupid whore? You are fucking pathetic!" He slammed the phone down. I stepped back and stared at the receiver, puzzled and a little disoriented. I looked out the window and saw a streak of silver hurtling down through the sky in the direction of the Pentagon. There was a flash and then flames and smoke. A wall of sound rushed across the river, slamming against the brick and reinforced glass and shaking the hospital complex like an earthquake. I stumbled and grabbed the bedside table for support.

Margeaux's death was lost in a sea of destruction and grief that immobilized everyone for weeks. On the afternoon of her burial, I stood alone beside her casket, a funeral home representative standing a discreet distance away listening to Oprah Winfrey's Yankee Stadium speech on a pair of black earbuds. Despite the distance, I could hear her voice ringing clearly through the stillness: "What was meant to divide us has brought us together. And we shall not be moved."

I felt guilty and hollow, as if my own grief, unconnected to Oprah's public outpouring, had somehow been contaminated by her steadfastness and her sincerity. I felt something die inside me; felt my soul turn black and hard as obsidian.

I stood immobile for a long time. *And we shall not be moved.*

As a young woman, Margeaux had worked under contract to Warner Brothers, chain smoking, drinking, and swooning with the likes of Jimmy Cagney, Paul Muni, and Edward G. Robinson. She usually played mobster's girls—'furniture molls' she called them—the kind of girls who perched on the arms of sofas or leaned against bars cracking wise and maybe getting slapped around by one of the boys. She once shared an apartment with Mae Clark, a bit player like herself whose claim to fame was that crazy breakfast scene in *The Public Enemy* where Cagney smashes a grapefruit into her face. Mae went on to have a long career in the business, but Margeaux, an inveterate troublemaker, was eventually fired and escorted off the Warner lot for public drunkenness.

Leaving Hollywood behind, Margeaux secured the greatest role of her life, that of the flamboyant third wife of a powerful southern preacher. Whether she married my grandfather for love or money is anyone's guess, but she attacked the role with a vengeance and she was the first wife to survive the good reverend's wrath.

Margeaux referred to their decade-long marriage as the "glittering détente," a phrase that, while typical of her irresponsible theatricality, also hinted at the relationship's violent undertones. The détente shattered one night in 1973 when Margeaux phoned her brother-in-law Tommy to tell him that "Wilson's gone downstairs to meet Jesus on the Carrera marble and I've only got one martini left," by which she meant my grandfather, uncharacteristically drunk, but characteristically enraged, had been chasing her with a baseball bat when he had stumbled on the stairs, flown over the balustrade, and plummeted to the marble floor below, crushing his skull, and shattering his spinal column. She once told me the sound was like a thousand blackjack dealers cracking their cards at the same time, a sound so violent and mercenary that it had made her spill her drink.

When Uncle Tommy and the deacons arrived, she met them at the door, handed her empty glass to one of them to refill, pointed to my grandfather's body, sprawled in a sea of dark, congealing blood, and said, "I guess I'll be going on for him in the morning."

And she did.

She took over the ministry for several months, giving drunken, incomprehensible sermons in her glittering couture gowns and teetering high heels. To the consternation of the deacons, she filled the churches and left her audiences breathless and penniless. With the pews and the collection plates overflowing, she took her final bow, selling the ministry to Uncle Tommy and the boys and stepping out of the limelight to watch them drive it into the ground.

And they did.

When a reporter from the *Atlanta Journal* called her for a response to the bankruptcy announcement, she said, "Sometimes great things come to an ignominious end."

But from the sprawling wreckage of the embattled Wilson Roberts Ministries stepped the blandly ruthless visage of my father, Reverend Vigilance Roberts. He rebuilt his father's lost empire, diversifying into television, futures trading, manufacturing, and agriculture. By the end of the twentieth century, the renamed Vigilance Ministries claimed a tithing flock that numbered in the tens of millions and the good reverend had a personal net worth that was estimated to be around fifteen billion dollars. Praise be unto Him.

❧

"Praise be, Joshua."

I look up at the sound of his voice. My father is standing beside my table flanked by a pair of crimson Cee Bees with side arms, muscles, and dark glasses.

"Hello, Father."

"What are you reading?"

I rattle off the title and wait for him to challenge me. He raises an eyebrow, but says nothing.

"What are you doing here?" I ask.

"I have a meeting nearby and thought I'd treat the boys to coffee. Want a refill?"

I shake my head.

My father hands the blond thug a card and nods toward the counter.

"May I sit down?" he asks.

"Sure." I push a chair toward him and he sits.

I look at the Cee Bee goon.

"He'll stand," my father says.

We sit in uncomfortable silence for a few moments.

"We live in trying times," he says finally.

"Yes, we do." I watch the blond Cee Bee lean over to stir sugar into two coffee cups. His pants stretch tight against a perfect, round ass. I look back at my father, but not before he realizes I'm looking at something, glances over his shoulder, and then scowls.

"You are going to be the death of me," he says.

"Or me," I say.

He sighs and shakes his head, laying his hands flat against the table as if he's about to push himself up and leave.

"I saw you on the news," I say.

He freezes and looks at me. "And?"

"It was a good sound bite."

"I'm setting the stage," he says.

"For what?"

"We have video this time. The techs are working on it right now, coaxing his face from the static like God coaxing the stars out of nothingness. *Fiat lux*, Joshua."

"Well then you'll catch him," I say.

"Oh yes. We're going to catch him, Joshua. And we're going to execute him publicly."

"He's a terrorist," I say.

"He's a dead man."

"Blessed are the peacemakers," I whisper.

The vein on the side of his neck pulses angrily and I can see the color of his skin shifting from pink to red to that dark, angry purple. He pushes himself up from the table and starts to walk away.

I look down at the table, trying to slow my pounding heart.

"You need to read further, boy." His voice again, close and soft.

"What?"

He moves even closer. I can feel his breath on my face. "You need to keep reading. The Sermon says many things, Joshua. Many things." He draws in a deep, controlled breath. "Blessed are ye, when men shall revile you and persecute you, and shall say all manner of evil against you falsely, for my sake."

I look up at him.

"They will not bring him down," he says. "This president will lead us to the Kingdom of Heaven."

"Right. And remind me. When is that supposed to happen? Soon? During his fourth term? During his fifth?" I raise my arms above my head. "I'm Rapture-ready right now. Where should I stand?"

My father's face tightens.

"There is only one place for the righteous to stand," he says.

"Now *that*, I do know," I say.

And then he is gone.

I sit for a long time staring at pages on the table before me. My anger rises until it dances hot and hungry behind my steaming eyes. I drop my head into my hands, clamping my palms over my ears, trying desperately to stifle the sounds of other people: the mumbled litany of prayers from the next table, the crying of a stroller-bound infant, the angry whispers of arguing women behind the counter. *I want them to be gone. I want them to be gone.*

"Josh?" The hand on my shoulder startles me so badly I jump, slamming my knee into the underside of the table and spilling the coffee.

"Whoa. Take it easy, man. It's just me." Peter smiles down at me. "Can I join you?"

"Fine," I say. I work to rein in my anger, imagining the blood pulsing back-wards through my arteries, receding into my pitch black core.

He sits opposite me, beautiful hands reaching out as if to touch me, but then shrinking back and lying flat against the table where my father's had been moments before.

"I saw the old man," he says.

"Oh, yeah," I say. "He's all over the news."

"No, I mean here, a minute ago."

"Oh, right–"

"What did he want?"

"Coffee, I guess. For his bodyguards."

Peter eyes me speculatively. "What else?"

"He said they've got clear video of the Inheritor's face," I say. I can feel my hands trembling so I put them in my lap, out of sight beneath the table.

"Do you think they really do?" he asks.

"I don't know."

"Maybe they already know who it is."

I glance around and drop my voice. "Then why not do something about it."

"How could they?" He's whispering now too, leaning close across the small table. "Think of what it would look like; the son of the Chief of Staff..."

"Then why not something... quiet," I say.

This stops him cold. "You sound like you want to die," he says finally.

"I'm not sure that's fucking possible," I say in a loud clear voice. Several people at neighboring tables glance in my direction.

Peter's face flushes. "I'm gonna get coffee," he says. "I've got extra rations. Want anything?"

I shake my head and watch him hurry away from me.

✺

The second time the fire engulfed me I accidentally took out the V.I.P. viewing stands at a public execution on the Mall near the Lincoln Memorial. But I learned from the experience. This time I could feel it coming and I reached out into the building energy, feeling around for control. As the outer edges of the explosion touched my skin, I was able to halt the reaction for a moment, burning off my shirt and sending shafts of light out of my eyes and mouth and nostrils into the surrounding crowd. The light began to swirl like a hurricane of fire. And out of the midst of the amber fire, out of the center the effervescing light and heat tearing through my body, came four words, delivered to me in Margeaux's voice. *The meek shall inherit.* Terror pulsed through the crowd, the bleachers quaked under the force of a thousand stampeding feet, and then I unleashed the power that had been building inside as an intense, deadly explosion.

Images of my transformation were broadcast live across the nation, but by the time the cameras located me, my skin was so transformed by amber light and swirling fire that I was unrecognizable. I saw the footage on CNN. The camera panned the crowd and then zoomed in on my bare chest and light-contorted face. I heard the words so distinctly, the words that everyone was talking about, the words that boomed forth from my throat like human thunder.

The meek shall inherit.

The media coverage started so quickly the government had trouble reining in the on-air speculation. The fact that this had occurred during a live national broadcast seemed to place it beyond the reach of government censors. The pundits were divided about the reasons for the Lincoln Memorial bombing, but they were unanimous in their assumption that it has been a suicide bombing and that it had been the work of godless U.S. sympathizers and secular humanists.

I began to experiment with my powers, bringing my body to the edge, letting the energy ripple along my skin and then backing off, absorbing everything back inside. I discovered that my body needed at least three days to fully recharge. I also learned to protect my eardrums, and in a bit of gratuitous theatricality, I learned to burn off my clothing layer by layer. I assembled a prototype of a flowing white costume with a large blood red cross slashed across the front to wear beneath oversized street clothes when I went to a performance. I thought of myself as a showman, orchestrating a series of theatrical extravaganzas in which I destroyed strategic government targets: office buildings, Cee Bee training facilities, an Army induction center, and finally the sprawling Homeland Security complex on Nebraska Avenue. When I reached the site, I would burn off the outer layer of clothes, let myself be seen in the costume, resplendent as a Medieval Crusader, and then, when I unleashed the final explosion, I would burn off the costume leaving myself unrecognizable in a pair of tight blue jeans and a T-shirt.

The media inflated civilian casualty figures and downplayed the strategic importance of my targets. The government used the ensuing panic to raise the domestic threat level to red. New Executive Orders extended the curfew, produced a new list of spot warrant capital crimes, and closed synagogues and non-Christian schools. The Cee Bees rounded up hundreds of known secularists and resident aliens, loading them into tractor trailers and shipping them south into Virginia.

Speculation in the press escalated as the bombings continued. The first person to assert that the bombings had been perpetrated by a single individual was a FOX News anchor who read a passage from the Old Testament on air and began referring to the bomber as Ezekiel. There was a hasty retraction issued by the network, but the damage was done. In the popular imagination, and among the more unruly media outlets, the group of bombers had become a single, indestructible super-bomber. Names were bandied about in editorials and on afternoon talk shows but the one that stuck was the Inheritor.

✻

I never intended to tell Peter that I am the Inheritor. We met about a year ago in a men's room at Union Station. He sucked me off and slipped me his number. In a country where an Executive Order has made it legal for deputized members of the Christian Brotherhood to kill gender traitors or suspected gender traitors in public, cruising has all but disappeared. There are no bars, no gay bookstores, no bathhouses or video stores. Most gays have either made a run for the border or hunkered down and married women. The fact that Peter was willing to go down on me in the stall of a public restroom when half a dozen Cee Bees were patrolling the train platform outside made me so horny I couldn't think of anything else.

And I couldn't *not* call him.

When I finally did call, he was wary, laying out an elaborate plan for our meeting. He sent me to a couple of false start locations and when we finally met in a Georgetown nightclub, I stood close enough to smell the expensive cologne that barely masked his fear. We had a lot of gin and he finally asked me back to his apartment. We've been meeting up to have increasingly violent sex ever since.

In Peter's mind, the periodic black eyes, stitches, and sprained arms have come to mean we're dating, that we're in a *relationship*. So I shouldn't be surprised that a couple of weeks ago when I headed out for one of my performances, he followed.

I arrived at the Homeland Security complex and walked the length of the block. The lawn was smaller than I expected and the common wisdom, which held that the lawn was heavily mined, was correct. I could feel them humming in the ground, like a horde of hibernating insects. If I was careful, I could use the power of the exploding mines to accelerate my own explosive force and substantially broaden the swathe of destruction. I sat at a bus stop across the street for a while communing with the mines as I watched the flow of buses and pedestrians in and out of the main gate. When I finally crossed the street and walked in the direction of the guard house, I did not see Peter coming down the block.

As I approached, one of the sentries raised his gun and several things happened at once. From behind, I heard Peter say, "What the hell are you doing?" The other sentry raised his gun. I felt Peter's hand on my shoulder as my outer layer of clothes burned away. My costume emerged, shimmering in the sunlight. The words erupted from my chest—*The meek shall inherit!*—and people began to scatter. Before Peter could remove his hand, I turned, enfolded him in my arms, and unleashed the explosion.

I awoke next to Peter. We were sprawled on the grass about thirty yards from the edge of the enormous crater where the Homeland Security complex had been. It was my greatest triumph yet. I wanted to stand by the side of the road and take a bow. Instead, I sat and watched the bloody second act unfold. When the military rescue vehicles arrived, I waved away an Army triage technician, telling him we were fine and pointing in the direction of a woman who knelt a few yards away clutching her eviscerated intestines with bloody hands. Peter finally sat up beside me. "Oh my God," he said. "You're him."

※

Peter comes back to the table with his coffee and sits down, taking the lid off to blow across the creamy brown surface. He gets up to get napkins, finally tastes his coffee, and then goes back to the counter for another packet of sugar. Watching him priss around with his coffee makes me feel dark and murderous. He crosses his legs, folding the right knee over the left, bouncing his ankle like a teenage girl, and meticulously smoothing the lines of his Oxford shirt.

"I have to go," I say, pushing my chair back and leaving without looking back.

Outside, the air that had seemed so fresh this morning is acrid and thick with smoke from the bombings in the suburbs. I pick a direction and walk. The sidewalks are bustling with pedestrians, hurrying to get their errands done before the curfew claxons sound. The streets, off limits to civilian vehicles, are mostly deserted. I push past a pair of teenagers and step into the street, shoving my hands in the pockets of my khakis and walking down the middle of one of the downtown lanes. Some people glance curiously at me from the sidewalk or from the open air cafes, but most people walk on in immobile silence, locked inside their own nightmares.

I can smell the acrid stench of pulverized stone and burnt textiles, rotting food and decaying meat before I reach DuPont Circle. I continue in my empty lane, walking around the circle to the police barricades that mark the northern perimeter of the crater.

Flowers and candles and photographs clutter the ground beneath the snaking line of barricades as far as I can see in either direction. I kneel down and look at a pair of photos tacked to the wooden base of one of the barricades. In the first photo, a blond boy of about seven hugs a blond girl of about the same age; they are laughing. In the second photo a blond man, handsome and shirtless, is wrestling with a golden retriever on an expanse of green lawn. I look at the next photo—an Asian girl of about eight or nine—and the next and the next. Rows and rows of laughing children, smiling couples, women in wedding gowns, men in military uniforms, and students in team jerseys or sweatshirts with Greek letters.

Who are all these people?

"They are the faces of the flock," a voice says from behind.

I didn't realize I'd spoken out loud.

I turn around to find myself staring into Margeaux's pale blue eyes.

"What're you doing here?" I ask, confused suddenly.

She takes a drag on her cigarette and shrugs.

And that's when I hear the whistling sound that precedes a Bluebird missile strike. The sound arcs down from a distance and ends with a huge explosion a couple of blocks west on P Street. I turn and start to hurry in the opposite direction, but the sound of another incoming missile stops me dead in my tracks. The second explosion is a couple of streets over on New Hampshire. There are people screaming and running in all directions now, shoving each other and finally spilling off the sidewalks into the wide open streets. I look around for Margeaux, but she's gone. I hear more whistling in the distance and take off across the circle, running east along P Street. Another explosion knocks me off my feet and showers me with papers, glass, and bits of hot plastic. I stagger to my feet and see several people disappearing into the basement of a church. I run across the street, vaulting the glossy black hood of a limousine and throwing myself at the closed door. It's locked. There are more explosions, detonations occurring so quickly they sound like a summer thunderstorm. I pound on the door with my fists, but there is no answer.

I run around to the front of the church, taking the steps two at a time, thinking maybe I can pry open the giant wooden sanctuary doors. If I can get inside, the towering stone structure might offer some protection. I am about halfway up the stairs when I hear a whistling Bluebird descending. The explosion lifts me and slams me against the great wooden doors like a ragdoll thrown by a petulant child. I slump to the ground, the world suddenly dark. I raise my hands to my eyes and feel the blood pouring down my face from a deep gash on my forehead.

I am wiping the blood from my eyes when strong hands grab my shoulders, dragging me across the cold stone into the sanctuary and closing the door behind me.

Receding footsteps echo in the emptiness.

"Praise be," I say. "Thank you for granting me sanctuary."

There is a long silence.

"The Lord works in mysterious ways indeed," a voice says from behind me. "How does it feel to be on the receiving end of an explosion, Joshua?"

I stagger to my feet and turn to face my father.

He is flanked by the two Cee Bees from Starbucks. A uniformed driver and a man in a business suit stand several paces behind him, obscured by dust and shadows.

The blond Cee Bee has an automatic weapon trained on me; the other one holds a black police baton. I raise my hands like a criminal surrendering in an old movie.

"Dad, it's me," I say.

"Yes," he says. "I know exactly who you are."

"Dad, c'mon." I pitch my voice high, letting the timbre convey fear I do not feel.

"So now you're calling me Dad. Do you want to try 'papa' or 'daddy' as well? Will it melt the old man's cold heart to hear his baby boy beg and plead?"

His face is smooth and expressionless.

A nearby explosion rocks the sanctuary, dust filtering down from the eaves, giant chandeliers moving slowly above our heads.

"I don't understand why you're acting like this," I say.

"I think you do," he says. "I think you know exactly what I'm talking about and you're wondering how much energy you have left after yesterday's explosion."

"I really don't know what you're talking about." Tears well up in my eyes.

"He's got you dead to rights," a voice says from the shadows.

"Peter?" I'm genuinely surprised.

"My name is John, actually, but yeah, you know me as Peter."

He steps out of the shadows, his familiar features rigid with anger. The navy, pin-striped business suit and red power tie seem out of place draped over the frame of a man who had, just days before, lay bruised and naked in my bed. His upper lip is split, still crusted over from our last sexual encounter. Flames crackle around my fingertips.

His business suit seems to fade before my eyes, transforming from pin-striped blue into Cee-Bee dress reds. I stare at the crisp red fabric in surprise. I notice he's wearing the insignia of a deacon.

"You're a deacon." I say.

He looks puzzled, but he nods.

"Well," I say to my father. "Your deacon likes to take it up the ass."

"The *president's* deacon will do what needs to be done to protect this country," my father says.

"This is so fucked up, Peter. You can't fake the kind of cum-guzzling glee you—"

Peter takes a step forward, but my father puts a restraining hand on his arm. His uniform fades from red to blue and then he's wearing the pin-striped suit again. I want to ask him how he did that, but he's saying something else now.

"Did you think I was fucking you for the company? Is that what you thought?" Peter asks. "Did you imagine there's enough humanity left inside you for anyone to love?"

"Oh no, I'm not talking about love," I say. "You weren't in it for the love, Peter. You were in it to get the shit beat out of you and then get your ass cored like a rotten apple."

The blond Cee Bee chuckles.

"Tell your father it was my fault," a voice says from beside me.

I look over at her. She's wearing a tailored white dress and she looks like she's about thirty years old. Her hair is long, wavy, and glossy, like Ava Gardner in *The Killers*. "Margeaux, let it go. He doesn't care about that."

"Of course he does, Joshua. Deep down it's the only thing that matters to him. He wants desperately to be exonerated. How can he face his boss if he thinks he might be at fault, if he thinks he might be responsible for your performances?"

"Dammit! He *is* to blame!" I shout at her. "He's fuckin' *completely* to blame. You know what he is. You called him that yourself..."

She's shaking her head and frowning.

"What's he doing? Who's he talking to?" The blond Cee Bee turns to look at my father.

I whirl on them and say, "This is all your fault."

"Who? Me?" The Cee Bee's eyes are wide; he takes a step back from me.

"No. Not you. *Him.*" I point at my father.

His jaw tightens. "You never could take responsibility for your actions," he says.

"A trait I learned from you, when I watched you kill my mother and then tell the police she fell in the shower."

"Joshua, don't." Margeaux lays a cool hand on my shoulder.

"I was there. I saw everything. I was awake, hiding behind the sofa and I saw it—"

"Are you fucking *incapable* of telling the truth for one goddamned minute!?" My father's voice echoes like a thunderclap in the enormous space. Peter and the Cee Bees step away from him.

"He didn't kill her, my darling." Margeaux's fingers are icy cold against my cheek. "You did."

"*What!?*"

"I *said*—"

"I'm not talking to you!" I shout at him, turning back to Margeaux.

"You know it in your heart, Joshua. Remember."

A barrage of images: my mother yelling and reaching for my father's belt; me throwing an ashtray; ashes and blood on the yellow linoleum, and then kicking and stomping and blood and . . . *Oh, my God*. My blood turns to ice.

"The truth is: you kill everything you touch," my father says.

"The truth is: I'm gonna kill you all," I say.

He walks over and wrenches the gun from the blond Cee Bee.

"I'm not afraid of you, Father."

"I don't want your fear. I just want you to stop killing people… innocent people, Joshua." His voice falters. "You hate me. You hate the government. You hate the Lord… so be it, but you're killing innocent people—"

"I'm killing the enemy. I'm killing the wolves."

I glance at Margeaux, but she is watching me in silence. There are tears in her eyes.

"You've killed over twelve hundred people of whom less than eighty were Cee Bees or military officers. Do you imagine you've been depleting the numbers of the Christian Brotherhood all this time? Have you been ignoring the parade of civilian casualties on CNN? For God's sake Joshua, you killed forty elementary school children yesterday."

"Numbers. Numbers. It's just a numbers game to you."

"I assure you, this is not a game."

My father holds the gun in one hand and strokes his abundant whiskers with the other. His ears begin sprouting fur, the tips of them becoming pointed and standing erect. His black eyes are moving closer together, his face elongating into a furred muzzle and a mouth full of jagged teeth.

"You're a wolf," I say. "A grievous wolf." My hands are shaking and my body temperature is rising. Sizzling droplets of sweat dance across my burning palms.

Margeaux touches my shoulder again. "For I know this: that after my departing shall grievous wolves enter in among you, not sparing the flock."

"No." I shudder involuntarily.

"Not sparing the flock," she says.

My father raises the gun. "You're the wolf, Joshua," he says.

"I'll kill you all," I say. I let a burst of energy leap out and burn away my clothes.

The Cee Bees both back away, but Peter steps forward. "He can't do it. It's too soon," he says. "This is just theatrics."

I am standing naked before them, my arms outstretched before me like a saint in a Renaissance fresco.

I hear Margeaux's voice saying over and over, "Not sparing the flock."

"There is only one place for the righteous to stand," I say. "Isn't that what you told me, Father? Only one place for the righteous to stand: against the king of lies. Against tyranny. Against oppression and violence. Against bigotry and war and…" I trail off when I realize he is talking over my words.

"Against innocent children. Against the Lord's plan. Against Christ himself. Against love and compassion. Against decency and against men and women who are living their lives in accordance with the Lord's teachings…"

I feel the energy building inside me again. I let it rise to the surface. My skin begins to glow. Amber flames dance across my naked body.

My father says, "Sometimes great things come to an ignominious end," and pulls the trigger.

I hear Margeaux screaming as the spray of bullets tears me apart.

AFTER BALENCIAGA
Marshall Moore

Marshall Moore is the author of three novels (*The Concrete Sky, An Ideal for Living,* and *Bitter Orange*) and two short story collections (*Black Shapes in a Darkened Room* and *The Infernal Republic*). He is also the publisher at Typhoon Media Ltd, which publishes under the imprints Signal 8 Press and BookCyclone. A native of eastern North Carolina, he now lives and works in Hong Kong.

Couture seemed to be having second thoughts, and none of us knew quite what to do about it. Coco had been working on the same dress for weeks, taking her bloody time, as if she wanted the thin stench of her fingertips to seep into the nubbly silk, ruining it. I didn't blame her. Fabulously rich and gifted in life, a pioneer, she must have found her resurrection beyond appalling. If the decision had been mine, I'd have animated her more fully. I was not the one pulling the strings, though, and it seemed our well-dressed puppeteer (we nicknamed him Couture, since none of us knew what else to call him) had his limits. All that being said, the dress was a wearable masterpiece: more feminine in its shape-flattering cutting than her businesslike classics, more modern than the collections that had made her name and established her fame. Even in death, we evolve.

Cristobal and Yves organized a two-man strike when they heard Couture meant to dig up Chanel's body. "You must not bring back that Nazi-loving whore," the Frenchman spat. Rage dripped off him like the sweat he could no longer produce. The brain cancer had been hard on him in life, and in death he still looked like a Madame Tussaud's wax likeness of himself left too long out in the sun. We were seven at the table: Christian Dior (Saint Laurent hated him, and seating them side by side guaranteed the utensils would fly), Gianni Versace, Gianfranco Ferre. "She deserves to rot. Let her feed the mice and ants."

"Would you want to feed them yourself?" Versace said.

This brought a moment—only a moment—of silence to the table. Seven large egos paused to reflect. I could see what Balenciaga was thinking: *It would be better than this.* Of course he was thinking it; we all were. Yet no one spoke up. Sometimes you just have to have a think first. Me, I've never been an arse-licker, but I've also never been brought back from the grave. So I shut the fuck up. We watched Couture tuck into the mound of sashimi his private chef had brought in from Hokkaido. A sip of the Sauternes in his glass. Back to the fish. He was like a half-starved alley cat.

"Two words," Couture tried to purr. His mouth was full, so the words came out more of a gurgle: wet knots in a silk handkerchief. He sparkled, crass with sequins and gold thread in the destroyed thing Versace had designed for him. Couture lacked both the taut body that Versace's clothing looked best on and the good taste to know the difference between opulence and vulgarity. And it didn't matter. When you have Couture's power, it's always 1992 if your favourite collections debuted that year. Besides, I had a feeling he was biding his time until someone more outrageous (than me) could be made to join us at the table. Gareth Pugh, perhaps, or Gaultier. Wiping a gob of tuna off his lower lip, he said, "*Vintage Chanel*. Do you know how much originals would fetch?"

He sounded like he was trying to convince himself. You can tell when a man cannot think around corners, when he is hitting the brick wall in his mind. The word *vintage* could be put before every surname in the room to achieve the same effect. Except mine, of course: I was too young when I hanged myself, making the death too recent. Apart from me, we all knew what he wanted from us. Couture could whisper of secret sales to rich eccentrics, but he still had the same clothes he'd dug us up to make for him. He still had no buyers. What's authenticity in a case such as ours, after all? To start with, where would the fabric come from? It had all rotted or been put to other uses. The best he could hope for would be to pass our originals off as interesting fakes. And why resurrect the dead for *that*, when half the Chinese economy is based on high-end bootlegging? This would have been a ghastly insult but for what we'd already been put through. It's possible Couture understood this, whether he admitted to it or not. After all, everything we had made so far was in his own size. Even the dresses.

"Lee, what do you think?"

"You'll do it whether we like it or not," I said. If I'd been cut out for diplomacy, I'd have joined the UN, not Savile Row.

"You're just jealous," said Couture.

How the living so often utterly fail to get it. Once you're dead, so much ceases to matter. Oh, there's plenty left undone. I still regret topping myself before Lady Gaga was even out of her twenties. And this whole death thing… *immensely* over-rated. I thought I'd be drinking chamomile tea with Mummy in the Café Hereafter. I thought it would be like Paris, only more so. White marble architecture instead of yellowish limestone, vast rococo buildings that would make Alain de Botton wince and *Monocle* wag a disapproving finger. Perhaps I even *had been* with Mummy, and now couldn't remember. There'd been an awful pulling sensation, like a sloppy dentist pulling out a tooth before the anaesthetic shots have taken hold. This was followed by a sort of heave: I thought I was on the runway for reincarnation, about to be launched into or out of a womb… and *voila*. There was Balenciaga, as soon as I opened my eyes:

perhaps the only Basque not to become famous for blowing things up. And next to him, poor Versace, that shocked *he-shot-me?* look apparently etched onto his face forever.

"Are we in hell?" had been my first question.

"No, Beijing," Couture replied. "Although I'm told it's getting harder and harder to tell the difference."

At first it seemed Couture had brought us back to spruce up his own wardrobe, or at least to consult. I understood this; the doubts had not yet taken hold. When you can make dead flesh knit itself back together out of the muck it's decayed into, why *not* speak to the industry's best? Stylists are a dime a dozen and half of them don't know what they're on about. Balenciaga had the hardest time of us all, I think. Although he and Dior got on well—they'd been on good terms the first time around—he couldn't tell what Couture wanted with him.

"I think he brought me back because he likes my name," he confided to me one night.

"Better that than for sex," I said.

He just stared at me for a moment, awful gears turning in his head. He didn't ask and I didn't tell.

❦

Life, or un-life, gurgled on for an interval of weeks. Couture asked Balenciaga what to wear and then ignored his advice, putting on whatever the *grands couturiers* had designed for him. Dior and Saint Laurent tried to make our master elegant, in a traditional way, following the styles of the times they knew best. It almost worked. Couture had supplied them with acres of good silk and lightweight wool, promising heavier stuff for when the weather turned colder. But he had waif-like proportions, all bones and angles and limbs like small children would draw. No matter what the puppets designed for him, he looked like a scarecrow dressed by the gods. Which might have been why someone told him to dig me up. I'd done my time on Savile Row, after all, and I had a bit of a reputation for managing difficult cunts. If you can come out of corporate LVMH still half sane, masters of the undead can be dealt with.

Then Balenciaga didn't turn up at the table one morning. The unhappiest of us, and the most vocal about it, he was bound to disappear first. Couture said nothing, and we didn't ask. When you're a bespoke zombie, it's hard to avoid mixed emotions toward your fellow dead. Had the Basque been released into freedom or delivered back to the dirt? Was there a difference? Gloom pervaded. And when poor rotting Coco finished the dress, the next day, like Balenciaga, she was gone. Second thoughts again.

"I have an announcement," Couture said, sweeping into the dining room with all the grandiosity one would expect from a supernatural villain dressed in authentic, custom-made Saint Laurent. His skirt and jacket had the austere elegance the moment commanded: squared-off shoulders, padded but not so much as to make a caricature of his chopstick frame; exquisite cutting that hinted at the existence of an inner drag queen. Yet there was a matronly aspect, too, as if Couture might purse his lips and glare down his nose at us. Here again, Saint Laurent's dress suited the occasion.

"There's been… a change of focus. A *new* focus." And with that, he directed us to rise from the table and follow him.

Yves and the Italians looked as apprehensive as I felt, but we could hardly risk open protest. Into a gallery we went, visiting for the first time yet another of the forbidden chambers in this overblown Chinese Versailles that was our prison and our home. On one vast wall, we beheld a single, spot lit painting.

"A Degas?" asked Ferre.

"Almost," said Couture. "But look closer."

I had been to enough galleries to recognize something different about the palette and the composition: slight differences in the tones; shapes more fully realized. This wasn't Degas, but the artists clearly knew one another's work.

"Who is it?" Versace asked.

"Someone I've always thought was sadly overshadowed by her contemporaries," Couture purred.

And with that, a woman walked into the room… in *new* Chanel.

"Gentlemen, may I present Mary Cassatt."

We designers exchanged glances, all cognizant of what this meant—of the writing on the wall, you could say. Couture could only keep so many puppets dancing at the same time… dancing, or sewing, or painting. We'd be replaced by Picasso, van Gogh, or Juan Gris soon enough. Oh, he'd keep one or two of us around for consultations, but before long the rest would inevitably, *gratefully* follow Chanel and Balenciaga back down into the dark.

THE THIRD ESTATE
Lee Thomas

Lee Thomas is the Lambda Literary Award and Bram Stoker Award-winning author of *The Dust of Wonderland*, *In the Closet, Under the Bed*, *The German*, *Torn*, *Ash Street*, and the forthcoming *Like Light for Flies*. Under a couple of other names he has authored several suspense thrillers for young adults, including *Mason*, *Shimmer*, and the *Wicked Dead* series (co-authored with Stefan Petrucha). Lee lives in Austin, Texas, where he is working on a new book. You can find him online at *leethomasauthor.com*.

Morgan Anderson walks into the conference room of the Fearing Oil Company at 10:37 a.m.—seven minutes after the board meeting has begun. With him, he carries a cardboard box: its contents are heavy and he struggles with the package, all but rocking from side to side as he waddles across the carpet and hoists it onto the burnished mahogany table in the room's center.

"What have you got there?" Edward Fonit asks. Fonit is a handsome man in late middle age, whose recent visit to a plastic surgeon in Dallas, TX has given him the taught, tanned face of a thirty-year old.

"It's a surprise," Anderson says, bouncing his eyebrows comically and smiling as he slides the box to the middle of the table. He looks at the package for another moment, and then takes his seat.

"You're late," Edleeta Dorcester says dryly.

Anderson smiles and waves his hands at the box sitting at the table's center, as if the delivery of the package should relieve him of all other responsibility.

"That's no excu…" Edleeta begins, but is interrupted by Mitchell Brown, who says, "Are we all here?"

As the Chairman of the Board, Mitchell Brown is often forgiven such rude behavior. Even so Edleeta chirps deep in her throat, a sound of disapproval.

Anderson cocks his head to the side and notes the placement of his peers in the room. He counts eight suits, three skirt-suits, and a revealing blue dress, draped over the ample tits of the secretary charged with noting the meeting's important moments.

"Something to say, Anderson?" Mitchell Brown asks, annoyed.

Anderson grins. "Surprise!" he announces.

Surprise indeed.

They don't know that Morgan Anderson isn't there. Not intellectually. Not emotionally.

I climbed into his skin earlier that morning (one of dozens of recent visits I've made to him). Like a fist bringing a sock puppet to life, I slid into his body and moved him around. Now I wear Anderson like a Halloween costume. Further, they don't understand the nature of the gift I've put before them, not even when Morgan Anderson removes a slender remote detonation device from his pocket and jabs the black button at its center.

Inside the cardboard box is a plywood crate in which two wads of C-4 explosives, each the size of a baseball, have been suspended. Surrounding the explosives are thousands of beads of birdshot, which in retrospect might have been excessive.

After Anderson depresses the trigger, all goes white and then black and finally resolves into a field of gray in a single heartbeat. The blast peels Morgan Anderson's tissue—his blood and bone—away from me; shoots me from the decimated boardroom with the scraps of debris.

The explosion vaporizes the board of directors, two temps who are performing data entry in an adjoining space, the secretary with the ample tits, and three pigeons sitting on the ledge of the window. The collateral damage results in the death of Renny Meltzer, an executive who was in line to replace Edleeta Dorcester on the board if she'd lived long enough to retire at the end of the summer.

They are dead, but I remain. Spirit. Consciousness.

I soar across the office space in the wake of destruction like the steaming mist of Mitchell Brown's spinal fluid. And then I right myself, and drop through the floors until I reach the lobby. Unseen, I make my way across town to the Chester Building and ascend to the penthouse where I find my body reclining on a leather chaise.

For a moment I admire the body as I might admire the body of an attractive stranger—not young but healthy and heavily muscled. The skin is tight, golden and unblemished. Snow-white hair grows in shocking relief against the almond flesh.

Cubs call me a Polar Bear. Twinks call me old.

I was born Trevor Charles, but I was born broken. Unlike you, I am not chained to my tissue or fluid. I'm a free spirit by the most literal of definitions.

I used to fight crime under the handle *Marley*. I'd slide into some lowlife's skin suit and walk him right into a police station, present the evidence of his crimes, confess with his throat and lips, and then I'd leave the felon sitting there, in cuffs, looking confused and babbling questions no one but I could answer.

That was *then*.

I cared then.

I thought there was something in this country to care about, but all of that changed.

Now, I'm *Legion*, and I'm changing the world, one atrocity at a time.

Sliding back into my body, I get used to the weight of skin and bone. Sirens wail distantly as I open my eyes. Standing I stretch my arms, flex my back, and then walk to the window. Smoke rises two miles away—a column of black, billowing skyward, carrying fetid souls into the atmosphere.

Soon enough, my partner Curtis will come home. The city will shut down as they always do. The "crime" has to be investigated, even though the police and the feds will undoubtedly recognize my handiwork. People will gather to gawk, to mourn, to sob.

Cry, bitches. You've brought this on yourselves.

Unfortunately, Curtis will also be upset, and I'll have to hear about it for two or three days. Few hate my alter ego with Curtis's intensity, and I can only imagine what will happen to his heart and his head if he ever discovers that the man he's shared his life with for the past two years is the architect of so much misery.

Why? He'll ask. Every fucking time, he asks *why?*

He knows the answer. Like everyone else, he's been told the answer. I've made Legion's motivations clear from the beginning. My dogma has been posted on half a million websites the world over and spoken by every broadcast anchor in the nation.

I'm sure my decree is already scrolling along the bottom of the CNN broadcast screen—a concise explanation to accompany digital images of the ravaged Fearing Oil Building.

※

In my office I watch the video clip I recorded earlier that day. It has already gone viral, as I knew it would.

Morgan Anderson's face fills the screen, but I am the one speaking, moving his lips, holding the gaze of hatred in his eyes. The limited-spectrum camera on his laptop frames him from brow to chin. His features are grim and shadowed.

"Fearing Oil is directly responsible for the deaths of innumerable men and women. It has destroyed hundreds of eco-systems. They have misappropriated funds from their employees' retirement accounts…" I fast forward through the list of crimes; I know them all too well. They have been catalogued and collated. The documentation necessary to support my allegations has already been delivered to a BBC News desk. I slow the recording again. "…you don't listen. You let them—this tiny fraction of the population—you let them destroy and take and consider your paycheck ample reward for the dissolution of our economy and our ecology. You reward them for failure and subsidize their crimes. You elect their puppets into government, and they legislate your downfall, and take payoffs to keep their families segregated from you: the bitter, the beaten, and the exploited.

"Fearing Oil did not fall in an act of terrorism. It was an act of revolution. The Third Estate must rise and reclaim this nation, and they must do so through blood and sacrifice."

I turn off the computer screen and lean back in the chair.

"And then what?" Curtis's asks.

Swiveling in the chair, I turn to find my partner standing in the doorway. His arm is extended, aiming a 9.mm pistol at my face.

"Curtis?"

"Tell me," he says, "how does your great revolution end?"

"How long have you known?" I ask.

"Does it matter? I *know*."

I stand from the chair, and Curtis takes a step back. His expression is a miserable stew of a dozen emotions.

"I was so stupid," he says. "Jesus Christ, how could I be so stupid?"

"This has nothing do with you."

"How in the fuck does this have nothing to do with me? My partner is a mass murderer."

"You don't understand."

"No shit, I don't understand. They don't exactly have an Oprah episode covering this one, and I'm guessing I won't find anything in the 'Relationship' aisle at Barnes&Noble."

"People have to wake up," I explain. "If these corporations were human beings, they would be caught, tried and executed for crimes against humanity. But they don't. At least they didn't, until now."

"You're talking about murder."

"I'm talking about destroying monsters."

"You actually think you're a hero?"

"The only difference between heroes and villains is how the media spins their shit. Now, put down the gun and let's talk this over."

Curtis shakes his head. He is on the verge of tears, but the gun doesn't waver. "How can you be so God damn calm? What kind of monster are you?"

"You want the origin story?" I ask. "You want to know if I was bitten by a radioactive demon or if I'm the disaffected spirit of Adolph Hitler? What? You think I know how I became this way? Maybe it was the Agent Orange the government showered on my father, or maybe it was the intricate chemical cocktails mommy created to make it through one fucking day after another. Barbiturates for breakfast. A little acid here. A few mushrooms there. Some heroin to take the edge off. Or maybe God just decided I was special. What difference does it make? I'm broken. The spirit and the flesh don't connect."

"That's not true," he says.

"Really?"

"You're connected to flesh," he says. "Not the bodies you possess. No. But if your *true* body dies, so does the spirit. You need it to survive. Legion can't live in a permanently spectral state, so if I shoot *you* and I kill *you*, it's over."

"You don't know that," I point out. "That's just one of Looking Glass's theories. It's not like there are a whole lot like me out there."

Unfortunately, I have very good reason to believe that Looking Glass's ideas about my permanent demise are accurate. He is the one motherfucker I could never get past. No matter who I occupied, he could see me for who I was. As superheroes went, he fell on the lame side, reading auras and shit, but he had made my life difficult until I'd slipped him in Atlanta and had gone underground.

"I could put a bullet in your head and then no one else would have to die."

"And you'd go to the lethal injection gurney."

He considers this. The clouds in his eyes and the sneer on his lips show me he hasn't thought his plan through.

"How could you do this to me?" he asks.

I try to find a moment from our past, something that might touch his heart and take his mind off of opening my skull. But I can't find a thing. Maybe it's the duress of having a gun pointed at my brow, but I think it's something more. The truth is, Curtis and I have shared little over the years except our bodies. We didn't share our desires or disappointments—outside of some perfunctory vent sessions. We didn't enjoy the same films or books or television programs. We didn't even enjoy the same people. I never blamed him. After all, I'm the freak in this equation. Still the realization unsettles me. He is a hot muscle cub and I am his daddy bear, and as I look at the cold hole at the end of the pistol, I begin to wonder if that is all we've ever been to one another—the right type.

It shouldn't have come as a surprise to me. I am Legion, and Legion is a master of the superficial.

"Put down the gun, Curtis," I say. "Put it down and walk away."

"No."

"I can make you."

"Not before I pull the trigger. Your body will go limp if you leave it. I'll have time before you reach me."

He is right. But can he pull the trigger?

"How could I have been so stupid?" he asks again. "How could I not have seen this? You're a fucking psychopath, and I never knew."

"I'm not a psychopath."

"Right," he says sarcastically, "you're a revolutionary. You and your Third Estate bullshit. What the fuck is that anyway?"

Christ, he couldn't even be bothered to *wikipedia* the phrase. Did he never watch the news?

"Before the French Revolution there were three estates: the clergy and the royals made up the first two, and the third estate was made up of the populace who suffered from the corruption and excesses of the first two. Now we have the corporations and the government as the first two estates; the third estate remains the same."

"Did you ever think people might be happy?"

"They aren't happy. They're trapped. They expect their elected officials to make laws to protect them, but they don't. Corporations possess the government the same way I possess anyone I choose. They make politicians construct castles of law, keeping them safe inside and keeping everyone else out. Enron should have been an epitaph, not a fucking instruction manual."

"So you're going to murder every executive in the world?"

"I don't have to," I say. Apparently, he *didn't* watch the news. "Last week a personal assistant to the CEO of NationBank poisoned the asshole's protein shake. Then she stapled the memo announcing his seven million dollar bonus to his lapel—seven million that came from the fed bailout for the bank's failure. Yesterday, three members of the accounting department of Ervine-Tyne Power in California presented senior management with evidence of misappropriation of funds and falsified expense reports. When the senior managers, including the CFO dismissed them with a smug, 'We'll look into it,' one of the accountants blocked the door, while the other two produced handguns and proceeded to assassinate every last one of them."

"And?" Curtis shouts. "Tomorrow someone else will step into those jobs, so what makes you think they'll do anything differently?"

"They may not," I admit. "But there's also no reason to believe they won't come to the same end. It's time for accountability, Curtis. Why can't you see that?"

"Murder is not justice."

"It's all we have left."

"It's all *you* have left, and I'm going to stop you."

"By murdering me."

"I…"

"You didn't come in here to reason with me. You didn't want to discuss the situation. You picked up a gun."

"It's the only way."

"On that we agree."

And then silence overwhelms us. We stand motionless, looking at the men we thought we knew, and perhaps Curtis realizes, as I had, that we know each other's skin and very little of what operates beneath it.

"How could you do this to me?" he asks again.

"Shut *up*," I say. "You made this about you, not me. I never asked for your approval or your assistance."

"You never cared about me at all."

"You might be right," I say. "But I stayed. Curtis, it may not have occurred to you, but I can be with anybody. Literally. If I want to be with a man—for an hour or a night or a month—all I have to do is slide into whomever he desires—a trick, a lover. Believe me, I did a lot of that when I was younger. But I didn't deceive you in that regard. You got the real me, for better or worse. That means something."

"It means I was stupid enough to let you use me."

"*You're* feeling used? This is my apartment, Curtis. This is my fucking *building*. Have you ever paid for a meal? You work to keep yourself busy, not because you need an income. You fuck your gym-rat conquests, and I never say a word about it. And don't play the offended innocent, because I saw it happen more than once. Hell, I was in three or four of them when it happened."

"You spied on me?"

I ignore the question, because the answer is obvious and irrelevant. "And did we ever agree to an open relationship? In fact, weren't you the one who demanded monogamy? Weren't you the one who said we could never have a truly intimate relationship if we were fucking around?"

"Stop it," he says.

"You got that one right, didn't you?"

"You're a murderer," he snaps as if that negates my observation.

"For fuck's sake, stay on topic. If you're genuinely concerned about all of the suited carcasses, quit whining about what I did to you."

"You have to be stopped."

"You're not going to shoot me," I say. "This isn't a villain's downfall; it's a break up. We're at the exact same place we'd be if you'd met someone else or if you'd caught me fucking around. It's over, Curtis. Don't ruin your life over it. Let's just walk away. I'll make sure you're taken care of. You can even keep the apartment. Otherwise you're going to jail for murder."

"I'm stopping Legion. The worst terrorist our country has ever known."

"Prove it," I say. "There is no evidence. Everything I bought or touched was done through the people I possessed. Nothing can be linked to me, and once I'm dead, even Looking Glass won't be able to confirm who the body belongs to. He'll see nothing but flesh and hair like anyone else, because my spirit will have been released for good. So how are you going to convince the police this was anything but a spoiled little muscle boy trying to snatch his daddy's estate?"

He considers this for a moment, eyes shrouded with thought. As he does so, I realize a few things myself. When Curtis accused me of being Legion, I didn't deny it, didn't so much as feign innocence, and when he pointed his gun at my face, I didn't do much to defuse the situation. If anything, I'd fueled his aggression.

Then, as my partner's eyes clear with what he must consider a solution, I understand that I want an ending– if for nothing else, then certainly for the relationship.

He speaks, and what he says surprises me, though I should have known he'd find it a rational enough solution.

"Looking Glass can identify you now, before you die. The police will believe him."

"You don't have enough time to get him here," I say, my voice low and dry.

He digs in his pocket with his free hand and produces a cell phone. He lobs it across to me. Reflexively, I catch it.

"Call him," Curtis says.

Ridiculous, I think. "No."

He jabs the gun in my direction. "Call him."

"Well look who's trying on his daddy britches," I reply. I give the phone another glance and then throw it to the floor, where it shatters on the tile.

Frustrated with the game, I start toward Curtis.

"Don't," he says.

But I do anyway.

"I'll shoot."

"Then shoot or walk away. I'm done with this."

"Did you ever love me at all?"

"I didn't hate you. That's as close as you're going to get."

"Stop moving!"

"Shoot or walk away."

And the motherfucker shoots me. The bullet tears into my chest, pausing my approach. Curtis's eyes grow wide and white, and then he fires again, ripping a hole in my pectoral, my ribs, my heart. I collapse on the tiles...

And then I slide through the floor, descending the many stories of the apartment building, and in the lobby I pause to note the panic on the doorman's face as he answers a call on the building's landline—likely a disturbed resident or Curtis himself, reporting gunfire. Down I go, through the parking garage and the basement storage units.

Down to an apartment no one but I have entered in nearly a decade. The walls are lined with steel to keep out the rats and poured concrete to keep out sound and moisture. The interior is sleek and contemporary, but bathed in gloom.

My real body lies on a hospital bed; wires and tubes sprout from my withered face and emaciated limbs like alien weeds. The *hiss-chunk* of a respirator echoes against tile and bare walls. Drops of nourishment plunk from the plastic sack into the IV tube. My heart rate, monitored by digital lines and cold numbers, is steady. My temperature normal.

I pause outside of myself, looking down in disgust.

No one has seen this monstrosity—the real me—in years, nearly a decade now. I will need to return to it soon. Walk it around, build up its strength before I possess another handsome disguise and set up a new alter-me in a new city.

But first there is Curtis. If I let him walk away, he will talk and some will listen. A minor problem, but one I don't need.

He's probably still holding the gun.

So I rise from my actual home, leaving my real body to accept technological ministrations, and I soar back toward the penthouse and Curtis—a beautiful casualty of my plans. They will find him on the floor next to the body I have recently vacated, a bullet in his head. Murder-suicide. Tragic. Romantic.

Revolutions devour the weak.

THE ICE KING
Tom Cardamone

Tom Cardamone is the editor of *The Lost Library: Gay Fiction Rediscovered*, and author of the speculative novella, *Green Thumb*, and the erotic fantasy novel, *The Werewolves of Central Park*. His short story collection, *Pumpkin Teeth*, was a finalist for the Lambda Literary Award. His fiction has appeared in numerous anthologies and magazines, some of which can be read on his website: *pumpkinteeth.net*.

The Ice King walked into The Bear Trap off of Twelfth Avenue and stood, allowing the patrons hunkered at the bar to size him up. He liked to be admired. The men mostly looked like him: overly masculine, large and in leather. Several shaved heads wrapped in aviator glasses regarded him and, though no obvious emotion was revealed, The Ice King knew he was lusted after. He always was.

Music pulsed. A few men pretending to be bored lifted drinks. Under the red lights the alcohol in the bottom of their glasses shone like diluted, bloody mucus. He stepped up to the bar and placed a boot on the rail. Men in jackets and leather pants turned to exhibit their hard-won physiques. The Ice King's chiseled musculature was strapped by a leather-studded harness that crossed his chest and back, buckling at the waist of his leather chaps. Everyone was dressed like him in his own way, but no one else wore gloves. Cracking his knuckles produced an icy vapor, imperceptible in the darkness of the bar.

When he takes off his gloves, people die at his frozen touch.

The Ice King put a leather finger to his moustache and smoothed his upper lip. He was thirsty, but not for alcohol. Under natural light it would have been more noticeable that his skin was completely white, but he was not an albino. He *was* ice. Flesh steely, like a distant mountain peak; beneath the permanent tundra cold, lifeless rock. Metallic blue pupils swirled around white irises. His arctic gaze could freeze anyone and anything.

The bartender eyed him wearily but The Ice King ignored him, absently stroking the long scar that marred his perfect bicep. The memory of that battle, the particular super hero who administered the punishment, bordering on total defeat, filled him with anger. And anger led to arousal.

He exhaled frozen breath. *The fools probably think I'm smoking.* He puckered and blew lazy smoke rings of chilled air toward the ceiling. A fair-haired twink sashayed by, giving him a long look. He had always liked blonds.

The boy cocked his hips as he walked; ridiculously tight vinyl pants shivered low across his shapely ass. He paused at the stairwell to the basement and looked back at The Ice King, his parted lips glossy, feminine. The Ice King followed. The music wasn't as oppressively loud toward the back of the bar. The lights were fewer. No one noticed the icy vapor rising from the snowy footprints he left on the floor. Numerous bars throughout the world were named The Bear Trap. The only thing they had in common was the type of men they attracted: ready and willing. Likely he had been to all of them. He couldn't remember the layout of this one though, and relished the anticipation welling up within; it was rare that any emotion broke through his permafrost of disdain.

He descended the stairs into a labyrinthine bathroom of doorless stalls and leaky urinals. A florescent tube hung askew from the ceiling and flickered weakly. The stale air stank of piss and cheap poppers and cigarette smoke. Now he remembered: there *was* a backroom. The broom closet concealed a gross curtain that led to an ancient basement, practically a cave, with an earthen floor to soak up the sweat and semen of desperate animal assignations. The Ice King stepped into the antechamber crowded with mops rancid from the sour scent of bleach. He could hear men panting, sucking and wallowing in the darkness. These men were the clay he would sculpt.

In bathhouses and backrooms, when the mood struck, he fashioned icy atrocities, orchestras of men frozen in acts of fellatio, masturbating strange flowers of arrested sperm arching in the air, mouths opened in screams of ecstasy or death, stalactites of sweat hanging off their chins. First he would observe the men, pushing away any who approached so he could better study the action of the room. And when the men reached a crescendo he thought aesthetically pleasing, he would take off his gloves and touch the nearest coupling. Walking through the room, he spread winter. All froze and he would pause by the door and exhale a final, wintry blast of satisfaction. Art wrongly considered a crime when discovered. He knew his vision was unappreciated by the masses, much less the authorities. Still, his only hope was that the police photographers accurately captured his work and preserved it for future generations. Possibly when the sun had dimmed and the world had grown colder, became a bit more like *him*, only then would his work gain the recognition it deserved.

The twink stepped from the shadows. The Ice King had seen enough. He grabbed the boy roughly by the back of his hair and jerked his mouth open. The boy gasped in surprise but fumbled eagerly for The Ice King's zipper. They kissed and the temperature in the room suddenly dropped. He savored the swirl of fear and excitement in the boy's eyes, and watched closely as they became cloudy with frost.

Winter came.

🟊

The Ice King slowly rose above the city on a cloud of ice particles. With minimal concentration he could successively freeze and unfreeze the moisture in the air in such a way as to propel him to serious heights and at great speed. Obscured by clouds, he traveled the world, delivering icy mayhem wherever he pleased. The cold hell he created in the back room at the Bear Trap should have given him immense pleasure, but he was left wanting. The scar on his arm ached as he considered its source: the Canadian hero, Light Stream. The one time they had grappled Light Stream prevailed. Yet as the embodiment of cold, The Ice King considered himself a harbinger of death, so to have been thwarted—rather than feel defeated, he felt challenged. He was drawn to the earnestness of Light Stream, though usually revolted by such sincerity, coming from the hero it seemed wistful, and also oddly familiar. The Ice King wanted to return the touch, leave his own scars before freezing the blood in those "heroic" veins. The way his long hair had whipped about his face as they fought, hand-to-hand, high in the sky... he had always liked blonds.

A new destination fixed in his mind, he turned and flew north over the city. Sirens wailed below. The Empire State building stung the low clouds. Appropriately, the landmark was lit white. Snow white.

🟊

Mother Bear lived in a simple cabin on an island off the coast of Maine. She owned the island, as well as property in the Rocky Mountains. She often shared the island with the occasional girlfriend, though Mother Bear was short-tempered and her lovers never lasted long. Mother Bear was one of those mutants the government worried so much about. Worse, she was fully dedicated to realizing their worst fears. As the founder of the Annihilators, she attempted to forge a group to counter the World Guardians; where the Guardians strove to ease the world's ills, the Annihilators worked to both spread and benefit from chaos. Unfortunately, the other Annihilators were jailed or dead. Only Mother Bear had escaped and, though she quietly scoured the world for new villains to re-assemble her team, she was battle-weary. She spent more and more time in bear-form, scavenging in the woods, fishing with her paws in streams or napping in dark caves. Of the villains she had originally approached, The Ice King was the only one who had refused to join *and* survived her formidable anger at being rebuffed. His cold fortitude had earned him her respect, and then begrudging friendship.

He landed on her island. Frost from his dispersing cloud mingled with the morning mist and painted a thick mat of pine needles white. The island was covered with pine trees. The rocky ground never really leveled, slowing any approach to the cabin. The cabin was built into a hill, one side on stilts, with firewood stored beneath. He listened carefully as he approached but heard only birdsong. Smoke rose from the chimney: she was home. He formed a snowball in the palm of his hand and lobbed it at a window—a direct hit. He saw movement and the window swung open. Mother Bear pushed the hair out of her eyes and gave him a casual wave. A rare smile cracked his face.

She was still pulling on a pair of old jeans as he entered the cabin. Her door was always unlocked. This was her island and anyone who entered uninvited did so at great peril. The cabin was one big room, toasty from the fire in the fireplace. She immediately opened more windows to cool the room on his behalf and then walked over to give him a great big bear hug. The constant cold that radiated from his flesh never bothered her; bears can naturally withstand low temperatures. He relaxed and fell into an old recliner. A four-poster bed under a jumble of flannel sheets consumed one whole corner. The walls were covered with shelves stocked with necessities. The floor was carpeted with deer-skin rugs, animals Mother Bear had hunted and killed herself. A giant freezer stretched beside an equally large refrigerator. She offered him coffee, black. He took the mug and blew on it until it was perfectly chilled. He realized that he was jet-lagged and malnourished; he hadn't slept or eaten in days.

"Your handiwork made the news." She blew on her own steaming cup of coffee and nodded toward the television. When she wasn't rambling in the woods for days on end, Mother Bear was glued to the television. She was a news junkie, constantly channel surfing for news of unexplained phenomena that might help her locate new, hopefully malicious mutants. That and she devoured true crime paperbacks. He often teased her over her choice of literature and yet he relished the facts she would spout about serial killers and Nazis.

"Yes, it was one of my better sculpture gardens." He yawned.

"You look famished, dear. I'm making stew." The light aroma of which had just reached him.

Dirty hiking boots much too small for Mother Bear stood idle by the door. A bloody bone protruded from one. He eyed her.

"Oh you didn't."

"Well she couldn't play cards worth a damn, and I was getting hungry." She exaggeratedly licked her lips and smiled.

The Ice King let out a short chortle. "You and your girlfriends. You'll never settle down."

She lifted the spoon to her lips and blew.

"Yes, I'm something of a nomad, but not as much as you. I can tell this is just a stopover, what are you planning?"

His eyelids grew heavy. "Something big, something really, really big," he yawned.

Sleep was an impending avalanche of shadows.

⚡

The Ice King woke in total darkness. It was well past midnight and the cabin was still. Through the open window stars were visible in the night sky. He felt rested and ready to leave, but knew that would be rude. Not that Mother Bear would mind, but he hadn't come all this way just to power nap. She snored and shifted under a mound of blankets.

He put his hands behind his head. Mother Bear was a large woman, what people would call "big boned." Crooked teeth and a man's chin were softened only by the thick brown hair which curled to her waist. Reading glasses also made her look less dangerous, more librarian than carnivore. Yet besides himself, she was the most treacherous criminal he knew. Likely they were drawn together because they were equally misunderstood; while often labeled "psychopaths," each had a natural understanding of what other people were to them: prey.

The room was still lightly scented from the stew. Though he didn't eat as much of it as she did—no one could put away food like Mother Bear—he savored the rawness of the undercooked meat, the naturalness of the sparsely used herbs and spices she had caringly gathered from the woodlands of her island. Both had laughed when she had momentarily gagged and then spat out a human tooth.

When The Ice King reflected on the difference between himself and others among the elite of the super powered, there was one singular factor: determination. Mutants were a genetic crapshoot, some with a less-than-fortunate outcome. None had purposefully sought power as The Ice King had. He had struggled in the industry of cryogenics. His willingness to experiment and take risks was frowned upon by the very management poised to reap profits from the outcome. That was lesson number one: the brightest are always managed by the dim, the weary, the weak. He was once weak. So he trained his body as he had trained his mind, consistently and toward two goals: strength and success.

In his experiments he asked himself a simple question. *If we can preserve a dead body by lowering its temperature, why not find a way to strengthen a living being with the same principles?* He thought it was ludicrous and limited that his field was focused solely on conservation, and not enhancement. Revolutionary ideas weare often dismissed as the ravings of madmen, so he kept quiet. He needed equipment and chemicals and research subjects, not peer approval. He still savored the memory of blowing out the windows of the laboratory. Shocked employees gathered in the parking lot. They thought the clouds smoke, the initial snow, ash. They were perplexed when they saw their breath. When the first frozen corpse of a security guard was hurled onto the pavement below, shattering like an icicle, they ran for their cars. He laughed as they fled. Testing his new powers, he conjured blasts of icy wind, strong enough to rip through the elevator doors and sever the suspending cables, dropping those trapped within to their doom. Going from office to office, he killed at random. Laughing, he commanded swirls of snow and ice to shoot from his hands and coat every surface. Desks turned into giant ice cubes. And if a luckless secretary huddled beneath it, so be it. He had made no friends at the company. That thought, in particular, had made him howl in delight. Everyone had called him the "ice queen," and not always behind his back. Now he had showed them he was, indeed, made of ice. *He* was in control, *he* was the strong one. A thin layer of ice frost covered his skin and hardened against the words, the snickering –he was finally, truly, impenetrably, cold.

Mother Bear shifted in her bed. The Ice King squinted, trying to discern what shape she had taken. Often she slept in bear form. A most peculiar aspect of her transformation: when she shifted, her animal form was male. Functionally male. Size-wise, *impressively* male. A massive furry paw kicked the covers away. The Ice King rose from the recliner and thought, *isn't it dangerous to disturb a sleeping bear?* He took a running jump and dove into the bed. Mother Bear, annoyed, desolately roared. She swiftly pinned him, bearing her teeth less than an inch from his face. He pulled on her fur. She batted him roughly until he rolled on his stomach. The claw marks that marred his back from their last encounter were permanent. He relished the scars, that she could cut through his icy layers. Her rising girth threatened his buttocks; she slashed his leather jockstrap to ribbons and bore down with all her weight. A mighty roar shook the nearby trees, overshadowing his whimpers of delight.

⚡

Light Stream flew high over Lake St. Claire. The sight of the desolate, choppy waters below cleared his mind. Though he spent most of his time flying between Vancouver and the newly erected headquarters of the World Guardians in New York, he relished his trips to Toronto. He loved the height of the city, and like the residents there, thought of it as a cleaner, more civilized Manhattan. And the Great North. To be able to dive off the top of CN Tower and rush across the mountains and over untouched forest was the only time he felt at peace. Above a large portion of the world without humanity, Light Stream was able to free himself from the confines of the word "hero." Sometimes he thought that if he ever wore a cape he would wrap it around his neck and choke himself; of all the members of World Guardians, he was the only one who seemed to *live* the mission. The others shed all responsibilities when they took off their masks. Well he didn't wear a mask. He was through with masks. In high school and college, well after he knew he had been blessed with the ability to fly and bend light, he never dared use his powers. He never acted on his desire to soar, to snap his fingers and spin lightning into the air. No, it took him a long time to know who he was and why he was here. That left no room for masks. His costume was designed strictly for aerodynamics. He had purposefully chosen a dark purple to help pilots see him at a great distance. His hair was long simply because he never thought to get it cut. He didn't think of himself as handsome and was amused by how the press portrayed him as vainglorious. As a flock of geese changed direction to avoid him, he banked low, giving them plenty of room.

Flying close to the lake, spray from the choppy water flecked his face. Whenever he was alone, feeling the pressures of his chosen path, he compulsively reviewed those moments in his earlier life when he had failed to grapple with his problems, the opportunities he had let slip away, needs that had gone unexpressed and unfulfilled. He remembered his first college roommate. They were both the skinniest boys in the dorm, the bespectacled outcasts. All that they had in common should have bound them together, but they never formed a friendship, rarely spoke beyond the bland pleasantries demanded by their shared space. Yet at night, from the bottom bunk, Light Stream could tell when his roommate was pretending to sleep, that they both were awake, aware of their barely clothed bodies, yearning to be touched. But they only touched once, the last night of the semester. After summer break he returned to the dorm room, having stored up the courage to confront his roommate about their mutual inclinations, only to find that the other boy had transferred to another college without so much as a goodbye. It was something he had always regretted, yet the moment was a catalyst. It was at that point that he decided to live deliberately and plot his difficult destiny.

He rose slightly to avoid a buoy and decided to head back to the city. *But which one? Wherever I decide to go there will be a problem I need to solve, an emergency to tackle. And wherever I don't visit, a crime will be committed.* Funny, now that he had finally come to terms with his powers and had dedicated his life to public service, gained the rock hard body such training and discipline demand, he still found himself attracted to the youngish, thin men who sheepishly asked for his autograph, their intelligence and interest shining through their thick glasses. He knew that his nervousness at their proximity came off as typical superhero aloofness; this in turn fueled their worshipful deference, meaning he slept alone most nights and, when in Manhattan, was forced to dine out with whatever character from the World Guardians happened to be available.

Just as he turned north, he noticed an unusual glimmer from within a dark cloud over Detroit. Even though he had flown all over the continent, he still found it unusual that an oddity of geography placed Detroit north of parts of Canada. The black cloud was stationary over the city. Light seemingly reflected off a new skyscraper from within, impressive at even such a distance. Light Stream decided to investigate.

I don't remember seeing a new skyscraper the last time I flew over Detroit. And Detroit was a shrinking city. It had lost population in the seventies and never recouped. Its crime rate made him a repeat visitor. New construction of this magnitude and speed was unbelievable.

Instinctively, Light Stream again flew low to camouflage his approach. He slowed his speed to better assess the situation and, as he did so, the hero noticed a considerable dip in the temperature. Large chucks of ice started to crowd the waters below.

But it's only September.

He was close enough to discern that the Marriott hotel, the tallest building in the city, had been engulfed by ice. Frozen towers shot up into the air, so much ice that the massive complex of skyscrapers known as the Renaissance Center that surrounded the hotel was consumed as well. Light Stream hovered and shivered, gripping his thick shoulders he marveled at the giant crystal castle; it was nearly a work of art. But within the frozen turrets he noticed little black dots. He floated closer. People. A man with a briefcase. A woman still in her robe frozen in mid-leap as she tried to escape the surging cold by jumping out of her hotel room window.

The Ice King.

Light Stream's frame glowed with an angry light. His powers roiled and halos of angry sparks ignited around his wrists. Immediately, he soared upward and sought a defensive position in the clouds. Just as the Ice King had planned. The blow from behind was powerful. The impact knocked the breath out of him. Light Stream exhaled and folded and would have fallen except for the cold arms that embraced him. Consciousness flickered and for a moment he relaxed into the arms that gripped his chest. The clouds were sheets and pillows and this was the way he wanted to wake up in the morning, caressed lightly, strong arms around him, protecting him, loving him. But the embrace was cold. The dull burn of frostbite bit through his costume and he was revived but at a loss. *Why hasn't the Ice King tried to kill me?* And with that he felt a slight nip on his ear, the tickle of a frigid kiss, and he was released.

Light Stream plummeted. The cold villain floating above shrunk rapidly, mockingly waving "bye-bye" as the hero fell. Light Stream struggled to regain flight but he was falling too fast; the cold of that kiss clung to him like a memory. *That last night in the dorms. It was hot and humid. Both boys slept on top of their sheets, or tried to sleep. The sound of his roommate shifting restlessly above, struggling against the oppressive heat, was just too much. In his mind he had climbed to the top bunk a thousand times and added his heat to that of his roommate's. He noisily shifted on his mattress and in a moment of frustration, he stripped off his sweaty underwear and threw them into the middle of the room. Startled by his own rash action, he froze as his roommate moved heavily above. The mattress groaned and he covered himself with the damp sheet as his roommate, too, tossed his underwear onto the floor. Both pairs overlapped—white flags of surrender on the threadbare carpet. Silence. Neither boy moved. And then from the top bunk his roommate dangled one leg, then the other. An excruciating minute passed. The young Light Stream reached out and tentatively stroked one fuzzy calf. Both boys shivered and in an instant his roommate had jumped down and turned to face him, proudly displaying his body, his arms above his head gripped the railing of the bunk bed. Shadows leaked from his armpits and painted his ribcage and thin waist in darkness.*

His roommate, who had always been so cold, never changing clothes when they were in the room together, now swayed alluringly just inches from his face. The young Light Stream was breathless. Worried that he would accidentally levitate, he grabbed the mattress and the sheet which covered his nakedness fell away. His roommate examined his body, first with his eyes, then with hesitant fingers. Both boys gasped as each simultaneously gripped the other's heat, sweaty palms demanding that they pull on one another and join, one boy on top the other, lips together, sharing the same hot breath yet never actually kissing, except for a furtive nibble on his ear.

Falling fast as a bullet, Light Stream blinked. He must have momentarily passed out. With a bust of adrenaline he summoned all of his power and braked hard. And The Ice King flew by as Light Stream hovered in midair to gain his bearings. The Ice King banked far below. Light Stream bobbed in the sky, the memories from college still fresh in his mind.

His roommate had always been so cold.

Perplexed, Light Stream levitated and watched as The Ice King approached within a black cloud trailing icy hail.

Impossible, he's so big. Well of course it could be him, why would I assume he'd still be so skinny. College was almost twenty years ago. Look at how I've changed.

And he realized that he had changed in all the right ways.

No matter my challenges, I always faced them. My old roommate had run away. And look at what he had become.

✖

The Ice King drew on the knowledge of their first battle, and surmised that Light Stream drew power from the sun. He kept the sky dark with thick snow clouds. Whenever the hero rallied, The Ice King would drop large formations of ice onto the dumbstruck crowd shivering in the streets below, using Light Stream's morality against him. Though the villain was proud of his strategy, and Light Stream certainly looked bested, his blond hair was matted to his back with frost and sweat, The Ice King couldn't help but feel that the hero was holding back. He craved more than an epic melee and flew closer, to better encase his foe in ice and bring the combat to more intimate terms. The weary hero prepared for the onslaught and turned slightly, so The Ice King would not see the ball of energy forming in his hand. But as he bobbed in the wind, he allowed the powerful globe of light to dissipate. He extended his hands, palms out, and tried another weapon.

The Ice King was upon him. Bitter cold lashed his cheeks as the villain raised his fists, now covered with frozen icicles, ready to pummel Light Stream.

"Kelvin, is that you?"

The Ice King faltered. The largest icicle protruding from his knuckles cracked and tumbled to the frozen waters below. No one had called him by his given name in years, not since he had gone cold at the laboratory. He'd thought that name was gone, dead, buried in the snow banks of his fury.

"It's me, William, your roommate freshman year."

A variety of emotions flashed across the tundra of The Ice King's face. Reflexively, he fingered the scar on his arm. Light Stream floated closer and looked into the eyes of this killer, this madman, the dangerous freak who had playfully decimated the community Light Stream has sworn to protect. They had known each other briefly, during an innocent yet formative time, when neither knew what it was that they wanted, except that such desire made them outcasts. Light Stream's gaze was met with frosty resistance that wavered with recognition, and then longing.

They kissed. And Light Stream held The Ice King as the surrounding storm cloud dissipated into harmless rain. His hapless former foe fumbled in the air and finally relented and clung to Light Stream, who continued to kiss him deeply, with a kiss of forgiveness, understanding and passion. And it was too late for the wide-eyed villain to disengage once he realized that it was one of those rare kisses hot enough to melt ice.

LESSER EVIL
'Nathan Burgoine

'Nathan Burgoine lives in Ottawa with his husband Daniel, where he tries not to summon any demons unless it's really important. His short fiction appears in *Fool For Love*, *I Do Two*, *Saints + Sinners 2011: New Fiction From the Festival*, *Men of the Mean Streets*, *Boys Of Summer*, *The Touch Of The Sea*, and *Night Shadows*. His non-fiction appears in *I Like It Like That* and *5x5 Literary Magazine*. His first novel, *Light*, is forthcoming from Bold Strokes Books. You can find him online at *redroom.com/member/nathan-burgoine*.

The first time, I thought I had been invisible.

It was an easy mistake to make. No one reacted to me, no one had even looked at me, and so the next time I felt that pressure in my head and noticed no one looking, I gathered my first pathetic attempt at a costume—black gloves, black turtleneck, black pants, and one of my mother's Mardi Gras masks, also painted black. My head throbbed as I walked to the mall. I'd been convinced that if anyone had seen me, I would have known. At the very least, they would have pointed and laughed. That I was used to.

But no one reacted at all, and I walked right into the sports memorabilia store and took the signed football I knew Erik Miller wanted. I walked out, went home, and took off my mask and gloves—God they were itchy—and sat in awe of myself while I waited for the headache to fade.

Me. Tristan Edwards. Meta-powered. Invisibility. No one was ever going to hurt me again. I stared at the football for over an hour, dabbing at my nosebleed, picturing Erik opening it on his birthday.

And then I turned on the television, and saw myself on the news. "A bizarre crime," they called it, where "a masked man walked into the store in broad daylight." I was perfectly visible on the cameras, and the newscaster related that, strangely, no eyewitnesses could recall seeing the thief, and that the only thing stolen was an autographed football.

I wasn't able to breathe. I hid the football under the loose boards in my closet, and burned the clothes and mother's Mardi Gras mask.

I wasn't invisible. At least not to the cameras.

I couldn't give the football to Erik Miller. I hadn't gotten to hear him say "thank you," or look at me with gratitude. My headache grew worse so I laid down in my room.

When my father came home and I wasn't at dinner the headache was too strong for me to make myself invisible again; I cringed and tried not to cry while he yelled about how hopeless I was. I went to bed long before my mother got home.

❧

My costume always sits a bit heavy on my shoulders. No matter the improvements or the variations I've tried in style or shape, putting in Kevlar adds more than a few pounds along with the protection. Not that Kevlar will help against

Aleph. Still, I park my car in the empty lot and wait for a moment, adjusting the straps and tightening my gloves. I glance in the rear view mirror and put on the half-mask, though it's not likely anyone is going to see us.

I become Psilence. Not a particularly terrifying name, but I prefer to be underestimated.

No doubt Aleph is already here. The drive-in is long abandoned, a large open space where cars used to line up to watch movies on warm summer nights. I wonder if it has any meaning to Aleph, or if it's just a convenient place for him to meet someone he doesn't trust.

I tap my finger on the steering wheel a few times, and then get out of the car. The door echoes like a gunshot when I close it, and I roll my eyes. Aleph can fly, of course, which is colossally unfair in the scheme of things. I have always envied the ones who can fly, or teleport, or move at super-speed. It has more dramatic impact than stepping out of a Mazda. I resist the urge to feel around with my mind.

The burst of light is nearly blinding even through the smoky lenses set into my half-mask, and I throw up a hand. Ozone crackles in the air. The white-hot energy that Aleph can generate has formed a perfect circle around me, nearly shoulder high.

He walks out from behind the dilapidated, shuttered concession stand. He's in his costume, too. His face-plate is a matte bronze, like most of the rest of his outfit, with the exception of the single white Hebrew letter in the middle of his chest: the aleph.

I'm a little surprised he actually came, even now. Did a message from some-one as pathetic as me even deserve a response? I was hardly worth his attention.

But then he must have wondered how I'd known where he was in the first place. I'd left a letter at his front door—to his real name. That was something a villain of Aleph's calibre would have to resolve.

"You're Psilence?" he asks.

I nod. "Yeah."

"I had to Google you," he says.

Ouch.

"I'm a subtle guy," I say. It's the best I can come up with.

"You must have a death wish," he says.

I swallow. It all comes down to this. I veil, and vanish from his mind.

❦

Watching Cinder land at the campsite made my stomach clench. He was lean, and tall, and never the one the magazines put on the cover. That "honor" usually fell to Lustre, with her statuesque beauty, large breasts, and that borderline scandalous suit of gold and white she wore, or Cirrus, with her genuine prettiness. If the media wanted beefcake they played up Noire's Cajun bad-boy looks and broad chest—and the tattoos—or Touchdown, who had the look of a military man and an attitude to match. Cinder is the leader, but he was red-haired and soft voiced and didn't like the spotlight.

A flyer, Cinder's body sent off waves of heat as he landed. He was wearing the mirrored visor. I wondered if his eyes are bothering him again, or if he was just trying to hide most of his face from me.

"I can tell you're here."

His voice was jarring, something I'd never expected to hear again. I took me a second to recover, to remember how to breathe. I hadn't meant to telepathically veil myself from him, and it had never quite worked all the way with Cinder anyway. It was something to do with the way he could feel heat, a sense I couldn't disrupt.

I stopped influencing his other senses, and he turned to look at me. He was wearing his black uniform. Covert ops—a strength of his.

"Hi," he said. That damned visor pissed me off. I couldn't see his eyes, and I couldn't bring myself to go into his mind. I didn't dare.

Instead, I tried to keep my face blank. "I got your message, Jeff."

His lips quirked at his name—his real name. "I'm glad you came," he said. "You look good."

That hurt. I cringed.

"I mean it." Cinder shook his head. "I'm clean, Tristan. They... undid everything."

I took a breath. *Why did he contact me?* There was only one way to find out. "What do you want, Jeff?"

❦

My father and mother stared at me, she sad, he—as always—just angry.

"You skipped school again?"

I opened my mouth to defend myself, but then closed it again. I had been at school. I'd even written the test. But then that asshole Jimmy Potts started to whisper behind me. He called me a fag. Told me he was going to kick my ass. I saw Erik Miller smirk and I wanted to hide. I wanted to be somewhere else, somewhere no one could ever find me. I wanted the earth to open up and swallow me whole.

And it happened again.

At first, when the whispering stopped, I thought maybe Jimmy had caught the teacher looking at him. I didn't care and was just glad it was over. My head ached again, and a red drop hit my test-paper.

Another nosebleed.

I raised my hand to be excused, mortified that everyone was going to see me like this again, but Mr. King didn't even glanced my way.

"Sir?" I said.

He hadn't so much as blinked.

My head had been throbbing, and my nose dripped again.

Fuck it, I'd thought, and got up. I walked right up to him.

"Mr. King, my nose is bleeding."

He didn't acknowledge me.

My head throbbed, duller than before—and then I heard something.

Tristan's absent again. It was Mr. King's voice, but he hadn't opened his mouth.

"What?" I'd said.

Going to have to tell his parents. I leaned forward, putting my hands on his desk. Some of my blood spilled onto his calendar. I stared at his lips, but they never moved. My head had felt like it was splitting. *I hope his father doesn't go off on him again.*

He'd known. He'd known about my dad, and… he was thinking about it. I stood up straighter, ignoring the pain in my skull. I had always been good at ignoring pain. Hearing someone's thoughts, not as much. I squinted. Looking into his eyes seemed to make it easier.

Poor kid isn't even that smart. He's got nothing, Mr. King thought.

I'd pushed off from his desk and walked out of the classroom.

No one had reacted at all—and I started to think I knew why.

But with my mother and father standing in front of me, fresh from their call with the school, I'd not quite gotten it together enough to concentrate. My head felt funny—sort of throbbing—but I hadn't heard what they were thinking.

"I had a nosebleed."

"Jesus, you're such a wimp," my father said. Then he clenched his fist.

I flinched. My mother took his arm but he shook her off.

"You're barely passing," my father voice dripped with contempt. "If you don't get good grades, what are you going to do? You're no athlete."

"Yeah, I know," I snapped back.

"You giving me guff, boy? Football got me through college. I didn't have parents willing to foot the bill. I'm not throwing money away on nothing."

"Jack," my mother said, touching his arm again. "He had a nosebleed."

"Pansy ass boy."

"Shut up!" I yelled. It exploded out of me. My head felt like it would burst with the pain, and my nose had erupted again. I leaned forward, gagging and pinching my nose, waiting for my father's tirade but it didn't come.

"Jack?" my mother's voice croaked with worry.

I looked up. My father's mouth was open as he stared wildly around the room.

"Jack? Are you okay?"

My father shook his head. He broke out in a sweat. His mouth moved silently.

I can't talk! His voice panicked inside my head. *I can't talk!*

He met my gaze, eyes wide.

I smiled.

✥

"Lewis Nicolas," Cinder said.

I hadn't expected that. One good thing about barely being a member of the team had always been having time to read the files. I still remembered most of it.

"Aleph?"

Cinder nodded. His jaw was tight.

I was confused. "I'm flattered you think so highly of me, but I'm afraid I can't rat him out for you. He plays in the big leagues, Jeff." I raised my hands. "We don't belong to the same golf club. I'm nothing."

Cinder looked at me, or at least I thought he did. Bloody visor. "Tristan."

"I'm nothing," I said.

✹

It had been weird seeing them up so close. I hadn't thought they'd ever been anywhere near our town, yet here they were, gathered around my favourite campsite up in the hills outside of town. Me—a twenty year old part-time gas jockey—and two agents from the North American Metahuman Defence Agency. Superheroes.

Cirrus had been pretty, her chestnut hair back in a ponytail, and up close I'd been able to see that behind the mask, her eyes were also brown. I'd always liked her simple costume—a rich blue colour with a white sash. Cinder was taller than I thought he'd be, wearing his gold and red costume, which I'd always thought was a bit over the top.

"Tristan Edwards?" Cirrus asked. Her eyes glanced at my left eye—which was puffy and swollen and an ugly purple colour.

I nodded.

Cirrus smiled. "Don't be nervous."

That made me laugh. "Right. I nearly killed someone."

"So you said in your e-mail."

I hugged my arms around myself. It was freezing up there in my t-shirt.

Cinder raised a hand, and the air in the small clearing grew noticeably warmer.

"Thanks," I said, my first words to him.

"What happened?" Cirrus sounded genuinely concerned.

"There were these guys who were shoving me around. I could tell they were bashers—they were thinking about beating me up." This had made Cinder frown a little, and I rushed on. "I think I'm a telepath." I bit my lip. I clearly remembered telling the first bruiser to pick on someone his own size, and he turned and started attacking his friend.

I took a deep breath. "I think I can make people do things."

⚡

"We know where Aleph is." Cinder's voice was quiet.

That stopped me. "What?"

"We know where he is." Cinder worked his jaw. He kept all his stress there. I always liked that about him. He ground his teeth at night, and had to wear a mouth guard. The man could fly, could project and manipulate heat and flame high into the Kelvin scale, but at night he tried to grind his teeth down to nubs. Sometimes I gave him a face massage when N.A.M.D.A. was on a heavy assignment and he was working insane hours. It had been a way he was vulnerable with me. I loved that.

He was also really warm. Most nights we'd managed with just a sheet.

"I don't get it," I admitted. Part of me itched to just go into his mind and make him tell me what he wanted. But I didn't.

Cinder pulled the visor off. Hazel eyes. Nothing special, but God they cut through me. Because Jeff looked at me with a mild kindness, and a little pity. No love.

"We know where he is," he repeated. "But we..." He swallowed. "We can't handle him."

I knew him well enough to know how much that had cost him to say. Especially to me. There was a coldness in the bottom of my stomach. "Jeff –"

"Aleph can manipulate energy like that," Cinder said and snapped his fingers. "He can collapse Lustre's lightfields, put out my fire and Cirrus's lightning, even block Noire's bolts. Touchdown can't get near enough to him. Every time Aleph's been knocked back even a little, it's been a telepath."

"I know," I said. "I do watch the news. Didn't Mentaliste almost knock him out cold last time? I'm sure she'd be up for it again. Go team, and all that crap." I'd raised one fist.

"Mentaliste's pregnant."

I couldn't help it. I laughed. "No shit. Touchdown gonna make an honest woman of her?"

Cinder's mouth twitched again. "They got married last month. On the sly. Vegas."

"Well, I'd ask you to pass on my congratulations, but…" I shrugged. "I hear she's not a fan of my work."

Cinder's smile vanished. Wrong thing to say.

"Tristan," he said. "You owe me."

⚡

Recon had become my code-name, not that it really mattered. I was unofficial. Everyone remembered Titiritero—the Mexican telepath who dominated others into committing crimes—and no one wanted the Agency to go public about bringing a telepath on board. It would have been a PR nightmare. I found that my first trick had been my best asset—making the minds of other people ignore me completely—and it had been the one I ended up using the most. Touchdown quickly grew tired of trying to teach me hand-to-hand combat, something for which I hadn't the strength or the aptitude. On the rare occasions when they brought me along, I mostly stayed veiled and used my telepathy to let them know what was going on inside a building with hostages, or force a surrender before things could become violent.

Noire thought I was creepy—I'd found that hilarious coming from a guy who could manipulate shadows—and though Cirrus and Lustre had always been polite, it had been obvious that I was in every way a "reserve" member. I was never on the posters or interviewed in the magazines. I had been strictly a back-up, a telepath that had been useful for a few types of missions, but mostly stayed at home.

That had all been okay by me. All I'd ever wanted was a place where I could be quiet. I'd been getting much better at reading minds—once I begun actively using the ability it seemed to grow stronger whenever I truly pushed myself—and in time, the challenge had instead become *not* hearing thoughts.

Which was how I figured out that I wasn't the only gay guy on the team.

Cinder had taken my accidental snooping well, and I redoubled my efforts to stop reading thoughts by accident, mostly succeeding. He was a calm guy, though I knew he carried a lot of stress around from being the leader, and also from keeping a part of himself hidden from the others.

By the time I'd been with the group for almost three years, I knew I had fallen in love with him. The arrival of the time-traveling Quantum—Colin Reichert—warning us of a villainous temporal incursion had put us all on the edge—I'd been constantly exhausted trying to help the temporally displaced hero figure out who was from our timeline and who wasn't by reading their thoughts. Maintaining a secret in that atmosphere had been impossible, and Cinder came out to the rest of the group. They were nothing but happy for him, which was nice. Colin stayed, and Quantum became a powerful new addition to the team. Jeff remained as quiet as ever, though he opened up to me a little more once we started to spend more time together on our own. When it was all over, and I finally worked up the nerve to invite him on one of my camping trips, I was pleasantly surprised when he accepted.

✺

"I assume you're not asking me back to the team," I said. I forced some amusement into my voice.

Cinder just looked at me.

"I wouldn't last a minute in a fight with Aleph, Jeff. Not without the rest of you to back me up."

His jaw clenched again. "He's worked with partners before."

It took me a second to realize what he was suggesting. Partners. I remembered everything I'd read in Aleph's file. And everything that hadn't been in there, except if you happened to notice. *Partners.*

I veiled.

Cinder reached out, but I already stepped aside. "Tristan... wait!" He turned his head, frowning. He knew I was still there. "Tristan, please."

I waited. At least while I was veiled he couldn't see me hugging myself and trying not to cry.

✺

"That was certainly more efficient than when I do it," I said.

Jeff smiled at me—a rare treat, and he looked so handsome. He made the campfire burst into flame with just a single pointed finger.

He looked good in the green t-shirt I gave him for his birthday.

"I don't think I've ever been camping before," he said.

"I love it. I've done it since I was a kid." I looked at him. "Thanks for coming."

He nodded, and then his jaw tightened. Unintentionally, I'd dipped into his thoughts. *Tell him.*

I felt my heart lurch to triple-time. Jeff stared into the flames, not moving. It was adorable: he was struggling to find a way to tell me. I hadn't been able to stand to watch the poor guy suffer. Not after how kind he'd been with me.

"Go ahead," I said.

He'd looked at me, surprised but obviously a bit relieved. "Oh," he said.

"I feel the same way," I took his hand.

He withdrew it. "Wait." He frowned. "The same way?"

My stomach had gone tight. "What were you going to tell me?"

"Quantum—Colin—and I are…" He blushed. I'd never seen him blush before. "We're giving it a shot. Dating, I mean." Then he frowned again. "But you feel the same way? You mean about Colin?"

My head throbbed. "Colin isn't even from our timeline."

Jeff's hazel eyes stared at me. "I'm…" Then he'd gotten it. "You meant me." His eyes filled with pity.

I rose. "I have to go." My voice was raw and weak, and I felt my eyes filling up.

Jeff stood. "Tristan."

"I'm an idiot," I said. "God, why am I such an idiot? I'm not special, right? I'm barely on the team. God—Quantum can bend time!" I shook my head, so angry at myself. "Imagine the sex."

"Hey," Jeff took my arm and looked me in the eyes. "I do like you. It's just… well, I think of you as…"

"Nothing?" I'd suggested.

"No," he said firmly. "You're my friend. I like you."

I stared into his eyes, and then did what should have been unthinkable. But it hadn't been. It was *easy*. I'd shoved hard.

"No, Jeff," I'd said, my head throbbing. "You love me."

���

When I stood across from him at the campfire, after what he'd said, I wondered if that's why he'd asked me to meet him here. The campsite. The scene of the crime, as it were.

"Aleph's partners were nearly as powerful as he is," I said. "And as I recall, they're both buried now."

Cinder turned to face where he heard my voice. "Yes."

"He's also a solo kind of guy. Both those partnerships weren't very stable," I said.

"I know," Cinder said. "Mentaliste thinks he's got trust issues."

I laughed.

※

We'd been fine until she arrived. Mentaliste, they'd decided to call her. Unlike me, she hadn't been a one-trick pony. Born in Quebec, Mentaliste had developed telepathic abilities like I had, though they were weaker—I'd allowed myself to be smug about that—but she was also telekinetic. My already small role became even smaller.

I didn't mind. I had Jeff, who loved me, though now and then I could feel some small part of him struggling with a detail or two, and every time I smoothed it out in his mind, it became a little easier to do. Colin—Quantum— had travelled into some random future, and Touchdown and Lustre made it perfectly clear who they blamed. But Jeff's loyalty had been total. We'd camped most weekends when he hadn't been on duty.

I'll give Mentaliste credit. I hadn't see it coming. Breaking into the mind of another telepath is a lot of work; she never gave me an outward sign of suspicion so I never read her thoughts. She had gone to Touchdown first—they had already become close—and the two of them had taken me by surprise.

We were in the kitchen, of all places. Jeff, Cirrus, Noire, and Lustre were out on an interview. It was just the three of us. That had been their only real mistake, looking back. People underestimate the weak.

"I know what you did to Jeff," Mentaliste said. That was all she felt the need to say.

They were on either side of me. I felt my arms press against my side, and my feet had slid together. Mentaliste held me still, telekinetically. I didn't waste time trying to play dumb. I'd been cornered again, trapped by people stronger than me.

But I knew better than to show fear.

"And?" I said. "So what?"

Touchdown became livid, like I'd hoped. He'd been at the mercy of Titiritero once. The "Mexican Puppeteer" had used Touchdown to knock bank guards into comas. One had died. Touchdown stepped close, his fingertips crackling with bio-electric impulses. He glared into my eyes and snarled. "You fucking freak! You as good as raped him!"

"Jay!" Mentaliste tried to warn him.

"I'm her, and she's me," I said, and pushed into Touchdown's mind so hard my nose bled. That hadn't happened in a while. He'd jerked back, and his eyes widened. Mentaliste tried to dodge, but Touchdown grazed her arm with one quick jab—his power threw her nervous system into a tailspin. She collapsed, unconscious. My arms and legs came free.

"Hold onto him," I said, and Touchdown nodded. "I'll get some restraints."

Then I walked out of the kitchen, down the stairs, and out into the street.

❦

"Trust issues or not, I really don't think Aleph will want to hang out with me, Jeff," I said.

He waited.

"Does the Agency know you're here?" I asked.

Cinder took a long while before he answered. "No."

It didn't surprise me.

"You've noticed his targets, right?" he asked.

I sighed. Jeff was right. I had noticed the pattern. Aleph was violent, and more than powerful enough to take down entire buildings—which he'd done many times. Churches, especially. Once, an entire jail. And a Log-Cabin Republican event. His list of murders had even included some members of the senate, federal judges, and more minor politicians than I could recall. People called him an anarchist, but when the body counts finalized, I'd noticed how the charred corpses of the right wing bodies stacked much higher, and how—here and there—there were targets a lot more like mine.

It was only obvious if you went looking for it.

"Yeah," I said, because Cinder was waiting for me to reply. "But just because we have a similar agenda, I don't think he's going to invite me along for his next crime."

Cinder put his visor back on. Then he pulled something from his belt—a memory stick. Information about Lewis Nicolas, I assumed. Aleph's location. He put it on the ground, then straightened. He looked directly at me. It was probably just luck. It might have been that heat sense of his. Either way, it made me flinch.

"So change his mind," Cinder said.

He leapt, and flew away. There was a flash of warmth against my skin, and then nothing.

✄

The e-mail on my screen had startled me; the sender name had made me feel sick. It was from Jeff. I'd risen, spilling some of my tea, and had rushed to the window to see if the rest of N.A.M.D.A. were outside.

I'd been careful for the last two years. I'd made a new costume, for the rare times I appeared in one. I was using a new name—Psilence—not that anyone had really known that Recon ever existed. I unleashed no grand schemes. I knew my limits, but the right thought in the right mind at the right time had always been a force to be reckoned with.

I'd not been idle.

I had wondered if anyone noticed how certain rich right-wing bastards started donating to kinder causes. I had known I'd been found out a couple of times—I'd gone too far with that so-called "church" that insisted on picketing at funerals. They had brought Mentaliste in to help my victims recover from their sudden desire to volunteer all their time to picking up garbage. I had taken some pride in how long it took her to fix the pastor, though, who had "decided" to takes vows of silence, poverty, and chastity; and went on a hunger strike. He looked better thirty pounds lighter.

And maybe it had been a mistake, but when that child molesting bastard in Oklahoma had gotten off on a technicality, I had him write "Psilence" in his own blood on the wall of his hotel room after he slit his wrists. No one was ever going to fix him.

But how had Jeff found me? I hadn't been using my real name since my days in the Agency—getting a fake ID had been child's play. I hadn't needed a regular job—it was easy enough to collect "donations" from some of my richer victims.

Still, investigation had always been one of Jeff's strengths.

"Shit," I said. I clicked the message.

All it said was: "Campsite. Tomorrow, 10pm."

I hit the reply button and agreed.

※

"I want to work with you," I say, trying not to let my voice crack. My eyes are watering from the glare of the energy curtain.

"Why would I work with you?" Aleph's voice is a sneer. "You're a bug compared to me."

I force myself to sound calm. To exude confidence. Behind his face-plate, it's hard to tell if he's looking at me or not, but it's not like he's given me much room in his little circle of death. "Every time you've been beaten, it's been a telepath," I say. He shifts slightly, annoyed again at not quite knowing where I am. "I can help you."

"I don't deal with ghosts," he snaps.

I drop the veil. I reach up and take my mask off, and I can feel the surprise in his mind. Sandy hair, hazel eyes, plain face. I've always looked younger than I am. I'm starting to work my way into his thoughts, though it's difficult to do it so slowly and without giving myself away.

Aleph raises his hands, and the circle of white plasma tightens to within inches of my feet, dancing around my body. It's hot, but it's not burning me. Yet. It takes everything I have not to flinch, not to try to make him turn it off. It's also nowhere near the worst he can dish out.

"I can handle the telepaths for you," I say. "It's everything else I suck at."

He snorts.

"I know the kind of people you go after," I say, hoping this won't tip him over the edge. "If you looked me up, you know how I feel about them. I'd like to help."

For that one moment, his thoughts open to me. He considers it. He's not going to kill me. But he's certainly not going to work with me. It's too bad, he thinks, that the first guy he meets who understands is someone so weak. I'm even a little bit cute. But I'm unworthy of his attention. I'm not a threat.

I'm *nothing*.

It's a small crack in his defences, but it's a crack. I've worked with less.

I push. He gasps, and for just a second the plasma burns blue-hot and leaps at my chest. I yelp, but I slam into his head and the energy winks out. He staggers back. His mind isn't weak, but he was unprepared. Smoke smoulders from my costume.

"Take off the mask," I grind out the words, ignoring the burning pain across my chest and feeling sweat form on my forehead. It's always been easier when I can look into someone's eyes. His hands jerk once, then shakily start to rise. He's fighting me, but if I lose, I die. When he grips his faceplate, he lets out a strangled cry before he tugs it off.

Furious brown eyes met mine. I pour into him. I feel myself tipping, and manage to sink to my knees without keeling over entirely.

He cries out. I hear him gag, then whimper as I dig through his mind and—as Jeff put it—change it. He even whispers "please," and for a moment I feel bad for him. But it's just a moment. He has killed so many, over the years, and never cared about bystanders. He would kill Jeff, and not lose a moment's sleep. He is evil. He's so much worse than me. I reach into his mind with everything I have, and tell him what to remember.

What to believe.

What to *feel*.

Blood erupts from my nose, and I keep going. There's a ringing in my ears, and the pounding in my head is worse than ever before, and I keep going. All I ever wanted was not to be hurt again. Well apparently, that's too damn bad.

Pain.

Then darkness.

After Cinder flew away, I turned the memory stick over and over in my hand. I hadn't been back to my hometown in years. I started walking, not really sure where I was going until I was at my old front door. My parents were long gone, but when I knocked on the door, the young woman who sleepily answered had a particularly open mind. It was easy to force her to let me in, even though her parents were away for the weekend.

She had my old room, but hadn't found the hiding spot I'd made under the boards in the closet. The football was still wrapped in a plastic bag, which cracked when I unwrapped it. I told the young woman I was never there, and she let me out politely before going back to her bed.

Erik Miller was still in town. He'd married, and had three children—all boys—all of whom had inherited his height and easy smile. I stayed veiled as I walked through his house, kept them asleep while I looked at each of his sons in turn. The middle one looked the most like him. I went to Erik's bedroom last, where he and his wife—a girl we went to high school with, though I couldn't remember her name—were sleeping.

His hair was thinner, but he was still in good shape.

I put the football on his bedside table. I slipped into his sleeping mind, and reminded him of how he'd wanted it as a teenager. In his sleep, he smiled gratefully.

Then I left.

❧

"Please wake up!"

Someone is holding my hand. It's such an effort to open my eyes. Aleph's face swims into view. He's pulled off his helmet completely. I don't know where we are, but I'm on a very comfortable bed. I'm still wearing my costume pants, though my Kevlar vest and uniform shirt are gone. There are a couple of red burns across my chest, but they're not terrible. They'll heal, in time.

Lewis Nicolas is looking down at me with worry. Now that he's not trying to kill me, I have the time to notice his face. He's got a strong brow and a shaved head, and his brown eyes are actually quite striking. He's got a five o'clock shadow going on, and though there's a scar that runs through his left cheek, somehow it suits him. He's almost handsome, and it surprises me. Even I assume the villains are ugly.

I swallow, aching everywhere. My head is pounding. "Where...?" My voice comes out cracked and dry.

"Oh thank God," he says, and squeezes my hand. His thoughts start to bleed into my mind, and I just don't have it in me to close them out. He's terrified I wasn't going to wake up. He's not quite sure how N.A.M.D.A. got the jump on him, but there's no way he's ever going to let it happen again. All the power he has, and he couldn't do anything but watch me as I lay there, not moving... He remembers a battle with Cinder and the others that didn't happen. He remembers me helping him.

"Tell me you're okay," he says.

I nod. "I'm okay," I say, voice working this time. "Where are we?"

"I brought you back to my place. I finally got you in my bed." He laughs, then shakes his head. "You scared me."

His place. Where they'll find him. I force myself to smile. "I'll be fine. Just need to rest. It's always like this when I push myself. Give me a second, and I'll get up."

"No," he says. He's worried about me. He leans over, and kisses me.

I kiss him back. It's a gentle kiss, but I can tell he'd like it to be deeper. He's just afraid of hurting me. No one has kissed me like this in a long time. He pulls away.

I breathe for a second. "We have to get out of here," I hear my own voice, and it sounds like it's coming from far away.

"What? Why?" He leans back.

Change his mind. Those were my only instructions, but I know what else was implied.

"They know where you live," I say. Just like that, I've made the choice. Keeping him here would be child's play. I could turn him over to the others. To Jeff. "Cinder. The rest of them. It's only a matter of time. I just need a second, and then I can get up."

He scoops me up, almost effortlessly. Aleph is strong. His hands are shaking though.

"We'll find a place," he says. He's already walking. "We'll lay low. You're right—we'll do it your way from now on. At least for a while. Jesus, I thought... I love you. Don't you dare do anything like that again."

"Okay." I close my eyes, and press my head against the hard armor that covers his chest. He loves me. It's not real. I know that.

Still.

It's better than nothing.

THE PLAN
Charles "Zan" Christensen

Charles "Zan" Christensen is a comics writer and publisher living in Seattle, Washington. He was the founding President of nonprofit LGBT comics organization Prism Comics, and is currently the publisher of graphic novel publisher Northwest Press. He was featured with artist Mark Brill in *OUT* magazine's "OUT 100" for 2011 for their work on the anti-bullying comic book *The Power Within*. "The Plan" is his first prose fiction work and is dedicated to the guy who turned him in to the police.

I remember rain like this. Thick, heavy rain, driving almost sideways in the wind, with drops so big that they hurt when they hit your exposed skin. Rain like this will soak you through in a just few seconds and chill you to the bone. But not us; we gave off so much heat that we barely noticed it. This rain always got us in the mood.

But you're not here with me now.

The city erected some bleachers in the town square yesterday in preparation for today's public relations lovefest, but it's way too early for anybody to be here yet. It's not quite dawn, and with the rain clouds covering up whatever dim light might be on the horizon, it's near pitch black out. I've already disrupted the power to the few streetlights on this block to make sure it stays that way. Darkness never bothers the mysterious Eclipse; my sleek, flexible black armor helps me blend into the shadows and I always see perfectly, thanks to my Infinity Lenses.

I've never told anyone the whole story of how I got them, since it doesn't exactly paint me in the best light. Still, you might have heard variations on the general theme: alien crash lands on Earth, entrusts almost magical technology to incredulous Earth man with his dying breath to use it to defend the powerless and mete out justice.

They actually weren't lenses when he pressed them into my hands. They were two small stones, diamond hard and clear, and they seemed to respond to my thoughts, as if they could become whatever I needed. I shaped them into a pair of obsidian lenses and discovered when I wore them, I had all kinds of amazing powers. I vowed to honor the alien's dying wishes and use my newfound powers for the benefit of all.

Well, that lasted all of about three weeks.

I discovered that being able to see in pitch darkness and move through walls and having the strength of ten linebackers and the agility of a jungle cat was actually not very lucrative when you spend all your time foiling bank robberies, intervening in gang wars and maintaining a full-time shitty office day job. So I switched teams.

Save your moralizing and your judgements; it's easy to brag about how you stuck with doing the selfless thing, but you weren't the one who was faced with missing another mortgage payment and losing your house. You weren't the one buried in credit card and student loan debt from getting a worthless masters degree.

It was one little heist at the start, just to settle the biggest debts, but then another opportunity arose, and another... Before I knew it, I got caught up in the challenge of it all. Yes, I admit it, it was fun. After we tangled a few times, they were calling me a "super-villain" and you were calling me your "arch enemy."

Speaking of challenges, it was pretty tricky to sneak into the Mayor's office and make a copy of the layout for today's event, but it turns out I won't even need it to know where the podium is going to be. Some helpful technician has marked the spot with gaffer's tape, so I know exactly where to rig the device so it will be right below you.

The rain's got me lost in memories when there's work I should be doing. So I get back to work laying my final trap for you.

❄

"Drop the bag and step away," came the booming voice from behind me.

I froze, not knowing how to react at first. I'd been careful, not leaving any evidence at the crime scenes and making sure to disable any security cameras. I wasn't trying to show off and draw attention, like a lot of "villains" did. Sure, I'd been taking some larger hauls, but I thought I was still going below the radar of the Justice Alliance. I mean, did they really watch collectible coin shops to make sure they're not being robbed? I thought a security guard might eventually stumble upon me or something random like that, but I wasn't really expecting to deal with a hero confrontation.

I hadn't even thought of a goddamn super villain name yet.

When I turned around to size up the threat, however, all my worries melted away. Established superheroes tend to have pretty slick outfits—they're on super-teams with big public relations budgets and design consultants—but it was obvious that this guy was just starting out, and fashion sense wasn't one of his superpowers. His costume was a mess of garish yellows and light browns in ill-tailored shiny spandex. He had added a wide black leather strap to some small yellow swimming goggles to cover his eyes. His cape was edged with brown feathers which had the unfortunate and not-at-all threatening effect of looking like he was wearing a wilted brown feather boa. The costume was bad enough, but when he told me his name, that pushed it over the edge.

"You thought you'd steal those precious coins undetected," he said earnestly, using whatever superhero gravitas he'd managed to pick up from Saturday morning cartoons and comic books. "But you didn't count on the keen eyes of The Eagle!"

I actually felt a little guilty when I laughed out loud. I couldn't help it; even though he'd obviously worked so hard on this getup, puckered seams and all, it was so predictable and literal. A guy dressed up like an eagle calling himself "The Eagle." Yawn.

"Look, buddy, I'm sure this is fun for..." I started to say, after I managed to suppress my laughter.

Before I could finish, he was hurtling at me, teeth clenched, apparently not too pleased to be mocked on what might be his maiden voyage as a superhero. I realized right away that he wasn't just some wannabe in a cape; he was actually flying through the air, and had he lost quite a few feathers when he pushed off forcefully from the ground. When I sidestepped to avoid him, he connected forcefully with the glass display case that I'd just emptied of its contents, compacting it into a pile of flattened metal and pulverized plate glass and making quite a dent in the wall behind it. Not only was he fast, but he was plenty strong and durable, too.

As passé as it was, the spandex certainly showed off his body; his muscles were on full display, tensed and rippling as he rose from the crushed remains of the showcase. He brushed off the broken glass—and the embarrassment—and squared himself to face me again.

Maybe his guard was down because he wasn't expecting me to be so direct, but for whatever reason, I was able to land a solid punch, right to his nose. Temporarily stunned and disoriented, he sank back down to the floor.

I took advantage of the moment and sent the mental signal to the Infinity Lenses to initiate phasing mode. I dissolved into an insubstantial black mist, feeling the odd sensation of my body being held together solely by my force of will. The fastest I'd ever managed to make the change was five seconds, which sounds quick but, trust me, it wasn't the kind of thing I would want to try in the thick of battle. I shuddered to think what would happen if something interrupted the process midway. Once the transformation was complete, however, there was no way anyone could lay a hand on me.

And the effect certainly was stylish.

Before I let my body dissipate to re-form elsewhere, I leaned in near the disappointed hero's face and whispered, "You'll do better next time."

And I don't know why, but I planted a ghostly kiss on his cheek.

        ✺

Villainy might not be an "honorable" line of work but, regardless, it's still work. I had to cut a chunk of pavement out of the street, wire and place the device, then put everything back exactly the way it was. I couldn't risk your "Eagle vision" detecting that something was amiss and ruining everything. And I did all this in a skintight costume while it was pouring down freezing rain. Why do I even wear this costume when there's nobody around to see it? Force of habit, I suppose.

Shortly after I finished and headed to my position on the rooftop, the prep crew that was scheduled for 8 AM arrived early to start setting up the stage and lights. If I'd stayed one minute later, I would have been discovered and my plan would have been foiled before it began. Talk about an anticlimax.

From my vantage point, I can see the workers scurrying about, ants preparing for the arrival of the queen. In addition, some citizens have shown up early, trying to sneak onto the bleachers and get good seats, but they're waved back and put into a line while the crew finishes their decorating and safety checks.

I watch carefully for a few minutes until I'm sure that nobody's noticed my handiwork, and then I sink down below the ledge and lean back to check my remote activator. Everyone is going to be on extremely high alert at the event, so I can't risk having the device active and on a timer, or even actively scanning for a wireless signal from a remote control. Its power signature or radio frequencies might be detected by one of the Justice Alliance's security devices. Instead, I used the Infinity Lenses to create a dimensional portal, just an inch in diameter, at the core of the device; I can open another portal, up here on the roof, and press the power button myself. If I don't pull back fast enough, maybe I'll lose a finger, but you'll lose a whole lot more than that. And that's the point.

✍

"Defeat your enemies, or your world is doomed!" the Arranger's crazed voice boomed out over the giant loudspeakers.

Everyone gets a kick out of watching heroes and villains slug it out, but they usually just watch the news to get their fix; the Arranger had taken voyeurism to whole new heights and kidnapped the lot of us to duke it out under his watchful eye. He claimed that we had to fight to the death or he would destroy the Earth, and so heroes and villains alike complied. We villains might be greedy, selfish bastards, but most of us are locals; at the very least, we didn't relish the idea of our playground being razed.

(The Arranger's threat turned out to be complete bullshit, of course, but we didn't find that out until years later. You start to take threats like these seriously, in my line of work).

By this time, The Eagle and I had pretty well established our friendly rivalry and were constantly running into each other. He'd been so stodgy and by-the-book when he arrived on the hero scene, with his goofy colors and awkward catchphrases, but he'd come a long way. I don't want to take all the credit, but I'm sure I played a part in his transformation; after a year or so of tussling with me, his costume was sleek and sexy as hell. The color scheme went darker, replacing the yellow with black and toning the brown down a lot, and his cape was streamlined to a simple black and gray three-point shape. There was even a time when he experimented with not using one, but that didn't test well, I guess, so he took it up again. It was made out of a high-tech nanomaterial that the Justice Alliance had concocted, and it hugged his body in all the right places. The change wasn't just cosmetic; The Eagle had definitely embraced a little bit of the dark side in his worldview as well. He realized that things were often more gray than black and white and dislodged that stick from his ass. At least a little.

Still, he never wavered from his core principles. Although I covered it up with snide remarks and dismissiveness, I developed an enormous respect for him because of that. For his part, he knew that I stole and caused mayhem for the thrill and challenge of it and that I wasn't a diabolical menace at heart. And

I think he understood even before I did that a lot of the needling and taunting was to get his attention more than anything, and he started to give as good as he got. Star-crossed through we were, I could tell he enjoyed it.

When the Arranger had nabbed us, we'd been in mid-battle. The Eagle had interrupted me after I broke into the offices of an "ex-gay" halfway house to clean out their safe—you'd be surprised how much money you can make preying on the self-loathing of others—and was finishing up by replacing all of their reading material with copies of "The Joy of Gay Sex". I considered that part more of a public service than a crime.

When he saw what I was doing, he looked almost pained to have to intervene.

"This isn't the answer, Eclipse," he warned me. "I know, in your own twisted way, you think this is some kind of justice, but you're just giving these people more ammunition to use against us."

"Maybe I'm just not as patient as you," I purred at him, opening to a particularly lascivious page in the book and showing it to him. "Though if I were, I'm sure I'd have the patience to get limber enough to do this. Care to give it a go?"

It was at that moment that the Arranger's teleportation beam locked on us and teleported us in the great hall of the Battle Complex, where the heroes and villains were assembling, all startled and disoriented. Luckily for The Eagle, the book I'd been holding hadn't made the journey with us.

When we weren't alone, our banter got a lot more formal. I could tell that he got uncomfortable when I flirted with him when the other heroes were around. Not so much because of the gay thing—he'd skyrocketed in popularity after he came out, and been linked to every hot male superhero from Volt to Captain Kinetic—but because I was a villain. Maybe he'd adjusted his thinking a bit to see what I did as less harmful in the grand scheme of things, but I was still wasting my talents on selfishness and was ultimately a moral failure in his eyes.

"Defeat your enemies, or your world is doomed!" came the voice over the giant loudspeakers, and we moved to the appropriate opposite sides of the room.

※

People are coming in from all sides, and the square is filling up fast; giving government employees a paid day off to commemorate the first annual "Eagle Day" goes a long way toward guaranteeing an audience.

It's coming up on 9 AM and you're not here yet, but people have gotten used to superheroes never being on time, given the nature of your work. After all, every minute you spend soaking up public accolades just takes away from the time you could be defending the status quo.

It looks like the city officials are anticipating a bit of a wait, because the deputy mayor has been given the podium to say a few words. You know they're desperate when they give him the floor; the high point of his administration has been a comprehensive review of the taxes on landscaping services.

Even though the risk of detection is low, I'm still hesitant to use the Infinity Lenses to reach out and check that the portal is still in place inside the device. I've never done this particular trick before, leaving a portal open when I'm not actively maintaining it. I decide to chance it and do a test run, summoning a tiny portal in the air in front of me. I slowly put my finger through, feeling the smooth, concave surface of the plastic button that will bring my plan to fruition.

I hear a piercing cry from behind me and pull my finger back quickly, lest I accidentally set off the device, and I close the portal at my end. I whirl around to see... a crow, perched on the ledge, looking at me with a puzzled expression.

※

I could never tell if all the birds that seemed to hang around when The Eagle was on the job were just some weird coincidence or if he had some telepathic link to them, or something. Do birds respond to pheromones? Or did he keep a flock of trained ones on hand? Having fifty birds spontaneously dive-bomb you when you're coming out of a jewelry store at 3am with your hands full is a pretty rare occurrence, and I assure you it can be pretty inconvenient. I'd managed to keep hold of the bags and get some undignified cover from the avian menace between some dumpsters, but their attack was forcing me to take a different route than the one I initially planned. The Eagle would probably be counting on that, so I needed to be on my toes.

I leapt from my hiding place and ran down the narrow alleyway, a few stray birds following me and pecking at my armor, chipping their beaks in the process. It's cruelty to animals to get them to do that, I think. I scanned the shadows with my perfect night vision, waiting for the telltale shape of my archenemy to appear. In true dramatic fashion, he stepped out into the light at the end of the alleyway and ran at me, putting himself between me and the next block.

Without slowing my pace, I gritted my teeth and concentrated on the shadows at the corners of the alleyway and they seemed to come to life, coalescing into a dark, amorphous cloud about five feet in diameter directly in front of him. I charged into the cloud, shifted direction abruptly, and passed him with a few inches to spare as he blindly reached out to try and grab me.

That didn't slow him down too much, though. He flew out the other side of the cloud and up in a wide arc, reversing direction to get back in pursuit. I did my best to stick the shadows, but his eagle eyes were in rare form that night. When I finally looked back to spot him, he was in the middle of a dive bomb. I almost made it clear but he clipped me, the impact knocking the wind out of me and sending me to the pavement. I took a breath, then sprang up again in a run, rounding the corner and hoping to find something to distract him. Not likely at 3am, but there was always hope…

I had to shield my eyes, which were adjusted to the darkness, to block out the bright yellow flames that were raging in front of me. The lower levels of an apartment building were ablaze and people were gathered in the street outside, but no fire trucks had arrived on the scene yet. There was heavy construction on this block and narrow streets; they might have been having trouble getting through.

The roar of the fire was so loud that it took me a moment to hear the screams coming from the upper windows. About two dozen people were still in the building and on the roof, trapped, with no way to get down. Maybe they'd had their exits blocked by the fire and made their way to the upper floors to buy some time, but the flames were moving steadily up the structure.

The Eagle caught up with me and made to grab me until he saw what I was looking at. Without a word, he disregarded me completely and flew to the top of the building to rescue some of the people from the roof.

I seized the opportunity to escape, racing around to the other side of the building. This would keep him occupied for at least five or ten minutes, and by then I would be long gone.

What I didn't count on was seeing two small children in a third floor window, just one floor above the raging fire. They were the only figures I could see; everyone else was on the roof or on the top floor and they'd been left behind. Their window was open and they were sitting on the windowsill—maybe because the floor had grown too hot to stand on—and they weren't crying or calling out. They looked stunned and very scared.

I set my ill-gotten gains down on the grimy alley floor and activated the Infinity Lenses. It took a full ten seconds to create a portal large enough to step through and another ten to open another in what I hoped would be the room they were in. It was hard to judge teleportation without a clear view of where you were headed.

I ended up a few feet off the floor and landed with a bit of a thump behind the children, startling them. The little boy leaned away from me, instinctively, and my heart jumped as I pictured him falling out of the open window. Luckily, his sister caught hold of his t-shirt before he fell, and I was able to cover the distance between us and scoop them up safely in my arms.

The floor was hot—I could even feel it through my armor—and the air in the room was very thin, most of the oxygen having been consumed by the encroaching fire. Holding them firmly, despite their feeble squirming to try and get away—I was an infamous super villain, remember—I headed back through the portal and stepped out in the alleyway again.

Rain had started to fall. The Eagle's teammate, Elementra, had arrived on the scene, hovering atop the building resplendent in her blue, flowing cape and long, black hair, arms outstretched; she was summoning a downpour to try and keep the flames from spreading to the neighboring buildings while he evacuated the last of the residents. The Eagle landed and leaned a very groggy man against a parked car. The man was barely conscious after being trapped in smoke for too long, and was calling out for his children.

I walked to the end of the alleyway and crouched to set the children down. They were still a little unsteady, but I aimed them in the direction of the crowd and hoped they could get there on their own. I shouldn't have worried; as soon as I set them down, they mustered the energy to race away from me and toward their father, who was overjoyed to see them.

The Eagle turned and saw the children, then looked directly at me, still kneeling, watching the reunion. Face flushed, I darted back into the alley to retrieve my loot, and he took off in pursuit after me.

I somersaulted up onto a parked car and bounced off onto a fire escape, making my way to the roof. Elementra's rainstorm had intensified. I thought the heavy rain might make it easier to elude The Eagle, but it turned out to mess up my vision just about as much as his. It was tougher to make things out by heat signature with the rain cooling everything down.

The second I made it to the top, I heard a high-pitched shriek and felt a shockwave that knocked me roughly to the tar and gravel roof. I tumbled forward, awkwardly at first, then managing to get my footing to turn the motion into a controlled roll. I'd forgotten about the Eagle's sonic screech; he rarely used it unless he needed to put someone down at a distance. He was much more of a hand-to-hand kind of guy.

He was playing rough tonight.

I realized with dismay that the jewelry bags had fallen from my hands when I'd been hit, and The Eagle had snatched them out of the air and set them on the rooftop. He'd return the stolen necklaces, rings and tiaras after the fight, but that was apparently a secondary concern.

I stayed face down, letting him think he'd knocked me out, and let him have it with a shadow blast from my Infinity Lenses when he got in range.

He staggered back, but I only had a few seconds to get to my feet before he came at me again. This time I threw a punch, but he met me with a concise judo move—our bodies pressed up against each other momentarily before he pulled me past him, where I slammed hard into a slim tree trunk.

A tree trunk?

The space was set up as a rooftop garden, with potted trees and decorative grasses and even rows of vegetables. It had not been tended too carefully, and was pretty overgrown, but it was thriving nonetheless; it looked like a little wilderness in the heart of the city.

That was the setting for our dance, the way heroes and villains dance. Throwing punches, ducking, weaving, using our super powers to our advantage when we could. As silly as it sounds, after that initial impact with the tree, we started to take special care not to injure any of the plants. Someone had gone to the trouble to set all this up, and it seemed wrong to destroy it.

But it had been a long night already, and both of us were getting tired. Sometimes I'd see an opening and have to give him a jab to get his mind back in the game. Other times he'd catch me getting a little too cocky and would give me a taste of the same thing.

The rain was still pouring down, and we were breathing hard with all the exertion, light steam coming off of our bodies. Our costumes were in shreds. The bobbing and weaving and sparring soon gave way to more clenches and wrestling—we were pretty evenly matched in the strength department—and soon we were face to face.

And then, we were kissing.

I don't know who started it—maybe we met in the middle. But it surprised me, this fierce passion that took hold of me, channeling all the fury from our battle into stoking a long-suppressed desire.

We broke the kiss and I studied his face. I released him momentarily, trying to give him an "out," a way that he could pretend that this was all my idea and put a stop to it, but he didn't take it. In a flash, we were all over each other again, stripping away the tattered costumes preventing us from pressing our bodies closer together, devouring each new bit of exposed skin to fill our boundless hunger.

All at once he was on top of me, my legs encircling him, his aim unmistakable. He hesitated for just a moment, giving me an opportunity to put a stop to it all, as well. Instead, I held his body tightly and bit into his shoulder to give him a little bit of the pain that I felt as he entered me—pain that gave way quickly to pleasure for us both.

The autumn rain pelted us, up there on that roof, animals lost in an urban jungle.

✳

You're a half-hour late.

The mayor is doing his best to entertain the crowd that's filled the bleachers to capacity and spilled down the city streets in every direction, but he's never been that good at impromptu public speaking and you can tell he's uncomfortable without his script. The election's coming up, and of course he was banking on this as a way to associate himself more closely with you to get more votes. This isn't about honoring you and your contributions as much it's about getting a good campaign video.

God, I hope he gets caught in the blast, too, the pompous windbag.

"The Eagle is a little held up," the Mayor continues, "Doing what he does best, helping the citizens of this fair city!" He waits for the audience to cheer at that, but they're reaching the limits of their patience and getting restless. Some of them have been here for over three hours, in the rain, and they are starting to worry that maybe you won't even show up. What if you're locked in battle with your arch enemy, Eclipse, and can't get away? What if you've gone on another cosmic adventure with the Justice Alliance and aren't even in this solar system?

I peek down at the crowd, and see one of the poncho-and-sunglasses-wearing security detail standing off to the side of the stage, near the podium. He's looking down at the pavement and speaking into a wireless headset, calling in some kind of an issue while the event continues as normal all around him.

To my relief, he pulls two teenagers out from under the stage, where they'd been hiding, thinking they'd have the perfect front-row seat to see you. He hasn't seen any sign of my plan.

The waiting is killing me. Hurry up and get here to get what you deserve.

✼

"So what do you think?" I asked tentatively, waiting and watching for his reaction. We stood on the same rooftop a week later with nothing standing between us: no sarcasm, no irony, no jokes to deflect the enormity of what was happening. And there were no Infinity Lenses blocking him from looking into my eyes and seeing that I was telling the truth. Every instinct told me not to face him without wearing them—without the Lenses I'm powerless—but I needed to show him that I was serious.

I'd contacted him through official Justice Alliance channels to arrange the meeting; their number was right there on the website and I couldn't think of any other way to reach him. To say he was surprised to hear from me would be an understatement.

"Um… would you tell him that Eclipse is on the line and would like to speak with him?" Surreal. He actually got on the phone with me, and I'm pretty sure he didn't have the call recorded because he was afraid I'd say something incriminating. I told him to meet me at the rooftop garden that night at midnight. There wouldn't be any fighting, and I wanted it to just be him and me.

So here we were, and I had just suggested that I would be willing to walk away from my old life to be with him. Floated the idea. What if I did that? What kind of possibilities would there be for us? I was sick of all the flirtation and subtext and assumptions; I just wanted to get it all out in the open.

The Eagle mulled over the situation, and I could tell that he felt that I'd put him in an awkward spot. He had rules he had to follow, and they didn't include starting a relationship with his archenemy, even if that archenemy suggested that he'd give up his life of villainy and work for the other side. He'd enjoyed the flirtation and the excitement, doing something that he knew he shouldn't be doing, for a change, but this was entirely too real.

There have been a few transitions from villainy to heroism in the past. Some stick, but most don't. Doctor Magnetic suffered some awful near-death experience which was followed by a period of sympathy, and then he got to transition into being one of the "good guys." Not me, I just made the leap. I leapt off a twenty-story building without a grappling line, sure there'd be a flagpole or awning or utility cable to keep me from falling to my death. I'd been fearless.

Bullshit, of course. It was easy to leap when I thought The Eagle would swoop down and catch me.

He leaned in and took my hand in his, looking directly into my eyes. My heart sank when I saw the mix of sadness and pity in his eyes. I was so stunned that I barely noticed when he attached the handcuffs to my wrist and took the Lenses out of my grasp. The roar of police helicopters preceded them coming up over the sides of the building, spotlights fixed on us.

Handcuffs. Jail. Twenty-one hours of my freedom lost before the remote teleportation node implanted behind my ear had powered up enough to function, allowing me to return to my lair.

Something had cautioned me not to wear the real Infinity Lenses, to hope for the best, but to plan for this eventuality. As a result of that plan, The Eagle had instead confiscated a very stylish pair of prescription sunglasses and was probably studying them at Justice Alliance headquarters, trying to figure out how to make them work.

I seethed for hours, barely able to think clearly, my head clouded with rage at The Eagle. As my anger cooled into steely resolve, the seed of a plan started growing in my brain. One final plan.

❦

"Hi everybody, sorry I'm late!" you say as you swoop in. You're wearing that impractical ceremonial cape that you trot out for special occasions; it's reminiscent of the first cape you wore, festooned with lustrous feathers but executed flawlessly, detailed with gold and silver. These things cost money, and there's no sense in them getting ruined. You only wear this when you know there's not going to be any fighting.

Perfect.

Even though you're over an hour late, the crowd erupts in cheers. They'll forgive you for anything. Even the weather seems to cut you some slack; the rain petered out slightly just before you arrived, and a sliver of sun is threatening to peek out from behind the dark clouds any moment to light up the event.

The people in the press box are delivering a collective sigh of relief at your arrival and the turn in the weather. They're adjusting their zoom lenses, taking practice shots of you to get the perfect focus and exposure, preparing to capture the big moment.

I watch you descend to the podium, hovering next to the smiling Mayor and looking out into the sea of adoring faces. You're saying something, but my heart is racing and I can't think of anything except what's about to happen. An aide is scurrying up onto the stage holding a giant golden key prop, which he'll hand to the Mayor to hand to you. All the camera flashes will be almost blinding.

I only have a second to hesitate and ask myself... is this really what I want to do? Do you really deserve this for what you did to me?

As you're about to take hold of the key, I summon the portal and push my finger through, triggering the device.

There's a loud crackling noise and, for just a split second, the stage is engulfed in a brilliant, blue light shooting up from the pavement, disintegrating the stage, the podium, your beautiful, ridiculous cape. The Mayor is standing close enough that he's halfway in the blast, which is good enough for me. Despite pulling my finger back as fast as possible, I feel a sharp pain and then a prickling sensation on my finger before it goes completely numb.

Tearing my eyes away from the scene below, I look at my finger, apprehensive. As I feared, the tip of the finger of my costume has been completely disintegrated, leaving my index finger intact but exposed. Goddamn it; gloves this sophisticated cost about two-thousand dollars to manufacture. Meanwhile, down on the stage, you're floating in the air above a giant hole in the stage.

Completely naked.

The Mayor is nearby, one foot on the solid stage and the other over nothingness, only having avoided falling into the hole by grabbing onto his aide for balance. The clothes have been disintegrated from half of his body and are falling off on the other side.

The flashbulbs go off, and at least one of us has our perfect photo op.

❧

It's snowing. The weather has been getting warmer so it's probably the last snowfall of the season, and it will only be seen here, high above the city. Down at ground level, it's a misty rain, giving the streets a wet shine that reflects the brilliant red of car taillights and neon signs, washing away the dirt that's built up over the winter.

"It's just so beautiful from up here," Conduit murmurs to his patrol partner, who is floating in mid-air in front of him. Not being able to fly under his own power, he's rarely been up this high, outside of a plane. "I can't believe you see things from this perspective all the time."

"I'm glad I could share it with you," The Eagle replies, floating in the air beside him and flashing him a smile.

"So… you never caught him?" Conduit asks tentatively, crouching on the edge of the rooftop atop the highest skyscraper in the city. "If someone pulled a stunt like that on me, I don't think I'd let him get away with it."

"He disappeared right after," The Eagle answers, visibly uncomfortable at recalling the highly publicized events of last year. "Hasn't been seen since. Frankly, with the kind of threats the Justice Alliance faces, pranks rate pretty low on the priority list." He pauses a moment, then chuckles and has to follow up with, "Even ones as spectacular as that."

"It was pretty genius, wasn't it?" Conduit laughs through his mask, before pulling it up far enough to expose his broad smile. "I didn't want to say anything until I knew you had a sense of humor about it, but you definitely have to give him credit."

Conduit, clad in a sleek, white bodysuit with blue accents, had burst on the scene a few months ago, operating solo. New as he was, he impressed hero and villain alike with his determination, ingenuity, and unwavering selflessness. He was one of the few heroes who'd ever turned down a Justice Alliance membership invitation, saying that it was still too soon and that he still had some things to work out on his own before he joined any kind of team.

A month ago, he'd finally relented and joined the team as a probationary member, and The Eagle had been assigned to be his mentor. They got along really well; Conduit had a twisted sense of humor and a playful, irreverent side that The Eagle appreciated. "So why did you take so long to join the Alliance?" The Eagle asks, taking a seat next to his partner. "I know I jumped at the chance when they offered membership to me."

"I just wanted to make sure I could do it on my own," Conduit replies, his voice contemplative. "When I started out, I thought I was trying to be a hero just to please someone else, to live up to his standards. After he was out of the picture, I understood that what I wanted most was a change in my life, not necessarily the man who inspired the change."

"And my takeaway from all that is…" says The Eagle playfully, "…you're single?"

"You're awful," Conduit responds with a grin. "Is it really Justice Alliance policy for your mentor to constantly flirt with you?"

The Eagle's face reddens.

"Relax," Conduit laughs. "Sorry, I can't help myself. You're such an easy target."

"I never got to ask you," The Eagle says, changing the subject. "How did you get your powers, anyway?"

"Well," Conduit answers. "There was this alien spaceship that had crashed, carrying a member of a force of galactic guardians. I came across the crash and went to help, but there was nothing I could do. He was dying."

"He gave me these Infinity Bands," Conduit gestures to the glowing blue bands that he wears on his wrists, "and with his dying breath, urged me to use them to defend the powerless and mete out justice."

"And that's what I've been doing ever since."

THE KNIGHTS NEFARIOUS
Rod M. Santos

Rod M. Santos was born in Manila, raised in the Bronx, and is currently lost in Yonkers. His work fluctuates between dark and lighthearted fantasy with frequent stops throughout the speculative continuum. His stories have appeared in *Icarus* magazine, *Beneath Ceaseless Skies*, *Cinema Spec*, *Myths and Magic*, and *Skulls and Crossbones: Tales of Women Pirates*. In 2008, he garnered an honorable mention in the Year's Best Fantasy and Horror (Datlow, Link, and Grant) for his story "In Earthen Vessels" (*Philippine Speculative Fiction, Vol. 3*).

Breaking into the Second Wind Nursing Home was easier than Muse expected.

An old woman sat up in her bed, eyes widening with each blink. "Hello, dear. Is it time for my meds?"

Muse was impressed—the sight of a man in a hematite half-mask and cobalt blue spandex hadn't made her scream. He pulled up a chair. "I'm just here to talk."

He could, alternatively, have gone to a bar or park bench or anywhere with people willing to engage in conversation. But he remembered how lonely his grandparents had been when they were alive, and thought to give back a little... while getting what he needed, of course.

The old lady looked at the back of her wrist. "Someone's stolen my watch! I bet it's that hag, Janet, across the hall. She huffs Ben Gay when she thinks no one's looking."

Muse spoke soothingly. "No, no, your watch is on the nightstand. It's a little after midnight."

She nodded absently while Muse laid a gentle hand on her arm and activated his powers. Tingling warmth passed from his fingertips into her body, travelling upward to fill the wellspring of her mind. For the millionth time, he regretted that he couldn't use his powers on himself.

Her sudden smile added wrinkles to her face. "What's on your mind, dear?"

"My friend's thirtieth birthday is next month—well, more of a lifelong crush than a friend—and I'm not sure what to get."

"Well, what does she like?"

Muse didn't bother correcting her reflexive choice of pronoun. "That's the problem. My friend doesn't really *like* much." Which was a nice way to say that he hated everything.

"Ooh, I have an idea," the old woman said. "What does she give other people for their birthdays? Usually you can tell what a person wants by the kind of gifts they give."

This made sense, but Dr. Schadenfreude was not known for his generosity. "He's not the gift-giving kind. More like the 'I will detonate a doomsday bomb unless all world governments bow before me' kind."

The old woman laughed. "Well there you go, just get them to bow to your friend." She paused, her brows furrowed, head bent. Muse waited patiently, until she started snoring.

"Ma'am?"

The woman woke and continued as though there had been no break in their dialogue. "Sometimes the best way to handle a problem is from the opposite direction. That's what my husband, Lord-rest-his-soul, used to say. If you can't give her what she likes, then take away what she doesn't."

Muse rubbed his chin. That list ran as long as a ski slope. He had known Dr. Schadenfreude since junior high, a simpler time when Muse was just Malcolm and Dr. Schadenfreude was just Edward. Even then, there had been no shortage of complaints: cafeteria food (gray lasagna was a staple), dress codes ("neckties are nooses"), and, of course, the bullies that plagued their teenage years. The list had only lengthened with time. But after a moment's consideration, Muse realized what topped all else.

Captain Stratagem. Defender of the mundane, he of super strength, lightning intellect, laser eyes, and tireless ego.

"He has a nemesis," Muse said.

The old lady patted his hand. "So why don't you just rub him out, dear?"

"This nemesis is... formidable. His mind's like a computer, with a database of all known super vill—I mean super-powered folk. He always wins because he's studied every known variable."

"Well, then you just keep surprising him. After all, birthdays are supposed to be full of surprise."

Overload him with surprises? Even so, the odds of success weren't promising.

And yet... he imagined presenting the hero, bound and helpless... the look on Dr. Schadenfreude's face...

Muse jumped up from his chair. "You've been very helpful. Maybe when it's all over,"—*if I survive*–"I'll come back and tell you about it." He leaned over and kissed the top of her head.

"Oh, no, dear," she said brightly. "Never on the first date."

The word went out, to every sleazy bar, back alley, sewer, and Tea Party convention:

Super villains wanted.

But not just any villains. Muse needed unknowns, those who had never made headlines or were only starting their careers. Criminals who lurked far beneath Captain Stratagem's radar.

For audition space, Muse broke into the now defunct Jean-Paul Sartre museum. The building had been closed down for safety violations when visitors could find no exits.

The interview room was actually a backstage dressing room. The wall painting behind Muse displayed Don Quixote charging against a tilted windmill whose top was a lighthouse beacon. A single smiling moth circled it. Muse didn't bother trying to interpret it, but he thought the lighthouse was handsomely painted.

He scanned the list of applicant names and sighed at the selection. *Captain Kookaburra? Dr. Oblivious? The Spinster?*

The first applicant walked through the door—literally—passing through like a wraith. A sweet sugary scent perked Muse's appetite.

In a thick accent, like Vincent Price playing a matador, the man announced, "I am El Fantasma que Sangra."

Muse rummaged through post-traumatic flashbacks of high school Spanish. "The fantasy who sings?" True, the man had a lithe physique and a handsome enough face—at least what could be seen behind his Zorro-esque mask—but it rang a bit egotistical to call oneself a fantasy.

The man gritted his teeth. "The *Ghost* who *bleeds*."

"Much scarier," said Muse. "But what do you do exactly?"

He demonstrated by oozing red through his costume. "A psychological tactic to unnerve the enemy. In reality, nothing can hurt me, for nothing can touch me." The sweet sugary scent filled the room more strongly.

"Why do I smell strawberry jam?" Not that Muse minded; he *loved* strawberries and everything that had them as an ingredient.

"It is blood, Señor Muse. I assure you. It would be an honor to serve on your team."

The last words sounded sincere, but Muse was on guard against flattery. "*Gracias.* Please wait in the auditorium for my final decision." The man bowed and disappeared through the door.

Heavy, clanging footsteps heralded the next applicant. Titanium armor covered him from head to heel, power servos revving menacingly as he walked. He'd barely stepped into the room before proclaiming in a buzzsaw voice: "I am not a robot."

Muse looked at the list of applicants and nodded. "I see you call yourself 'Armored Suit Man'—"

"Yes! Yes, that is what I am! A man. In an armored suit. Not a robot."

"Tell me about yourself."

Glasteel eyes whirled, while an oval LED at his chest beeped and blinked. "I was manufactured circa 2051, before my lab-crèche exploded hurtling me back through time."

"Hmmmm." Muse tapped his fingers on the table. "And your powers?"

"Accessing database, please hold," he said. After a pause: "Flight. Ability to press ten tons, extreme durability. Assorted arsenal, including lasers and flamethrower. Built-in GPS."

Useful. Strength and fortitude would definitely be needed against Stratagem. It may have been premature, but Muse made a decision. "I'd like to welcome you to the team."

"Fine," sputtered Armored Suit Man. "If that's your attitude, just because I look like a robot—which makes you a bigot—not that robots can help the way they were made—then you can take this job—"

"I said, '*Welcome to the team.*'"

"Computing." A sound like a drunken fax machine echoed in the room. Then, "Thank you. I will make you proud."

Before the metallic footsteps faded, Muse was already having second thoughts.

The next few candidates proved less than stellar—a satanic mime, a lady who called herself the Butterfly Whisperer, among others. Muse wrote big X's next to all their names.

The following applicant entered whistling *Puff the Magic Dragon*. Middle-aged, a few pounds shy of portly, thick brambly beard to offset a balding pate. He wore a tan trench coat—with no hint of shirt or pants underneath. Muse sighed and rested his chin on steepled fingers. "Before we start, you understand that exhibitionism is not a power?"

The man grinned and shrugged. "Depends what's on exhibit."

Muse hoped he wouldn't need an eye-scrub after this. "A work of art, I'm sure."

"Because I dig your groovy vibe, I'll let that slide. From the looks of those other dudes out there, I'm guessing I'm the only one here that's done hard time. Three months. Indecent exposure."

"I'm glad you didn't say concealed weapon."

The man snickered. When asked about his powers, he said, "Name should give you a clue."

Muse glanced at the list. "Flash Forward?"

"Time for show and tell."

Before Muse could avert his eyes, the man threw open his trench coat with practiced ease. Three impressions assaulted Muse: wanton, hirsute, and jelly-baby.

Then something weird happened.

Light flickered across the man's body, skin like a movie screen. Kaleidoscopic visions shimmered like a first class acid trip. Images leapt off, more striking than any 3D movie because they incorporated all the senses. In one scene Muse saw himself walking on a Peruvian beach, arm in arm with a handsome, somehow familiar stranger. A second image showed Dr. Schadenfreude, face contorted in anger, screaming at… him? A third vision nearly overwhelmed Muse: he was alone, fleeing through thick vegetation from something—some*one*—far more powerful than he.

Mercifully, Flash Forward closed his coat. "Sorry. Didn't mean to awe you so much."

Muse loosened his death grip on the table's edge. "What was… that?"

"Your future. Likely parts, anyway."

Muse's mind continued to spin. "How reliable are the visions? And when does the vertigo stop?"

"It's major mojo. Years ago, I flashed a grumpy, old gypsy woman. She said she'd make me truly revealing, but no one would care about my body because they'd see more important stuff instead. It stings, you know? People not seeing you for yourself."

"You can't just turn it off?"

"Nope, it's in my skin. I can't even look at myself in the mirror. One thing you should know though. The things you saw—could be years from now, so don't lose too much sleep, *capeesh?*"

"I w-won't," Muse said, still frazzled. Dr. Schadenfreude mad at him? Perhaps his friend was just having one of his cranky days. Muse hardly noticed when Flash Forward excused himself out.

A young Asian man wearing a brown bunny suit hopped into the room. He looked around, tentatively.

"So... would you like to tell me about yourself?" Muse asked.

"I was bitten by a radioactive chocolate bunny."

"A chocolate bunny? But they don't have teeth."

The man paled, his reply a choked whisper. "*Radioactive ones do.*"

"Ah, and can you tell me why you're here today?"

"My therapist said to be more sociable. Join groups."

Muse was still feeling sour from Flash Forward's visions. "So... what's your power? Melt in the sun? Have your ears bitten off?"

"I create chocolate bunnies. The regular kind, not radioactive ones."

"Naturally." Muse tried to imagine some possible utility for the power. Fending off starvation, perhaps. "Well, thank you for coming today. I don't want to waste any more of your time, so—"

The man thrust his hand out and a dark blur bulleted from his palm at supersonic speed. A podium near Muse exploded. Sawdust and the scent of chocolate filled the air.

"Ahhhh," said Muse.

Chocolate Bunny Boy nodded, and then hopped out the door. Muse drew a smiley face next to the applicant's name.

A short parade of colorful but useless candidates followed. Eventually, *thankfully*, the last applicant entered.

Light slid from beneath the door, and Muse sat at attention. When the man came in, Muse had to remind himself it was impolite to drool. A silver-lined toga swathed the applicant's chiseled physique. A laurel of ivy crowned luxuriant brown hair.

"W-welcome," Muse said. "Would you like to sit down?" *Or stay standing. Perhaps turn around a few times, then touch your toes.* Muse noticed that the man was not on the list. "May I ask your name?"

"I? I am Robigus. I am a Roman god."

Undeniably. "And why are you interested in joining a team, Robigus?"

"I'm immortal. I'm bored."

"Ah, well, I'll definitely do my best to keep things exciting. What sort of abilities do you have?"

The god showed his first sign of hesitance. "I'm… a protector."

"And what do you protect?"

He scratched his nose, mumbling behind his hand. Muse was certain he heard wrong. "Did you say 'grain'?"

"Yes. My favorite crop is corn. A pity the Empire never grew it."

"Corn? As in 'on the cob'?"

"Yes," Robigus said, more loudly.

"What do you protect it against?"

"Mostly diseases, but also weevils, aphids, and vagabonds. Anything really."

"Orville Redenbacher?" Muse quipped.

The lights of the room suddenly flickered, and the temperature plunged twenty degrees. Robigus's face twisted with rage. "Never again will you utter that name in my presence!"

Muse swallowed and shrank back. Some part of his mind wondered how Captain Stratagem would cope against this level of fury.

"My apologies. And my sincere gratitude for coming today. If you'd like to take a seat in the auditorium, I'll be out shortly."

Muse's gaze followed the god as he left, admiring the view. He wasn't entirely sure how a deity of corn would help, but at the very least he would be good for morale.

❦

The applicants fidgeted in their chairs as Muse took the stage. The final roster had been easy to pick, and after thanking all for attending, he called out the names of Robigus, Chocolate Bunny Boy, Flash Forward, Armored Suit Man, and El Fantasma que Sangra.

Grumbling rose immediately. One reject jumped up. "You will rue the day you denied me! So swears the Numerologist!" Muse dismissed the threat. The man's sole power was to guess what number you were thinking.

"Those who were chosen, please come up." The five super villains gathered as the rest shuffled out the exit with mutters and raised shaking fists.

A large folding table had been set up on stage. Not exactly the war room in Dr. Schadenfreude's subterranean fortress, but it would serve.

"So what's our first mission?" asked El Fantasma.

"We could knock off a liquor store," Flash Forward suggested.

Armored Suit Man's chest light blinked. "Or pillage Best Buy."

"Or plant corn," Robigus said, oblivious to the confused stares of the others. When he finally noticed, he flexed his chest muscles at them.

Muse shook his head. "I've already decided our first undertaking. We're going after Captain Stratagem."

Silence fell over the group.

"Dude, undertaking is right," Flash Forward said. "As in undertakers, who we'll need after the fight."

Chocolate Bunny Boy raised his hand. "My therapist told me suicide is permanent and that things do get better if one stays positive–"

Muse glared. "This isn't suicide."

Gears whirred from Armored Suit Man's direction. "My databanks indicate Captain Stratagem has bested such foes as Hades, King Catastrophe, and the entire Venutian space armada."

"Only because he'd studied their powers and tactics. He'll have no clue what we're capable of."

"With all due respect, Señor," El Fantasma said. "*We* don't know what we're capable of."

Muse had had enough. "I know I didn't pick a bunch of cowards. And I don't think any of you signed on to rob lemonade stands. We're going to make history by taking down one of the most prominent heroes of all time. The decision has been made, done, finito. If the thought of fighting him makes you uneasy, you can go home now."

When nobody moved, Muse restrained a sigh of relief. "Good. And don't worry. We'll have at least a week to learn each other's powers and practice attacking in concert–"

"We must attack tomorrow," Robigus announced.

Everyone's head turned. Dr. Schadenfreude would have fumed at the interruption, but Muse was too taken aback. "Why tomorrow?"

"It's my feast day. The one day in the year where my power is increased tenfold."

"You couldn't have mentioned this earlier?"

"I'm immortal. I lose track of time." The god laughed. "Besides, surely it's marked on your calendar? Normally I celebrate in a grove, where sheep entrails and wine are offered in sacrifice. But clouting a self-inflated mortal will suffice."

Muse felt each chamber of his heart palpitating. He took a deep breath; breaking down at their first meeting simply would not do. "Okay. Okay. Tenfold?" *Would it be worth it to rush the schedule?* He recalled the god's fury during the interview. *Probably.*

"Before we start brainstorming a battle plan, I'm going to use my powers to inspire each of you. We'll need as many good ideas as we can get."

Muse made his circuit around the table. But when he reached for El Fantasma, his hand went through him.

"Sorry, Señor Muse. I prefer not being touched." The sadness in his voice rang clear. Even through the small holes of El Fantasma's mask, Muse could see the apology in the man's eyes.

Dr. Schadenfreude would have demanded the man to solidify, but Muse didn't have it in him to make such an order. *Perhaps I'm not as ready to lead as I thought.*

Flash Forward offered his palm. "Slap me some skin, for inspirayshin."

Muse did so, and struggled not to imagine all the things that hand may have touched. He moved on to Robigus, who thought he was getting a massage, and Bunny Boy, who complained it tickled.

To Muse's surprise, his power even proved effective on Armored Suit Man. *Perhaps there is a man beneath that armor.*

✺

The brainstorming went well. "You all have your preparations," Muse said. "We'll reconvene tomorrow at seven a.m." Flash Forward groaned at the command, and Muse made a mental note to give him a wake-up call.

As they dispersed, El Fantasma asked Muse for a private word.

"I apologize again, Señor. I was of little use today, and likely will be so again tomorrow."

"Well… every bit helps."

"I will try. For you."

"For me?" Muse stared, for the first time wondering about the man behind the mask.

"Your name is spoken in circles that matter. Granted it is always attached to Dr. Schadenfreude, but it is spoken with respect even when his is not."

Muse bristled that the compliment included an insult against his friend.

El Fantasma continued. "So I value your opinion. Please do not think I'm a ghost because of cowardice. Sometimes it's just easier not to let anyone in, to withdraw."

Muse was touched by the man's openness, yet uncomfortable, too. Using his best Dr. Schadenfreude tone, he said, "Enough. I didn't pick the Narcoleptic or Mr. Migraine or those other rejects. I picked you, and you should be thankful."

The man smiled; not the effect Muse expected to his scolding.

"Muchas gracias," El Fantasma said. He turned to walk away, then added, "One thing more. The group you've assembled... it would be well to look beyond their powers, to see the strengths and foibles in their personalities."

"I'll take that under advisement," Muse said, though he had little intention of knowing them on anything but a superficial level.

When El Fantasma left, Muse took a deep breath and started working on a way to catch Captain Stratagem's attention.

The next morning, Muse pulled up in his car, pleased to find the newly assembled team waiting at the rendezvous point. Even Flash Forward was ready, gargling black coffee before swallowing it. Muse said, "Everyone, if you'd kindly gather. I've chosen Iowa to be our battleground."

"We're going to drive there," asked Bunny Boy, nervously, "in an '83 Chrysler Cordoba?"

"We're going to *fly* there." He turned to Armored Suit Man. "And *you* will fly us."

The scent of strawberry thickened in the air. Muse grew alarmed when he caught El Fantasma breaking out in a red sweat. Was the man acrophobic?

"I will need to solidify to stay in the car," El Fantasma said, a quiver in his voice.

"You can do that, though, yes?"

"I… could." The man's hesitance grew, and Muse could foresee where this was leading. "Perhaps it's better if I stay–"

"You made a commitment, and you will abide by it. As I would expect from any man of his word."

El Fantasma recoiled as if slapped. The comment had stung, just as Muse hoped. "Very well. As long as I don't have to sit next to the more… unwashed… members of our group." He glanced sidelong at Flash Forward.

"Shotgun's all yours," Muse said.

Robigus, Flash Forward, and Chocolate Bunny Boy crowded into the back. Flash Forward guzzled down the rest of his coffee. "Hey Bunny Dude, can you make Peeps? I got a craving."

"My name is not Bunny Dude," Chocolate Bunny Boy said as he clicked his seatbelt. "And Peeps are lethal. At least the radioactive ones are."

"Really?"

The car lurched as Armored Suit Man hefted it into the air. His leg thrusters ignited and soon they were soaring heavenward.

Flash Forward rolled down the window and yelled. "How fast can you get us there, dude?"

"Oh, what, I'm supposed to be able to calculate our arrival time just because I look like a robot?"

"Well, gee, your ears are metal. Your teeth are metal. Your eyebrows are—."

"That's facial profiling!"

"It would be best if we rest up and avoid further conversation," Muse interrupted.

Flash Forward suggested singing a song to pass the time. "How many bottles of beers do you think we need to get to Iowa?"

A dozen kegs, at least, Muse thought.

Robigus fidgeted in his seat like a child needing to go potty. "*Etiam advenimus*?" he muttered.

"No," Muse sighed, the tone of the question requiring no translation. "We're *not* there yet."

The note Muse had sent to Stratagem was concise: *Go to Grundy County, Iowa. As of 10 A.M. today, I am effecting my surrender.—Dr. Schadenfreude.* The supplied coordinates would lead the hero to the cornfield where he, Robigus, and El Fantasma lay waiting in ambush. Most of the team had tied corn to themselves, partly as camouflage, partly to court Robigus's blessing on his Feast Day.

Armored Suit Man stood watch, disguised as a scarecrow, his telescopic eyes scanning the blue sky. Bunny Boy patrolled deeper in the cornfield, his every hop clearing the eight-foot tall stalks. When Stratagem arrived, the first thing he would notice was a giant bouncing rabbit.

A soft beep sounded in Muse's earphone, and Armored Suit Man's voice cut through. "Attention Dorothy, the Wicked Witch has arrived... and is veering on a course towards Toto."

"Acknowledged, Tin Man."

"I am not a Tin Man, I am a Scarecrow."

Muse ignored him and contacted Bunny Boy via his comlink cuff. "You've been spotted. Hightail it to the Lion."

A startled squeak came over the speaker. "Lion? You didn't mention lions."

"I mean Flash Forward," Muse said with a sigh.

"Why didn't you just say so?"

From where Muse lay, he could see the clearing where Flash Forward lounged smoking a joint. The moments ticked by, then a heavily-breathing Bunny Boy hopped into view. Flash Forward snubbed out the joint and put it in his pocket.

A strong wind stirred the stalks, and a sound like an incoming missile shattered the clear Iowa air. A figure set down in front of Flash Forward and Bunny Boy, sending a cloud of grit into the air.

Stratagem. Muse's heart thudded in his chest. All he could see was the hero's back, but even so, the man cut an imposing presence—gold cape billowing, silver spandex clinging lovingly to bulging muscles, red epaulettes on broad shoulders, and bare arms that could toss skyscrapers without strain.

Stratagem sniffed the air. "Under Iowa Code section 124.401, you are hereby charged with the unlawful possession of marijuana." His rich baritone resounded with authority.

Flash Forward snickered. "Don't see no Mary-Jane, Daddy-O. Could be I have a joint in my pocket. Too bad you can't see no proof."

Excellent. Muse had worried the exhibitionist would flub his lines.

Stratagem's head bent slightly forward, and Muse knew the hero was using x-ray vision to investigate Flash Forward's statement. Exactly as Muse predicted. The x-ray vision would also reveal Flash Forward's nakedness, and then…

Stratagem stiffened, then staggered, clearly mesmerized by the sun-bright kaleidoscopic patterns exploding on Flash Forward's skin.

"Now!" Muse shouted, and everyone burst from their hiding places and charged.

Bunny Boy kicked out at Stratagem's knee, to no visible effect. Armored Suit Man fared better, landing a kidney punch that elicited a pained grunt.

And then Robigus was there. With a roar, the god swung, his blow hurtling the hero through the air and deeper into the heart of the cornfield.

Muse cursed under his breath. The plan had been for Flash Forward's powers to transfix Stratagem while the rest of them pummeled him into unconsciousness. But the god's last punch had proved too strong. "Hurry, we have to press our advantage!"

Armored Suit Man craned his neck. "At last measured velocity, our target should be approximately 93 meters away. Motion detectors are not picking up anything. He may be down."

"Let's not assume. Robigus take point."

The god scoffed. "What I've seen thus far has hardly impressed."

"Don't underestimate—"

Parts of Armored Suit Man started beeping. "Boss! I'm detecting movement. Speed: 110 mph. Bearing: Us!"

"Evasive!" screamed Muse, throwing himself to the ground as a whistling whoosh keened louder. A yellow tractor blurred through the air smashing into Robigus like a bowling ball making the spare. The projectile clipped Armored Suit Man, spinning him away, while Chocolate Bunny Boy hopped high, barely clearing it. Only El Fantasma stood his ground, the vehicle passing harmlessly through him.

In the distance, Captain Stratagem rose into the air like a spirit of vengeance. Red light blazed from his eyes as he sped toward them.

Muse scrambled to his feet. Robigus lay unconscious on the ground only a few yards away. *Damn*! Even from a distance, Stratagem had managed to identify his greatest threat.

"Knights Nefarious, assail him!" When the team just stared, Muse added, "That's us! Attack!"

Bunny Boy raised his hand. "I don't remember voting for that name—"

"Hush! And Attack!" Muse's voice was turning hoarse, unused to shouting orders.

Bunny Boy leapt high, shooting a burst of hollow-point bunnies. Armored Suit Man released a laser blast from his chest.

Stratagem dodged the latter, but found himself pelted with the barrage of chocolate projectiles. He raised an arm to block them. "You're assaulting me with Easter Candy?"

"Launch the largest bunny you've got," Muse hissed at Bunny Boy, then turned to Armored Suit Man. "Ready your flamethrower."

Bunny Boy took a series of quick breaths that would have impressed the strictest Lamaze coach. A chocolate bunny the size of a VW Beetle began materializing before him.

Muse waited a second, then ordered, "Flame it! Bunny Boy, shoot!" The flamethrower in Armored Suit Man's forearm scorched the chocolate bunny as it rocketed forth.

Stratagem had braced himself to shatter the object with a punch. It left him unprepared for the wave of molten fudge that crashed into him. Disoriented, he tried to fly up, but plunged headlong into the ground, gouging a huge furrow through the rows of corn.

"Stockpile!" Muse shouted.

They rushed forth, corn cobs swinging from their clothes. Flash Forward whooped, happy to finally join the action.

The group ganged up on the prone hero, showering him with punches as Bunny Boy bounced up and down on his back. El Fantasma, unable to engage in a physical assault, threw demoralizing taunts instead.

Stratagem's arm suddenly swung out, slapping Flash Forward and Armored Suit Man into the distance like toys flung in a child's tantrum. He caught Bunny Boy in mid-descent by the throat. "I... am not... a trampoline."

El Fantasma darted away, the movement catching Stratagem's attention. Laser beams streaked from the hero's eyes, only to burn the stalks on the other side of his target.

Muse charged from behind hoping for a sneak attack, but Stratagem whirled to throttle him with his free hand.

"Let them go!" El Fantasma cried.

"Or what? You'll walk through me? I've fought the Red Spook and Poltergeist and other intangible cretins. You're even more useless than your teammates."

Muse saw the shock and wounded pride on the El Fantasma's face. "I am sorry, Señor Muse," he said, his voice betraying only the slightest tremble. "The *Capitan* is right. I should never have bothered." He slowly sank into the ground, and with him, Muse's hopes.

"Another one gone," Stratagem said. "Now before I knock you and the Easter Bunny unconscious, would you care to explain why you're draped in corn?"

"They're... protection."

Stratagem smirked and systematically used mini-blasts of his laser vision to target the corn cobs on Muse's body. Each exploded in a burst of popcorn, each bang like point-blank firecrackers as Muse yelped and squirmed.

"Enough!" came a thunderous voice, and Muse turned his head, hope swelling at what he saw. The cornstalks parted like the Red Sea to give Robigus passage.

The scent of rich earth invaded the air. A dark cloud veiled the sun as the enraged god spoke. "I have heard the screams of my children, their stalks snapped and roots ruptured from *Terra Mater*! Quake now, and know the vengeance of the corn!"

Bunny Boy took advantage of the distraction, planting a kick right into Stratagem's solar plexus. Stratagem released his captives just as the Roman god fell upon him.

The two combatants rained blow after blow on each other, each impact sending a shockwave that made Muse's bones shudder. Divine light limned Robigus. Stratagem met each attack, unflinching. Muse could imagine the battle raging forever.

And then, between punches, the taunts began. "Your fetish for corn is appropriate. Quite a pitiful little crop. Did you know corn caused a pellagra outbreak in the late 19th century? Nutrient deficiencies, not surprisingly."

To Muse, the ploy was transparent. "Don't listen to him!" But Robigus was already snarling, his rage making his attacks wild. Stratagem weaved deftly under frenetic punches, returned with several solid jabs.

To his credit, Chocolate Bunny Boy jumped in to help, bunnies streaming out so fast that smoke issued from his palms. When Robigus pressed the attack, Stratagem caught his wrist, and judo-flipped him hard into Bunny Boy. The god was unhurt, but Bunny Boy fell to the battlefield and lay still on a bed of broken cornstalks.

Muse heard rustling behind him and spun to find Armored Suit Man approaching, his right hand slung protectively over his left side.

"What's wrong?" Muse asked, rushing over.

Armored Suit Man said nothing, his metallic face turning a pinkish sheen.

"Are you injured?" Muse persisted, then noticed the coils and wiring poking out of his teammate's "wound." Muse understood then. Armored Suit Man could no longer deny what he was.

A choked cry grabbed both their attentions. Robigus stood behind Stratagem, a muscled arm wrapped tight around the hero's throat. Hope bloomed in Muse's heart. It would only be a matter of time before their foe lost consciousness. Robigus gave a startled squawk when Stratagem suddenly launched into the sky taking the god with him. Muse gaped, and Armored Suit Man blared, a sorrowful sequence of beeps. Aerial combat would yield only one winner because, for all his power, Robigus was a god of the soil, of the earth—-a god who could not fly. The two clashed unseen in the clouds, their presence only known by the thunder of their blows.

And then silence.

Robigus's limp body plummeted through the clouds, speeding until it blasted a crater in the earth with an ear-splitting boom.

"We're toast," observed Armored Suit Man, as Captain Stratagem floated down without haste.

"No," Muse said, "not without a fight. I can't stand against him, but you can."

"Me? I'm not even a... a man."

Muse slapped him in the face, a move he instantly regretted. He gritted his teeth against the throbbing in his hand. "Do you think a man is only the materials he's made from? Flesh or metal, bones or gears? That's just the housing. It's what's inside that counts."

"But—"

"Yesterday, at our meeting… my powers actually worked on you. They wouldn't have unless there was something inside you to inspire. You have a soul, my friend. And you have *life*. Are you going to waste that bemoaning how you're different from everyone else?"

A gleam shimmered in the Glasteel eyes, a spark so bright Muse thought it would set the world aflame.

"You're right," proclaimed the buzz-saw voice. "It's not others who are the robophobes, it's me. Well, no more. Say goodbye to Armored Suit Man." Leg thrusters ignited, and Muse watched him skyrocket on a collision course with Stratagem, a battle-cry on his metal lips: "And say hello to Robot Man!"

Stratagem's laser beams lanced out and cut him in half.

"I'm glad you cleared that up," the hero said. "No guilt, then, in using my lasers at maximum."

"You monster!" Muse cried, stunned as the two halves of Robot Man fell to the earth.

"I believe it's your turn, Muse," Stratagem called down.

As a desperate ploy, Muse shouted into his comlink. "Stratagem's in position, launch the missiles!" As his foe readied to meet the imagined assault, Muse made a break for it. Hearing no sounds of pursuit, he glanced back.

Stratagem had risen higher, scanning the fields. But how long before he saw through the ruse?

Muse stumbled, a sense of déjà vu nearly crippling him. *This* was what he had seen when he'd first interviewed Flash Forward—himself, crashing through vegetation, alone and fleeing a foe he had no hope to defeat.

He thought of his friend, the man he had hoped would one day notice his love. *I'm sorry, Edward. It looks like I'll be missing your birthday.* Muse's arms stung as he batted away the jungle of cornstalks. A shadow fell over him as Stratagem swooped down and blocked his escape.

"Cute tactic. All this time, I'd believed Schadenfreude was the mastermind and you the henchman."

Muse wanted to slap the smugness off Stratagem's face, but it was pointless. *'Suicide is permanent,'* Bunny Boy had said. "I surrender. But don't be surprised when Dr. Schadenfreude breaks me out of jail."

Stratagem's laughter rippled through the cornfield. "Will he? If you were held hostage, what ransom would he pay? He's as selfish as any villain I've fought, and I've fought thousands."

Muse flushed. "Apparently you don't know him as well as I."

"Really? If you lost your power tomorrow, would he keep you around?"

"Shut... up."

Stratagem laughed again, then stopped, his attention swiveling to the right. Muse heard it now, too—rustling through the stalks, something being dragged, and heavy panting.

Stratagem clapped his hands once, the tremendous shockwave enough to flatten the cornstalks around the source of the noise.

El Fantasma stood there, back towards them and sweating jam.

"You should have run," Stratagem said.

"I shall, but not alone," he responded, then spun aside. In that same movement, he ripped open a trench coat to reveal the naked, unconscious form of Flash Forward.

Muse had the quicker presence of mind not to look, but either bewilderment or overconfidence made Captain Stratagem stare one millisecond too long. His mind snagged once more onto the psychedelic lightshow.

Muse could only imagine what visions assailed him. Strain and sweat marred the hero's face, a look of apt concentration, and Muse feared the hero might soon build enough willpower to turn away.

El Fantasma called out frantically. "We must run. Now!"

Muse nodded, but when he saw Stratagem standing there, too engaged to defend himself, Muse paused, wishing for even a fraction of Robigus's strength. *But I can't do a damn thing.*

Or could he? He couldn't harm Stratagem physically, but perhaps...

"What are you waiting for, Señor?" El Fantasma cried, nearly pulling his hair out.

Muse activated his power on Stratagem.

Those who had been on the receiving end of Muse's ability had described it in a variety of ways. Puzzle pieces of light shaping to form the big picture.

A tornado of fireworks that illuminated the mind's darkest recesses. Sparks birthing bonfires birthing suns.

How would that affect a psyche already besieged by mind-staggering visions? Muse had never before tried to use his power for offense, but he did so now, stimulating Stratagem's mind with a deluge of insights, inventions, and new modes of thought. *Just how much data can that computer brain of yours juggle before it crashes?*

Muse could actually feel Stratagem resisting, raising psychic walls as formidable as a mountain range. But the attacks of Robot Man, Bunny Boy, and Robigus had taken their toll. Muse fought on, eroding Stratagem's psychic mindscape, stirring dust, disturbing pebbles, then stones and boulders, till the mountainsides sloughed down in violent landslides.

A soft groan escaped Stratagem's lips, his face grew slack, and he toppled at last to the ground.

Muse dropped to his knees. *Was it over?* He felt drained, so much so that when he heard a sharp beeping, he was shocked he had enough energy to flinch.

Out of the cornstalks crawled the head and torso of Robot Man. "Bravo! If you can find my lower body, I should be able to fix myself enough to fly us out of here."

"You... I-I thought you were dead."

"Only cut in half. What do you take me for... some fragile human?"

Muse laughed with relief, and even a measure of pride. A hand rested on his shoulder, and he was shocked to find it was El Fantasma.

"The others do not appear seriously hurt, except for Señor Robigus, but he is healing rapidly."

"Good. And thank you. If you would be so kind as to help me to my feet, we can search for Robot Man's better half."

"An important thing to search for," El Fantasma agreed.

✿

In the darkness of the lab, Muse could hear the breathing of his teammates. A balloon popped, making him jump. "Sorry, my bad," Robot Man said.

"I don't really like the dark," said Bunny Boy in a small voice.

Robigus asked, "Will this be much longer?" and Muse wondered how an immortal could be so impatient.

Then they heard Dr. Schadenfreude's footsteps. The door opened and the lights went on.

"Surprise!" they yelled, Muse's voice loudest of all.

Dr. Schadenfreude's hand was a blur as he drew his laser pistol and began blasting away.

"It's me!" cried Muse, and the gunfire stopped. Several balloons were vaporized and a stray shot had grazed one of Bunny Boy's ears, but Muse was relieved to see no one disintegrated.

Dr. Schadenfreude froze at the showpiece laid out on the central laboratory table—Captain Stratagem, trussed, gold cape fashioned into a bow, corncob in his mouth. Flash Forward had suggested a different orifice but Muse insisted this be a classy affair.

"How?" Dr. Schadenfreude screeched. "And who are these people?"

"They helped me get your birthday present. And don't worry, he's heavily sedated."

Dr. Schadenfreude looked from face to face, his expression growing more disgusted. "I'm supposed to believe these misfits accomplished what's eluded me my whole career?"

"Awkwarrrrrd," El Fantasma whispered, the r's rolling like a red carpet.

Muse blinked. "Guys, please wait outside?"

They shuffled out reluctantly, though not before Bunny Boy stuck his tongue out at Schadenfreude.

The heavy lab doors hadn't even shut before Muse spoke. "I did this for you."

Schadenfreude stood there in his black cape and purple lab coat, eyes fixed on Stratagem. His expression was that of a young child who'd unwrapped his Christmas gift... only to find the toy broken. Muse was moved by the depth of disappointment. He wanted to reach out... to offer comfort.

Schadenfreude's face hardened. "Was this to upstage me? Revenge because I've never returned your little crush?"

Muse felt his face turn hot. "You knew... all this time? You never said anything."

"I had no interest raising topics you yourself kept buried in silence."

Muse searched Schadenfreude's face for any sign of warmth, regret. It was a handsome face, confident and passionate, but it could not mask years of anger and pain. Muse had dreamt of bringing a smile to those lips with a kiss, of softening those harsh lines with a caress. But familiarity and fascination had blinded him. Bravado wasn't confidence. Mania wasn't passion. Pain suffered was no excuse for pain unleashed.

And there was only ever one reason why Muse was allowed to touch him.

"I'm sorry," said Muse.

"Your apologies mean nothing—"

"You don't understand. I'm sorry for making you, for feeding your madness."

Dr. Schadenfreude's eyes widened, and his body tensed like a coiled viper. "You? Made me?"

"You were in remedial Algebra for goodness sakes. You flunked Physics. Your Spanish was even worse than mine—"

"Worse than yours? Impossible."

"Yes, worse! How could someone with your GPA create the Slaughter Cannon or the Extinction Overdrive Calibrator? It was me, using my powers to turn every delusion of grandeur into reality. Pouring every iota of inspiration I could give because I wanted you to... to like me." Even now, Muse hoped Schadenfreude would show some hint of reciprocation, some sign that he'd kept love hidden for fear.

"You clingy little bug! How dare you take credit—"

"Stratagem was right. You only cared about my power, not me."

Dr. Schadenfreude leveled his laser pistol at Muse. "I thought you wise enough to consider the cost of insubordination. It appears I was gravely mistaken."

"We both were." Muse couldn't move, wouldn't fight back. If losing his life was the final cost he'd pay for loving a maniac, then so be it.

A ghostly figure rose from the floor, interposing himself between them. "I hope you don't mind, Señor Muse. The Bunny could hear things were amiss. And as for you, Dr. Schadenfreude, I would caution against any rashness."

"You dare? A piss-ant nobody—"

"I am El Fantasma que Sangra."

Dr. Schadenfreude cocked his head. "The duck who thirsts?"

"See!" said Muse. "Worse than mine."

The lab door burst open and the rest of the team ran in. "Freeze!" shouted Robot Man, his flamethrower shooting a small gout of flame in the air. Bunny Boy hopped protectively before Muse.

Dr. Schadenfreude had not lowered his gun. "The day I cower from a motley crew of fetishists and freaks—"

"We took down Stratagem," Muse said.

Schadenfreude hesitated. His eyes locked with Muse's, and for a moment, they were the only two people in the room. A single twitch on Schadenfreude's face marked the end of the staring match.

He lowered his pistol. "If I ever see you again—"

"Happy Birthday," Muse said, then led his team away.

❧

Not a week had passed before the news stations reported Captain Stratagem's escape. Apparently, he had absorbed the energies from the torture device he'd been strapped in, enough to recharge his prodigious strength and turn the tables on a shocked Schadenfreude. A newscaster spoke over footage of the Doctor being carted to an omega-level detention facility. Muse had never seen him look so defeated.

Muse took a last swig from his beer bottle. He changed the channel, but the broadcast of Schadenfreude's capture was everywhere.

Muse closed his eyes. Last night, he had broken into the nursing home again, had cried upon the old lady's shoulder. She had comforted him despite having no idea what he was talking about. "Did your friend not like the birthday gift?" she had asked. In the end, he could not help but laugh.

His cell phone rang, and he nearly jumped. It was El Fantasma.

"Buenas noches, Señor."

"Is everything okay?" A long pause ensued, and Muse began to worry. "Hello? Are you still there?"

"I... Señor, I was wondering if... you would be interested in going... in doing me the honor... of having dinner with me."

The next pause was Muse's. "...but... you'd have to be tangible to eat, right? And to sit on a chair..." Muse realized he was babbling.

"I already do all those things. But it might be nice not to do them alone. Unless you are busy—"

"No!" Muse glanced at the empty beer bottles on his table. "No, I could use some company, too."

They agreed upon a place, a quiet little Peruvian restaurant the next town over. Muse expressed concern they might not recognize each other unmasked, but El Fantasma stated he'd wear a corncob tie tack. After the call, Muse found himself lost in a tumble of emotions. He shut off the television and hurriedly undressed to shower.

As hot water washed over him, he questioned the wisdom of dating a team member. Was he just rebounding from unrequited love? Schadenfreude had been his world for so long. How meek El Fantasama seemed in comparison. Meek and kind... and sane.

Muse vigorously shampooed his hair and basked in the jets of steaming water. He became joyfully aware of his own smile, and the unexpected prospect of a delightful evening.

An evening that might just end with the taste of strawberry jam.

SNOW AND STONE
Stellan Thorne

Stellan Thorne lives in Manchester with his partner, several cats and a chaotic stack of comic books. He always wanted to be a super villain, but suspects he's either too nice or too lazy.

They stepped down from the plane onto sun-warmed tarmac; it was mid-summer, late in the day, and the sky was blue and bare, save for the subtle aurora-shimmer of the force field, domed high above.

Edward surreptitiously loosened his tie. His hands were sweaty, slick on the handle of his briefcase. He wasn't the last off the plane, but near to it—he'd been crowded to the rear with the other second-stringers. Out in front were the broadcast people: he saw Cal Ingram from *The World Today*, grinning in his trademark tweed, and there was Patricia Lean from *Lean and Mean*, a carrion bird in powder-blue.

A man he did not recognize leaned over to him. "Where are you from?"

"I'm Edward Stone," he said. "From the *Victoryville Herald*."

"Oh yeah?" He grinned, holding out a hand. "Good to meet you. I'm Tim Carvell."

He knew the name: Carvell had written a book about the coup. Edward had a dog-eared copy in his briefcase. "Nice to meet you," he said weakly.

Carvell cleared his throat. "Do you think we're–"

The sentence hung unfinished—loudspeakers whined suddenly, slicing into their conversation. Then a song started to play, tinny and bombastic: the national anthem of Prometheus Isle.

Soldiers in immaculate uniforms herded the crowd along the runway; there was a podium at its end, a great marble slab, black speakers high as a man on either side.

Carvell leaned close again. "The welcoming committee."

"Do you think—is General Snow going to be here?"

"Probably." Carvell smiled, thin and chilly. "He likes making an appearance."

The sound cut out suddenly with an echoing screech. Edward jumped a little, along with half the crowd. They waited in the buzzing silence.

Then: one moment, the podium was empty, with the soldiers milling round, automatic rifles loose in their gloved hands. The next, General Snow stood there, leaning down like a vulture. His uniform was black, gleaming with medals; the mask that hid half his face was white and severe, like the statue of an ancient emperor.

The murmur of voices died out. General Snow watched them with pale eyes, and when he spoke it bypassed sound: it burrowed into the brain like a half-remembered song.

Welcome to Prometheus Isle. You are all my guests. No—

(This came sharp as winter wind, cutting off Cal Ingram's indrawn breath.)

—*questions. Yet.*

His eyes swept the small crowd. They rested for a moment on Edward, who held his breath. There was the suggestion of a smile, behind his mask.

First, you are all invited to dinner.

❧

The news came late on a Friday afternoon, with the office still stinking of long, boozy lunches. He'd stayed in to type up his interview with Blue Simoom, a low-watt metahuman who did some hero work on the riverside. They met in a dim wine bar, where she got giggly after a few spritzers and made a small whirlwind appear in the peanut bowl.

It wasn't earth-shattering reading—but he'd liked her, with her home-stitched costume and earnest eyes. He hoped Louise would run it. Better someone like Blue than another sponsored meta, with strings of corporate logos silkscreened on their cape, or a posturing vigilante with a hard-on for *Guns and Ammo*.

Speak of the devil: Louise had emerged from her office. Edward looked up at her and smiled, but she didn't see him; she was buzzing with purpose. She held up her hands and loudly cleared her throat. "Pencils down, all of you. Come here—I need a word."

Edward flicked his monitor off and stood up, near the centre of the half-circle forming around her. After a moment, she nodded, more to herself than any of the others.

"Well, now that we're all here–"

There was a conspicuous creak: the office door opened, and Gerry Gates came in. He smiled at them, not quite sheepish. "Sorry."

Louise raised one corner of her mouth. "Thank you for joining us, Gerald."

"I was just finishing–"

She cut him off with one of her smoker's coughs, then fixed them all with bloodshot eyes. "Right. Yesterday, the government of Prometheus Isle announced they will be allowing a select group of journalists access into the country, and... an audience with its President-for-life."

"No," Gerry breathed. His eyes gleamed.

Louise continued. "The Promethean embassy has issued invitations to fifteen news organizations: one spot on a plane each." She coughed a laugh. "An all-expenses paid trip to Prometheus Isle. God only knows why we've been invited, Victoryville isn't exactly Washington. Still, we're not going to turn a gift like this down. One of you will be going to interview General Snow."

The office was very quiet for a moment. Edward watched them, from the corner of his eye: who was shuffling backward, who was leaning forward?

After a moment, Gerry stepped forward, ran both hands through his hair and grinned. "Well. Shall I pack my bags?"

Louise's brows raised, just a little—the only expression that showed on her botox-smooth face. "I can't fault your confidence," she said, "but you won't get a Promethean visa, Gerald. They're not issued to anyone with a criminal record."

His grin fell away. "That was civil disobedience."

She shrugged. "Doesn't matter. I'll have to send someone else."

"Have you got another Hillman prize winner here, Louise? Because if you do I can't see them."

Again, her eyebrows raised; she said nothing. With a heel-clicking turn, she looked at Edward.

"Stone."

He blinked at her. "Yes? Sorry?"

"You've got good experience with metahumans. And you've got a valid passport."

Edward's mouth opened, but before he spoke there was a humourless laugh from Gerry.

"Eddie Stone? *Eddie Stone*? From the *hero gossip column*?"

Louise closed her eyes a moment and pressed a fingertip to her forehead. "Gerald, can I see you in my office, please?"

The door slammed behind them. With slow steps Edward made his way to his desk and sat down. There was a soft tinkle of voices around him. He turned on his computer, typed in *General Snow, Prometheus Isle*.

Louise's office door showed two silhouettes through watery glass, like puppets in a shadow play. He glanced back to his screen. Gerry's voice cut through the door.

"—my career is fine, Lu. I'm thinking about us, about the Herald."

He focused on the screen. There was a propaganda picture of Prometheus Isle, all greenery and carefully restored buildings—there, crowded up against it, a blurry cell phone snapshot of a headless corpse. He read:

Since General Alberic Snow seized power two years ago, all Promethean media has been under tight state control—

"Because this isn't a goddamn puff piece!"

Too loud. Gerry always spoke too loud.

"No, no, that's not what I meant! I'm just saying–"

Edward kept himself still, concentrating on the soft click of his finger against the mouse, on the words scrolling by on the screen. He felt the weight of eyes on him.

—metahuman Elisa Reid (also known as 'Paragon') speaking for the League of Metahuman Peace Officers, says the League will abide by UN directives regarding Prometheus Isle, but warned of the risk from unaligned, or 'vigilante', metahumans—

"Come on, Lu, be serious. Think of his safety. He'll be lucky not to be shot on sight."

Her reply was measured, muffled—there was a burst of laughter from Gerry.

"Just as long as he knows he won't get airlifted out if he breaks a nail."

—the extent of General Snow's powers are unknown, but they are known to include near-invulnerability, enhanced reflexes, and telepathy, perhaps with minor 'mind control' elements. In addition, his scientific acumen has allowed him to—

The door to Louise's office slammed open. Edward forced himself not to look up. He heard Gerry breathe out sharply, heard the sizzle of a match as he lit a cigarette. He ambled over to Edward's desk.

"Look," he said, and took a drag. "Look. You're a little out of your depth here, but Lu tells me we've got no one else that fits the bill. So I'll brief you. Even prepare a list of questions. We can share the byline."

Edward breathed out slowly. "Awful generous of you, Gerry."

"Come on, Ed." His smile was distant. "You do all right on the freak beat, but this isn't Captain Rainbow or Rat-Girl talking about how their grannies inspired them and where they get their tights, or whatever. Let me help you."

Edward stood up, and smiled. Gerry leaned backward, just a little, lips twisted, as if he tasted something spoiled.

"Thanks very much, Gerry," Edward said, keeping up his well-crafted smile. "But I think I'll be all right."

✿

The presidential palace was a great, squat folly, a remnant of the old regime. The old monarchic crowns and devices had been buffed from its façade, but the rest of it was untouched—a museum piece, draped in the severe white banners of the militants. They were gathered at a dining table that could have seated a hundred; a handful of journalists, and a few Promethean nobles turned hard-line loyalists—allowed to keep a measure of their former power.

The General, of course, sat at its head. Watching.

The mood was sober. Normally, any four of the guests together—at least the journalists—would have been drinking and arguing in an eyeblink, but here, each sommelier and butler carried a sidearm. They looked down at their empty plates, trying not to notice all the gleaming guns.

There was a sound; half the table jumped. It was Tim Carvell, clearing his throat. "Well," he said, "I guess no one tries to rob the wine cellars."

A nervous thrill of laughter passed around the table. Edward tried to catch Carvell's eye; the writer wore a frantic kind of grin.

Snow cocked his head. He'd not joined with the laughter, but his pale eyes seemed amused. *An armed society is a polite society, I find. But... ah. Here comes the first course.*

He tracked the progress of his staff over folded hands. They slid silent and efficient, every button of their uniforms gleaming. Snow waited until every plate was heaped and every wineglass full. Then he took off his half-mask.

Below the patrician arch of his nose he was skinless: it was as if the meat of his jaw has been stripped away, leaving only bone and teeth. He was half a skull.

One man—Edward thought it might have been Cal Ingram—made a soft, retching noise in the back of his throat, quickly stifled.

Bon appétit said Snow, and his lipless mouth grinned—but then, it grinned constantly.

❦

After dinner, Edward tried to catch Carvell, to talk to him—but they were separated by uniformed attendants at their sides.

"Sir?" His escort was a young woman, with a port-wine birthmark on her cheek. She touched him lightly, at the bend of his elbow. "Come with me, please."

He glanced down at her gun, gleaming in its holster. "Do I have a choice?"

Her lips showed the ghost of a smile. "Always, sir."

His room was no worse, and no better, than any midrange hotel. It was cream-coloured and generic; there was even a small picture over the double bed, a workmanlike charcoal showing Mount Prometheus, the volcano at the center of the island, coiling smoke into the sunset.

He sat down on the edge of the bed. The mattress was ergofoam: one of Snow's inventions. It gave gently under his weight, then recoiled to prop him up. Back home, ergofoam was banned—officially—but no few managed to get their hands on a pillow or mattress here and there. Gerry Gates had boasted more than once about his own ergofoam chair.

He laid down for a moment, cradled by the mattress, and half-closed his eyes. An image flashed behind them: General Snow's skull-grin.

An hour or so later, he woke to a soft knock on the door. Sleep had snuck up on him, stuttery and dreamless. He dragged himself upright.

"Who is it?"

The door opened a crack; there was no lock. Carvell's face appeared there, grinning, a sheen of sweat on his forehead.

"Can I come in? I don't have much time."

Edward rubbed the sleep away from his eyes. "Time…?"

Carvell came in and leaned against the door. An unlit cigarette hung between his fingers. "Well, I had my 'interview'. Two questions I managed, before I got the boot." He brought the cigarette to his lips, and laughed. "Trying to quit."

"So, what do you mean, you 'don't have much time'?"

"They're hustling us back to the plane, one by one, when he's done with us. No more presidential hospitality, I'm afraid. I told my minder I had to take a leak. Took seven doors before I found you."

"What—"

"Look." He talked around the unlit cigarette. "They scan you for recording equipment. But I slipped this through. A meta friend of mine made it. It records his telepathic voice."

He reached in his coat—took out something small and sleek and white, like a tiny egg. Two steps, and he was sitting beside Edward; his hand slid into Edward's coat, and dropped the egg into his pocket. The touch was warm and startling and too quick; Carvell had an illusionist's hands.

Edward sucked in a breath. "Why me?"

"I like you." Carvell's smile was quick as his hands. "I like your work. You did good stuff, before you joined Louise Moorcock's rag." He paused. "And still... you never mock. You never go cheap."

A sour indignation rose up for a moment—did he know how he had to fight for every column inch, did he know how many times he'd heard *can you just freak it up a little*, or *remember, people like to* laugh *at these guys*—. The little white egg felt like a stone in his pocket.

Carvell straightened up. "Ask the bastard about the daily executions," he said. "Ask him—"

He cocked his head. There were footsteps coming closer, and someone calling out his name.

"See you on the plane, Stone," he said, grinning, and slipped out just as quick as he'd arrived.

🗲

He heard the march of footsteps back and forth—once, he thought he heard Patricia Lean's voice, rising in one of her shrill execrations. Then it was quiet, until they came for him.

He passed through a line of scanners, and a tall man swept every curve and plane of him with a black, pulsing wand. His eyes watched the on-and-off blink of its single green light. Carvell's gift remained snug in his pocket, unfound.

Before they let him into the old throne room—of course, Snow was quartered where the murdered king once ruled—a woman with a clipboard read off, in a thick accent, a list of rules, topics he was not to broach. He barely heard them; the blood in his ears rushed louder than her voice.

Then they pushed him inside. There were no minders, no mediators. He was on his own.

The great marble throne was empty. Two chairs of equal height had been set, facing each other, with a small table between then. In one of the chairs was General Snow, masked and immaculate.

Welcome.

He rose, and held out his hand. Edward hesitated for a moment before extending his own. The ruler of Prometheus Isle had a firm, friendly grip.

Please, sit. He indicated one of the chairs.

Edward sat down. It was a little too narrow for him. He squirmed into a comfortable position. He felt naked without a notebook in his hand.

"So." He grinned nervously. "How do we start?"

You ask me questions, of course. Snow sat down opposite him, hands lightly folded. He seemed amused. *Isn't that how it usually goes?*

"You'll have to forgive me," Edward said. "I'm not used to interviewing dictators–"

He swallowed reflexively. For a moment, there was a chill silence. Then, Snow laughed. His telepathic laughter was like fireworks, like biting down on something bright.

Fair enough. He crossed his legs. *I'll readily admit I am a dictator, but I also see myself as a liberator.* The lingering suggestion of a smile danced in his pale eyes. *I hope you will come to understand that.*

Edward coughed. "The free world doesn't seem to see it that way."

The 'free world'.

The phrase was loaded with a palpable contempt, sour as bile in Edward's mind.

I call it the sick *world, where children starve, in tents and in fine cities; where blood and money run like twinned rivers. Here, it is simple. I am the only atrocity I will permit within my borders.*

Edward had read the analyses, the pseudonymous blogs and thick grey-jacketed tomes. Narcissistic, grandiose, god complex—the words came to him easily, so easily that he had to bite his tongue. They were all true, they were all incomplete. Snow's colourless eyes fixed him like twin needles.

On Prometheus Isle, no one is without the necessities of life. No one is forgotten. Our crime rate is the lowest in the world. I admit, we are no democracy, but must democracy be the only way?

Edward took a steadying breath. He felt the subtle weight of Carvell's egg in his pocket. "And how would you respond to the claim that Prometheus Isle has executed more of its citizens on average than any other country in the world?"

Snow laughed; this time, it did not arrive in Edward's head like a recalled song. It was a real sound, a harsh, lipless guffaw.

I would say it is true. I do not suffer fools.

Edward stared at him. For a moment, the words would not come. Then: "You execute people for being *foolish*?"

Come now, Edward.

It was the first time the General had used his name. It sent a shiver through him. It was like feeling a soft whisper in your ear, then turning to see no one there.

I am trying to make a better world. I do not have the time to find a cure for ignorance, beyond a swift and sharp one.

Edward's mouth had gone very dry. "And what counts as ignorance?"

Snow moved in a blur. There was a clatter as his mask fell to the ground, a moment after his lipless mouth came level with Edward's eyes. He was leaning down, one hand on either side of the chair.

His fingernails, Edward saw, were black—the colour and sheen of chipped obsidian. Then Snow's hands were on him, pressing on his chest, and his skull-teeth were very close to his cheek. Edward could feel the subtle pulse of breath on his skin.

"Are. You. Scared?"

Snow's voice was soft, words carefully chosen. They hissed out from between his teeth.

Edward felt his heart massive within him, beating out a march in double time. "Yes."

"Hhh-hhh-whhhhhy?" That word came out rough and halting. A fleck of spittle landed on Edward's cheek.

"Because–" He swallowed. "Because you could kill me."

"Yessss." *But not*, came his mental voice, cool and restrained, *because of the way I look, yes? There you are: ignorance, shown by its counterpoint.*

He moved again, with lightning grace, and retrieved the mask. He stood by the window, now, gazing down on the courtyard. A quick adjustment of his uniform, and it was as if he had not moved at all. Then he opened his hand: resting there on his palm was Carvell's egg.

A bead of sweat, cold and slick, made a slow journey from the nape of Edward's neck to his lower back.

No need for such aides-mémoire. Snow closed his fist, and with a quiet snap crushed the thing to bits. *You'll remember this.*

Edward's voice was small but steady. "Are you going to kill me?"

Hah. He plucked a speck of dust from his coat. *You have only been a* little *foolish. Besides, it would be such a waste.*

"A waste?" He blinked up at Snow.

You and me are more alike than you know. He took a few slow steps closer, and brushed the edge of a black fingernail against Edward's cheek. *We are... rare beasts.*

"Alike..." Edward laughed shakily. "Pardon me for saying so, but *I've* not led a coup lately."

Perhaps you should have. He tilted his head. *Do not think my rule so terrible, Edward. Here, the men who beat Andy Flynn would never have raised their fists again. Here, Tonia May Greene's killers would have been brought to justice.*

At that, Edward went still. He slowly rose from his chair. "How dare you." His voice came cold and flat; his fear had gone, leaving anger in his wake, so fierce he nearly shook with it.

I am only telling the truth.

"I'm done with this." He turned away. "Send me back to the plane, General."

Of course. He sounded almost sad. *I will send you back immediately.*

Edward's shoulders shook. Snow had no *right*. Andy, Tonia—those were *his* friends. His failures. He hadn't been able to save them, and no hero had stepped forward in his place.

But first.

Look at me.

There was something almost hesitant in the thought-voice, something like a shyly dangled lure. Edward clenched his fists.

Look at me.

When he turned to face Snow, a shock went through him; it drowned the buzz of his anger like a thunderclap. Held between the general's careful fingers was a flimsy, cobweb-thin old paper. The headlines were blurred, the pictures grainy. He knew it, though. Knew it like a bad dream.

Don't you think I would have found out everything about you, before inviting you into my home?

"You didn't invite me," he said, voice distant. "Your embassy sent—"

Don't be a fool. I knew who the Herald would send. I wanted you, Edward Stone. The others are mere distraction. I wanted—

—this.

He threw the ancient paper at his feet. It fell open. Edward kneeled down, and saw his own photograph—editor in chief, it read. What a joke. Beneath him was Tonia, in shadowy profile. She always hated having her picture taken.

Their edition ran to a hundred on a good day, if they could afford the prices at the copy shop. Slogans were pasted haphazardly across every page: *Queer/ meta solidarity! Resist the superpowers-that-be!* They were going to change the world.

He was still on his knees when he felt Snow's gloved hand on the back of his neck, stroking him like a cat. A proprietary touch. The words below him swam in his sight.

Did you think it had all been lost?

"It was a long time ago."

And you all had different names, then.

Of course. And in his own picture, he'd worn a mask—looking more like a thug than a hero, but God, his eyes were so young.

You had your powers muted, didn't you? It's an easy procedure, if the subject is willing. Easy, and easy to reverse.

"They were not useful to anyone."

Oh, I don't know. I could find use for them, those powers of yours.

"I couldn't fight."

I could teach you.

He looked up into a mask of imperial white, into eyes like water, colourless and bottomless. Snow's hand on him was his only anchor, and Snow's voice sparked like fireworks in his head.

You could be my agent. My scalpel in this sick world, cutting away the rot. You could be my hero.

And when your work is done, you could come home to me.

He blinked away the blur. He felt his heart beating, under Snow's insistent fingers. "Do I have a choice?"

Snow laughed. He discarded his mask, and bent down to press a hard, lipless kiss on Edward's mouth. A benediction.

Always.

SCORNED
Jeffrey Ricker

Jeffrey Ricker's first novel, *Detours*, was published in 2011 by Bold Strokes Books. His writing has appeared in the anthologies *Paws and Reflect, Fool for Love: New Gay Fiction, Blood Sacraments, Men of the Mean Streets, Speaking Out, Riding the Rails,* and others. He is currently finishing his second novel and pursuing an MFA in creative writing at the University of British Columbia. When class is out, he lives in St. Louis with his partner, Michael, and two dogs. Follow his blog at *jeffreyricker.wordpress.com*.

"You're new."

Marcus Harris had never seen the woman standing in the visitor's vestibule adjacent to his cell, but her white coat, worn over a charcoal business suit, blared "psychologist." She wore glasses and kept her curly blonde hair shoulder length. Sitting in the plastic chair reserved for visitors (who never came), she crossed her legs and settled a clipboard over her knees. When she smiled at him, it was completely unconvincing.

"I'm Dr. Emily Wheeling," she said. "The warden asked me to come see you this morning and ask you a few questions."

"Oh, is it morning?" Marcus asked, sarcasm edging into his voice. "It's so hard to tell in here since I don't have ready access to a clock. Or sunlight. Where's Dr. Mathis?"

Dr. Wheeling looked down at her clipboard. "He had an unfortunate encounter with a homemade knife in one of the other wings, but I'm told he'll make a nearly complete recovery."

"That's a pity. So why does the warden want you to speak with me?" Marcus asked, even though he knew the answer.

Dr. Wheeling tilted her head so she was looking over her glasses. "I think we can both say we know why, so let's not start off like that, shall we?"

Marcus smiled. He liked her directness. "Please convey my apologies about his badge."

"He was a bit more displeased with the second-degree burns to his chest."

"I know he was attached to that badge, though."

"Well, fortunately the surgeons were able to remove it successfully."

Marcus said nothing in response. She was tapping her pen against the clipboard, whether out of nervousness or boredom, he couldn't be sure. It was a felt-tip pen, of course. They were taking no chances with him now, it seemed. It also seemed like she wasn't going to speak again unless he did first. He held out as long as he could stand the silence, which wasn't long.

"So," Marcus said, painfully aware that she had succeeded in waiting him out, "aren't you supposed to ask me questions?"

She narrowed her eyes at him. "How are you?"

"How do you think I am?" he asked, not even bothering to mask his anger with sarcasm.

She leaned forward, clasping her hands on top of the clipboard. "Not well, Mr. Harris."

For some reason, hearing her say his name—his regular name, not Megawatt, his alter ego—sent him over the edge. He launched himself at the barrier and slammed his palms against it. From past experience, he'd learned that open palms made much more noise than fists.

"*What the hell do you expect?*" he shouted.

To her credit, Dr. Wheeling didn't flinch beyond a raised eyebrow. She made a note on her clipboard and said, "I expect you'll want to have a seat now."

His chair had fallen over. When Marcus reached to pick it up, he noticed the tiny arcs of electricity on his fingertips. Jaw clenched, he silently willed the charge to remain—a pointless effort, since it always faded no matter what he did. They made sure of that in this place.

He slumped in the chair—he wasn't particularly interested in making a good impression with correct posture—and stared at Dr. Wheeling. All he wanted at the moment was for her to go away—odd, since the solitude of his cell was often unbearable.

"I don't really feel like talking right now," he mumbled.

"That's fine. I can come back later."

After she got up and walked toward the door, he said, "I still won't feel like talking then."

Without turning around, she replied, "Everyone feels like talking eventually, Mr. Harris. I've got time."

✒

Marcus didn't have visitors. He was allowed to, but no one ever came. The only one who'd made the effort was Alan—and lord knew *that* hadn't gone well. His family, never close, hadn't tried to contact him in years, and after he tried to destroy (even inadvertently) the largest city in America, he certainly couldn't blame them. What he *did* blame them for were the interviews they gave to the press after he was arrested, when his real identity was revealed.

Couldn't they have just kept their mouths shut?

He probably shouldn't have tried to electrocute his father over the phone line, though. That was how he'd lost his calling privileges.

And then, not long before his trial, when he'd blown up the common room television in an uncontrolled fit of rage, the prison staff realized they had a problem on their hands as long as Marcus was within range of an electrical current. He soon found himself in solitary confinement.

The TV had been an accident though. He hadn't meant to do it, but it had been shortly after his arrest and the news was still all over the cable networks, and he'd let his temper get the better of him.

That had always been Marcus's problem. Alan told him as much during his one and only visit.

"You never could exercise restraint," he said.

Marcus laughed. He was wearing the electrical dampening harness at the time, his wrists secured with zip ties. "I seem to be doing pretty well with restraint now," Marcus quipped. "Mind you, I'm getting a little help with that."

Alan shook his head. He was wearing his Altitude costume, his mask concealing most of his face. He dwarfed the plastic chair with his bulk, but to Marcus now, it seemed like he was overcompensating, trying to look the part of the superhero. As if being able to fly weren't enough and he needed that cartoon-character physique.

"I wish you'd take this seriously–"

"Take what seriously?" Marcus snapped. "My crimes or the fact that I'm never getting out of here alive? Or do you mean being betrayed by you? Because I take that extremely seriously."

"I did not betray you," Alan said, jumping to his feet. In his own anger, he inadvertently flexed, and for a moment his feet hovered a couple inches off the floor. "It just didn't work out with us, that's all."

"Was that before or after you started screwing Billy?"

Billy Lightspeed was a young speed demon from somewhere out in the Midwest—Kansas?—who was short but blond and buff with an aw-shucks attitude that made Marcus cringe a little. Alan, on the other hand, fell for it. When Billy joined the National Heroes Union, he sought Alan's advice on almost everything, from whether he should keep his alias (his real name was Gerald Matthews—Alan said Billy Lightspeed was just fine) to whether his costume was okay. (The design motif: lots of thunderbolts.)

Marcus chalked up Billy's personality to youthful exuberance and didn't notice the growing attraction between him and Alan until it was too late.

"You know that's not how it happened," Alan said.

"Oh, please. He's not even old enough to drink. Do you have to get him home before curfew on school nights?"

"Stop it. You're being so unreasonable—"

"*Unreasonable?*"

Fifty feet above them, there was a pop, followed by a dimming of the light and a gentle rain of thin glass. They both looked up at the socket where the light bulb had been. Marcus shouldn't have been able to do that with the dampening harness on.

He looked back at Alan with a wolf-like grin. "So much for restraint."

Marcus's life had contracted to a ten-by-twelve-foot cell made entirely of concrete save for the Plexiglas barrier. The bed was wood, with a memory foam mattress—no springs. The chair was plastic, as was the small table where he kept a clutch of books, magazines (staples removed), some paper, and a felt-tip pen. The ceiling, now seventy-five feet above him since they raised the roof, only made the room seem that much narrower. It was like living at the bottom of an elevator shaft.

There wasn't an ounce of metal in sight.

Every other day a guard brought in the dampening harness. It was all fiber optics, plastic buckles, and nylon straps, and when he wore it, he couldn't even hear his own body's electrical current.

Once suited up, he was led to a small exercise yard, which was really another pit-like room but, instead of a ceiling, it had a skylight. At least he could see a patch of blue along with the occasional cloud. And, one time, a bird.

After he was transferred to these chambers, he never saw any other prisoners. Sometimes, he could hear them, the low buzz of many conversations happening at once. He wasn't allowed to interact with the general population—too dangerous, the warden said.

Still, he heard their voices sometimes. The background crowd buzz was kind of like listening to the hum of current, which he missed even more than people.

The guard who brought him his meals and shuffled him to and from the exercise room was named Barry. He was a little older, a little chubbier than Marcus, who'd never been in the best of shape, even when he'd been in the

National Heroes Union. Even so, Barry looked physically more imposing, with his veined arms and rough, meaty hands. He didn't like to spend any more time in Marcus's presence than absolutely necessary, and never any closer than required. When Marcus mentioned this to him, Barry said, "I seen what you done to that kid."

"'Saw what you did.'"

"Huh?"

"'I saw what you did to that kid,'" Marcus clarified. He knew he sounded like a prissy substitute teacher, but the hell with it. "And he wasn't a kid. He was a murderer and had every bit of it coming."

"Don't make it right," Barry said. "Besides, he threw that bus in front of you and you was the one who blew up all them people."

"'You were,' not 'you was.' For God's sake, did you even finish high school?"

After that, Barry cut short the exercise period and herded Marcus back to his cell.

Dr. Wheeling returned the next day. If Marcus didn't know better, he'd have sworn she was wearing the same suit as the day before.

"So, Barry doesn't seem too keen on you," she said without preamble.

Marcus stared at the ceiling. He'd been lying on his bed when she came in, and he didn't feel like getting up for her benefit.

"No, he's not exactly a member of the fan club," Marcus said.

"Oh, that's right. There actually *was* a fan club, wasn't there?" She smiled, more in mockery than mirth, and Marcus felt the overwhelming urge to burn her flesh off. Not that he could, not in this place, at least. And anyway, burning off someone's skin had been the start of the downhill slide that had landed him in prison.

He kept his eyes on the ceiling and tried to ignore how close the walls were. This must have been how trapped miners felt.

"You miss it, don't you?" she asked.

Marcus looked over at her. He hadn't expected her to say something insightful. Nor had he expected to be unable to tell her no.

"Do I miss being appreciated, being thanked for helping make the world a safer place? Yeah, I miss that."

She had not written anything on her clipboard. Marcus wondered what, if anything, was in her case file on him. He looked back toward the ceiling.

"Sometimes I don't know if I ever deserved it," he admitted.

"Probably because you didn't," she said.

"I—excuse me?"

She set her clipboard on the floor and stood up. "Come now, Mr. Harris, a fan club? T-shirts with your face on them?" She walked toward the barrier. "That name you went by, Megawatt? The costume? It was all a bit too pop star, wasn't it?"

Marcus swung his legs over the edge of the bed and stood. "It was ridiculous, but it wasn't my idea."

"You went along with it, though, didn't you?"

"Look, what's your point here?"

"You were being worshipped—if that's not too strong a word—for something you were, not something you did. It was a gift of fate, or God, or whatever you care to call it. I can imagine it must have been a seductive experience, given how much discrimination you likely experienced prior to that. But, viewed a certain way, that adulation was just as discriminatory. And when you didn't live up to their prejudices, they turned against you."

"Who's this monolithic 'they' you're referring to? Society?"

She tilted her head, the equivalent of a shrug. "Your fans. Your family. The Union. Altitude."

At the mention of Alan's alter ego, Marcus crossed his arms and looked at the floor. "I'd really rather not discuss him, if you don't mind."

"Eventually, I think we have to," she said matter-of-factly. "We might as well start now."

Marcus went to his desk and picked up a magazine there, a month-old *New Yorker*. "And why is that?" he asked, trying to be casual as he flipped through the pages without actually reading anything. With no staples to hold them together, the slick pages slid against one another and fell out of his hands.

"Don't even try to read anything into this," he said as he gathered up the pages.

"Of course not."

Once he'd returned the magazine to the desk (the pages were out of order, but who cared), Dr. Wheeling returned to her seat and picked up the clipboard. Apparently, her insights were over for the moment. She flipped through her papers.

"What I still find odd," she said, "is that your parents didn't know about your abilities until you were arrested."

"Well, I wasn't about to tell them until I had to. What good's a secret identity if you tell someone? I knew that if I told my parents, they would tell the rest of the family, and the Harrises are a gossipy lot."

"That's not exactly what I meant," she said. "My point is that they must have been exceptionally oblivious not to have noticed."

"The other thing we're big on is denial."

Thinking of the awkward teenager he'd been could still make Marcus cringe and want to curl inward. It was bad enough that he'd always been chubby no matter how hard he tried not to be, but the first time someone called him "fatty faggot" in seventh grade, the nickname stuck until he was halfway through high school and his growth spurt, late in arriving, finally took his pudgy body and stretched the weight out vertically. After that, they were more likely to call him plain old faggot.

Sophomore year of high school was also when Marcus discovered that, at moments of high stress, he tended to blow every fuse in the house. Studying for a biology midterm and realizing he was destined to fail spectacularly, he'd touched a light switch and plunged the entire house into darkness. When he did it a second time—at school, in the middle of the test—he started to think something might be wrong.

The first time he really used the power, he hadn't intended to. He was fifteen, and it was the year Scout died for the first time.

The dog was in the backyard when Marcus came home from school, and as he poured himself a glass of water from the pitcher his mom always kept in the kitchen, she called downstairs asking him to let Scout back in.

Scout was down at the back of the yard, and when he called her name, the German Shepherd bounded up the lawn. All he could think at the time, when her front legs folded under her, was that it looked like she was trying to do a somersault. She planted her face in the grass, and when she tried to stand up again, she gave a confused whimper and keeled over.

"Scout!" It seemed to Marcus that he was down the stairs and at her side before he heard his water glass shatter on the floor behind him. He lifted her head into his lap. She looked up and panted, her eyes unable to focus. And then it all stopped.

"No," he said, the tears starting to catch in his throat. "Please, no." He said the word over and over as he rocked her in his arms. Scout was the one thing he felt he could count on. The thought of not coming home to her was more than he could take.

At the time, he thought he heard thunder even though the day had been cloudless. When he opened his eyes, he noticed first the nimbus of electricity still around his hands; second, that Scout was licking his face.

"How touching," Dr. Wheeling said once he'd finished the story.

God, you're a bitch, Marcus thought, and again wished he could melt her face.

"After all that, they still had no clue at all?" she asked.

"I got in trouble for breaking the glass, and Scout got to live for a few more months before finally passing away in her sleep. I figured it was a fair trade."

"It must be such a strange experience for you now, then," she said, "not having any power."

"You could say that. After twenty-five years, it's a bit odd to be so—" he searched for the right word "—mundane."

Dr. Wheeling tapped her pen on her clipboard. "Well, you *do* still have some power over the Union, at least. You know all their identities, I assume, not just Altitude and Billy Lightspeed."

Marcus smiled but said nothing. The Union members had all expected him to blab about who they really were. They never understood him any better than his parents had. In a gossipy family, he was the one who learned how to keep a secret. His parents had already dealt with one unpleasant revelation from their disappointing son. He couldn't very well have followed up with yet another, one that would have driven the wedge separating them even deeper. So he didn't tell his parents until his cover was blown, and at trial, he didn't give up anyone else's identity. That knowledge may have been his one last scrap of power, but it had no purpose that he could see, either.

"I hope you don't expect me to 'out' them to you now," Marcus said to Dr. Wheeling.

She smiled and shook her head. "Interesting choice of phrase though, I must say. At least acknowledge that you are not completely powerless, even in this situation."

"For all the good it does me," he muttered.

"That's your choice, though. Even your other powers, they're still a part of you. They just don't have a channel for expression, as it were, in this place."

"What would be the point in exposing them? It wouldn't get me out of here, it wouldn't get me back in the Union, and it wouldn't change anyone's opinions about me. The public's been pretty much against me since—since the accident with The Arrow of Armageddon."

Dr. Wheeling, who'd been tapping her pen again, stopped and looked over her glasses at him. "You don't accidentally flay someone, Mr. Harris."

Despite the ominous and somewhat pretentious name, The Arrow of Armageddon had been nothing more than a twenty-something hipster named Yuri from Russia who was really good at physics and engineering. He built himself a nuclear-powered suit of armor and then proceeded to loot every bank in town. He had no qualms about putting people in harm's way, like the metro bus full of commuters that he threw in front of himself to deflect Marcus's barrage of electricity. No one had survived.

Even then, Marcus would have been able to control himself if Yuri hadn't laughed at him. Called him inept. An amateur.

So Marcus shredded him, pulling in every surrounding watt of power to peel away Yuri's so-called indestructible armor. And when the once-fearsome Arrow of Armageddon lay defenseless in the middle of the street, Marcus didn't stop, and every light in the city went dim.

Public opinion started to turn against him after that. Even Alan had begun to look at him differently. After the Union held an inquiry into the incident, they voted to let him remain a member, barely.

Whatever Dr. Wheeling felt about his actions, her expression betrayed no indication of it.

"How do you cope with that?" she asked.

"I don't," Marcus said. He didn't realize that was the case until he said it out loud, but then something else dawned on him. "There's nothing to cope with. People expected me to feel remorse over it, but honestly, I still think he deserved it."

"Did he deserve it for causing all those deaths, or did he deserve it for humiliating you?"

Marcus held his tongue despite his rising anger. He had to give himself credit for that; normally he would have let his temper get the better of him.

Maybe he was improving.

✹

Or maybe not.

Each Monday, Marcus received a delivery of magazines and newspapers. Unable to listen to the radio or watch television without being a potential menace to the rest of the inmate population, to say nothing of society at large, print media was his only means of keeping up with what was going on in the world. He took the Sunday *New York Times*, the *Washington Post*, and the *Guardian* from London, along with the *New Yorker*, the *Atlantic*, *Time*, and *Wired*. Barry always dropped them off while Marcus was asleep, waking to find them in the pass-through drawer.

This time, Marcus awoke to the sound of whistling. It was Barry, who was just closing the door behind him. He was not the whistling type, typically. What put him in such a good mood?

The answer was on the cover of the topmost magazine: *People*, which Marcus usually had no interest in and did not receive. He picked it up and stared at the glossy color image of Alan and Gerald's smiling faces—well, they were wearing their masks, but still their grins practically burst off the page. Underneath them were the words "WEDDING BELLS!"

Marcus took the stack and retreated to his bed, where he set aside the others and opened up the issue of *People*. The wedding would be in the fall, a private ceremony limited to family and close friends so that they could make their vows without having to wear their masks—everyone from the Union, of course, would also be in attendance. The President and First Lady had accepted an invitation as well.

Gerald and Alan had made no secret about the fact that they were dating, but this… it stung more than he wanted to admit. Alan had wanted to keep it a secret when he was dating Marcus–"discreet" was the word he'd used. He didn't even want to tell the rest of the Union. It would be a distraction, he said.

Clearly, he didn't mind the distraction now.

"I do not fucking believe this," he muttered.

"Believe what, Mr. Harris?"

Marcus looked up. He hadn't heard Dr. Wheeling enter and take a seat. She sat there—same white coat, same clipboard, same felt-tip pen—looking completely innocent.

He flung the magazine to the floor. It skidded across the concrete and lay curled against the clear barrier. He wished he could have thrown it at her.

"Did you do this?"

She leaned forward to scrutinize the magazine cover. "I've published several scholarly articles, but a byline in *People* is not among my credits, Mr.–"

"*You know fucking well that's not what I meant!*"

Again, his outburst elicited no more from her than a raised eyebrow.

"Yes, I knew they were getting married. I didn't think it was prudent to convey that information to you at this time." She nodded toward the magazine on the floor. "I can see I was right. I certainly didn't arrange for that to be delivered to you, if that's what you're asking. If I were you, I'd turn my suspicions toward someone who isn't a member of your fan club."

"Barry?" When she didn't answer, he clenched his fists and growled in frustration. "I want to murder that fat old bastard. I swear I'll–"

He stopped, the absurdity of his situation leaving him suddenly drained of hope. He couldn't even make a dent in someone as old and out of shape as Barry. The fact that the warden didn't bother to put a stronger guard on his detail, even after what Marcus had done—it was insulting. Overcome with impotent rage, he banged his fists against his desk, yelling incoherently.

"Mr. Harris, you really should–"

"*I should what?* What the hell do you want from me, Doctor?"

"For starters, I want you to keep your voice down. It's still quite early."

"Afraid someone will overhear?"

"No, Mr. Harris, I just don't enjoy being yelled at before breakfast."

"Really? I thought the idea was to get the patient to open up. For a psychologist, you've certainly done a lot of the talking up to now."

"I follow an eclectic modality," she said.

"Oh, is that what you call it?"

She gestured at the magazine on the floor. "So is that why you tried to kill Billy?"

Marcus threw up his hands. "No. Why does no one ever believe me when I tell them that?"

"Perhaps because of your temper," she said drily.

"Well, regardless of that and whatever the prosecutor said at the trial, it wasn't premeditated. I didn't know I was going to try to kill him until I knocked him down."

"With a million volts of electricity," Dr. Wheeling pointed out.

Marcus sighed. "Yes, that."

The police had contacted the Union when an anonymous caller threatened to blow up a Coastal Power and Light substation. Marcus hadn't known Billy would get to the scene first. As the prosecutor indicated, though, it wasn't a stretch to assume the fastest man on the planet would beat Marcus there. Marcus also didn't realize trying to fry Billy wouldn't do a thing. All it did was make him talk really fast for a few days.

If he could, Marcus would have taken it all back, every misstep, every lapse of judgment, even his relationship with Alan. But they couldn't find any trace of a bomb or bomber, and then Billy, the little man-stealing upstart, started telling him what to do. Marcus let him have it.

Unfortunately, as Marcus drew all the energy he could from the city power grid to wipe Billy off the face of the earth, he also shorted out the cooling system in CP&L's nuclear reactor on the far south side of town. If it hadn't been for the rest of the Union, half the city would have been destroyed, and the other half would glow in the dark.

"So, you didn't lure him there just to try to kill him?" Dr. Wheeling asked.

"No! Have you been listening?"

"I have, but if you could set aside your anger, you might start asking yourself some more challenging questions. If there was no bomb, then it must have been a hoax, yes? So the next question is, who made the call? You did say Billy got there before you, correct?"

Marcus was silent for a moment. "You don't think... seriously? I can't imagine that naïve little pipsqueak would be that devious."

"You'd be surprised what people might do."

"But he'd already won Altitude. I was out of the picture. Why would he need to frame me?"

"To make sure you didn't re-enter the picture?"

Marcus looked at her, dumbfounded. All this time, he thought it had been his anger that had gotten the better of him, and to learn now that it had been Billy… he wanted to rage at the injustice, but he didn't have the energy.

"I don't believe it. I'll kill him." Even he wasn't convinced by his own words.

Dr. Wheeling shook her head. "Incarceration has given you a lot of time to think, Mr. Harris. But as far as I can tell, you haven't put that time to good use."

Marcus rested his head in his hands. "Well, I'll have a lot more time to improve on that, won't I?"

"While it is true you're here under a life sentence, parole is still a possibility within twenty-five years, dependent on good behavior. So far, your behavior hasn't been what anyone would call 'good.'" She smiled. "Certainly, the warden would not."

"In twenty-five years, I'll be sixty-six," he said. "What kind of a future is that to look forward to?"

"A dim one, I suppose," she said, her tone conveying no sense of encouragement. She walked up to the glass, her voice low. "Maybe it's up to you to seek out an opportunity to make a better future for yourself."

"And just how am I supposed to do that from in here?" he asked.

"I'm acquainted with some people who might be able to help in that regard." Dr. Wheeling went back to the chair and picked up her clipboard. "My job, after all, is to help my clients address the issues preventing them from having a full, well-adjusted life."

"So I'm your client now?"

"Technically, the Board of Prisons is my client. But I'm not here to diagnose them, am I?"

Marcus went back to his bed and lay down. "Well, I hope you charge on a sliding scale, because I have no way to pay you at the moment."

She smiled. To Marcus, it looked almost predatory. "I'm sure we can work something out."

❦

After breakfast, Barry came in with the dampening harness. Marcus looked for any trace of expression in Barry's face that might betray his guilt. When he saw nothing, he pointed at the magazine and asked, "Did you put that in there?"

Barry actually smiled. "What, you didn't like it?"

Marcus narrowed his eyes. "Clearly, my reading standards are a bit higher than yours."

Barry tossed him the harness. "Just put the damn thing on, already."

Marcus started to latch the harness in front, but the plate wouldn't go in the buckle. He tried again, and his thumb ran along the edge of the buckle opening, feeling something stuck in there. It was a piece of paper, tiny, folded several times. When he pried it out, there was writing on it.

He looked up. Barry, true to form, remained over by the doorway, as far as possible from Marcus, and wasn't looking at him. Marcus unfolded the paper and read it.

"My associates will collect you after you make your exit. I'll collect my fee later. Meanwhile, you have a wedding to attend this fall. Be powerful, Marcus.—EW"

Eventually, Barry turned to look at him. "Hurry up already, will ya?"

"Sorry," Marcus grumbled, though he wasn't sorry at all. He tucked the note in his pocket and buckled the harness.

Power surged through him.

It was so unexpected, Marcus jumped a little, as if shocked—which was impossible, at least literally. When he touched the straps of the harness, though, he could sense the threads of metal in them, strands that hadn't been there before.

"Hey," Barry said, actually looking a little concerned, "you OK?"

Marcus smiled and said, "Never felt better."

He pointed a finger and blasted Barry through the cinderblock wall.

The sirens were already blaring when Marcus stepped over Barry's lifeless body. "Sorry, Barry," he said. The man's sightless eyes stared up at him. Marcus really was sorry, a little.

But not much.

He had no escape plan beyond getting out of the cell. He knew breaking out of the prison would now be elementary. Even if they cut power to the entire complex, he had enough of a charge that he could pull more power from the very air. Once he got beyond the prison walls, if Dr. Wheeling was to be believed, there were people waiting. He wasn't sure he wanted to go with them. He did know that if he saw Dr. Wheeling again, he'd pay her generously for her assistance.

She wouldn't like it.

In the corridor outside his cell, he could hear the hum of current all around him, even with the sirens wailing. That was the thing he missed, the steady background noise of the world, its latent power, power that he knew how to tap. He felt it bending toward him. It wanted him to use it. It wanted to be part of him.

At the end of the corridor, the armored door swung open and three guards entered, guns drawn.

Marcus grinned and let the arcs of electricity curl around his fingers.

"Hello, boys."

YOUR CHANGING BODY: A GUIDEBOOK FOR BOY SUPER VILLAINS— INTRODUCTION BY MR. POSITIVE

Matt Fagan

Matt Fagan is a writer and artist raised in the wilds of Oregon, where he climbed trees and sometimes wore pants. His stories have appeared in *McSweeney's*, *Little Engines*, and *Thought Magazine*. He wrote and drew the *Love Omnibus*, a collection of comics about a gay couple living in Chicago, and the underground sensation *Domestic Partner of Frankenstein*. He is also the artist on an ongoing comic series called *Monster Dudes*. Fagan currently resides in Chicago, where he owns and operates Brainstorm Comics, and lives with his "special friend". He has a dog named The Doctor.

When I was thirteen years old, I spent an afternoon in the restroom of a public library that changed my life forever. What I learned that day set me on a path of self-discovery leading inevitably to this place. Writing the introduction to this book. What you hold in your hands right now is a source of great pride for me, and composing its introduction is, in a very real sense, my destiny. It is also one of the final actions that I am likely to undertake of my own free will.

Commissioning this collection of testimonials, advice and scientific analyses was a decision prompted by the decline of my criminal career, but the book has its roots in my childhood, long before I adopted the name Mr. Positive. Long before I became, as they say, "evil". While there is still time, I would like to contribute what little I can by telling my story. How I came to be this man, and why I believe this book is so important.

Things could have gone so much worse for me if I hadn't grown up in the country. In the chapters that follow, many of today's premier super villains share their most intimate stories, including how they first discovered their own powers; early exposure in urban environments is an emerging theme. At the age of nine, Skullkick was observed punching his furniture into atoms... by a woman in a neighboring Atlanta apartment building. He spent the rest of his childhood in hospitals, military schools and finally prison, all *before* he ever wore the mask. My family's little house was situated in the woods on the Oregon coast, safely away from prying eyes. When I wasn't in school, I was playing in the forest, climbing trees and exploring, and matching wits with my imaginary enemies. I enjoyed turning the woods into a tropical jungle, where I might search for a valuable stone or priceless jeweled artifact, with my archrival just one step behind.

And that's just where I was, the first time it happened. Deep in the woods on another bright, overcast morning, standing on a log over the shallow creek that ran maybe a quarter mile behind our house. At the top of the embankment on the other side was a cave. In reality, its clay walls extended no more than eight or nine feet into the hillside, but for me it had served as an entrance to Aztec temples, military prisons, the kingdom of the Mole People, and an interdimensional gateway to an alien world. I was eleven years old and anything was possible.

On that historic day, I had fought my way past cannibals and dinosaurs and a man-eating plant to get there: the Lost Caverns of Froon, legendary resting place of the Siamese mummy! As I crossed the familiar log—this time around, a rickety rope bridge—I decided that I would arrive just in time to discover that my nemesis, Professor Francois Buchard of the Royal Institute, had beaten me to the punch. I pictured him emerging from the cave and into the light, a smirk on his smug continental face when he saw me coming, too late once again. I felt a pang of anger at his imaginary arrogance.

But that familiar fake emotion, which had always faded as easily as the imaginary rope bridge, did not fade. I could almost see Professor Buchard, and my anger was suddenly, unusually real. My chest seized. I couldn't catch my breath, which terrified me. I felt my knees bending, and the bark scraping under my feet. The sky seemed to darken.

Long seconds later, I heard myself gasp. I was finally taking a breath, and as I listened to myself draw it in, I realized that it was the first sound I'd heard since this started. Was this a seizure? I had seen my aunt Janet have a seizure at a family reunion two summers earlier, but she had been twitching uncontrollably.

Not me. I was still. *Unbelievably* still. The spongy damp of moss against my legs told me I was straddling the log. I could hear the sounds of the forest now, and the sky was bright again. My chest though... the pain was gone, but I could still feel something there, as though I was being pulled. The panic was rising. I really could feel something grabbing my chest and pulling. Toward the cave?

I looked up then, and for the first time I saw the thing that would change the entire shape of my life.

Of course, it wasn't much to look at. Not yet. Hardly more than an unsettling dark stain across the creek, floating above the leaves and sticks that carpeted the ground. A stain in the air, like an oily drop of ink in a clear bowl of water.

"Overactive imagination". It was a refrain I had heard more than a few times, and maybe it was true. But I knew the difference between what was real and what wasn't. Logic told me that what I was seeing couldn't be real. Something had to be wrong with my eyes, like when the sky had appeared to darken a moment ago.

The trouble was that I could feel that dark spot, a connection, as if my own nerves ended in its shadow. The stain just hung there, I could see the mouth of the cave right through it and I could feel it tugging at my chest.

Seconds later, the stain was gone. I was snapped like a rubber band, knocked backward and rolled off the log. I didn't remember falling, but my knees were in the creek. The abrupt pain of rocks cutting into my kneecaps brought my mind back into focus. When I opened my eyes, I was looking down at the dirt on the bank. I smelled my own vomit, and took comfort that I could smell again.

✻

Somehow I knew that what happened to me wasn't normal. I loved my family, but instinct told me that I was better off keeping this incident to myself, so when I ran home I only admitted to falling off the log.

"It was nothing, really! Wet moss and soft bark, that's all."

And gravity, added my mother, tying her hair back with a quick motion. She gave me a smile, and then turned to grab the first aid box she always kept to the left of the sewing table. Whenever she wanted to talk, or spend time together, or bandage my knees, my mother always took me into her sewing room. That's what she called it, but the room was really much more special to her than that. The sewing machine was beside a long table that held all of her little projects, and they both faced a picture window that looked out over the woods. She loved to work in there. Two walls had large shelves filled with fabrics, sewing notions, art supplies and other things that I grew up thinking of as "Mom stuff"—because if you needed something, she always had it. The shelves also held her books, which included many photo albums, and a growing collection of mementos from my childhood. What I remember most vividly of that room, though, is the other wall, loaded with family photographs. My grandparents were represented here, with all of their children, every wedding, every birth. Most of these photos captured moments that happened a long time ago in distant places, but she told their stories so well that I felt like I knew each of these people as well as my own parents.

The sewing room was a comforting place where I always felt important. All of my school pictures were given positions of prominence; each moment of my life was valuable to her. She had framed images from every ultrasound. In my innocence I wondered if I was an only child because there would never be enough room for pictures of two of us. Once upon a time I had even asked, but Mom only picked up an ultrasound and gazed at it for some moments. "There would always be room for more," she said, "but it just wasn't meant to be for us."

Surrounded by such love it was hard to keep the truth to myself, but I did not know what had really happened, much less how to explain it.

It would be a long time before I ventured back into those woods.

✄

I was changed that day. Terrified that the incident might repeat itself, I avoided the two things that my eleven-year-old logic regarded as triggers: the woods, and my own mind. I was afraid to play. I became a very serious boy, keeping few friends and limiting my leisure time to activities like watching television, which discouraged imagination. In this way, I delayed another occurrence until I was thirteen, when my unbalanced hormones made it impossible to keep myself under control.

The worst part of my teenage school day was the mandatory PE period. A thin kid with no interest in sports and no social circle was fair game, and in PE the girls weren't around to keep the jocks from going too far. The best I could hope for was to hang back and try to be inconspicuous. That's what I was doing that Wednesday, sixth period, on the football field.

My goal was always the same: stay as far away from the ball as I could. Despite seven years of public school, and being born a male in the USA, I had never learned the rules of football and I wasn't about to start now. I stood near the edge of the field, many yards away from what I believed might have been called the "line of scrimmage," watching my classmates struggle without really knowing the point. Then, out of nowhere, it happened again, almost exactly the same as before. The sky darkened, and I was dragged forward by my chest. I fell across the twenty yard line and watched as the sun reignited. The familiar grip on my chest did not release, and I looked toward the source. Toward the boys at the line of scrimmage.

I was scared, but mostly I was just so sad that it had happened again. It was almost two years since that day in the woods, and I'd begun to think I had made the whole thing up. But I hadn't. Directly in front of me, right behind the players, was that cloud of ink again. Not quite a shape, maybe darker than last time, but I could still see the other boys through the shadow.

Again, only a few seconds passed before I was opening my eyes, face-down on the football field. I barely threw up this time. Since it had appeared behind most of my team and lasted so briefly, nobody seemed to have noticed the shadow. But some of the boys had seen me faint, bringing a lot of unwelcome attention my way. I was sent to the school nurse. In half an hour I was on my way home, diagnosed with mononucleosis, which guaranteed me several days off from school. Now that my condition had returned, I was determined to use those days well.

✺

I needed to know what was happening to me, but I was afraid to ask anyone. So exercising my best National Honor Society instincts, I waited for my parents to leave for work, and then I hopped on my bicycle and rode to the public library.

I held onto a dim hope that my situation wasn't as unusual as I feared, and that this trip to the library would end with the textbook explanation I needed. There are plenty of things that people don't talk about, but surely the books would divulge what I sought. Maybe adults just kept the weird stuff under wraps, because they don't want to frighten their children with all the bizarre things our bodies might do to us. Or maybe it was simply that a surplus of hormones can cause delusions, and they would eventually pass. The only good thing about not knowing was that I wasn't sure, yet, that I was some kind of freak. Not completely sure.

Even the card catalog embarrassed me. Somehow, I thought, the librarian could see that I was looking up the word "puberty". I slunk off toward the stacks, grabbing a couple of other books along the way, not even looking to see what they were. It didn't matter. I just needed something to hide behind.

I found the section I needed, uncomfortably close to the main reading area. Crouching, I tried to shield the embarrassing shelf with my body while reading the titles off the spines. There were few books that seemed to deal directly with my predicament, and a cursory inspection revealed little to recommend one over another. If I was going to choose, I would need time to examine them more carefully, and privacy to do it in. I took them all, sandwiched them between the decoy books and tried to look nonchalant as I meandered a circuitous route to the bathroom.

Once inside, alone, I locked myself into a stall and began to pore over the indexes and chapter headings, searching for some kind of explanation. But even the promisingly-titled *What's Happening to My Body?* offered nothing pertaining to mine. These books were all the same. After spending hours in the bathroom I had found only hormones, hair, and growing pains. Nothing about recurring hallucinations, cardiac seizures, or apparitions.

Another thing the books had in common is that they all recommended that any farther questions be addressed to a parent, doctor, school official, clergy-man or other trusted adult. As much as it pained me, I resigned myself to taking just this step. I would talk to my father.

My father and I, we didn't have a lot in common but I always knew he had my back. I can only imagine what he thought when I came into his den and asked if we could turn off the football game. When I recall the way I told him that "I need to talk to you," my own grimness almost moves me to laughter. Any child that serious must seem comical to an adult mind. But Dad stifled the smile and obligingly muted the television. He gave me a chair and if any part of a smirk remained, he didn't let it extend beyond the borders of his mustache. He asked, "What's on your mind, son?" When I think of his voice, I remember only the sound of concern.

As I sat down, I realized my mistake. Putting all my effort into finding the courage to talk to my father, I'd forgotten to figure out what I was going to say.

"Something's been happening to me," I told him, with great effort. "Something I don't understand. These... feelings. They make me sick. But I don't seem to have any control over them!"

My father started to nod, and for a moment I felt hopeful again. Like he knew what I was talking about. Like he was going to tell me the secret that the library books wouldn't share.

"These feelings," he asked. "Have you had them long?"

"Only a couple of times," I confessed. "The first was a long time ago, and I thought it was gone, but then it happened again this week! It was during PE. I was standing in the field watching the others play football when it hit me."

"Son, I can see that this is hard for you to talk about, and I think I know what you're going to tell me. It must have been scary for you, realizing how it made you feel to look at those other boys. You're so young, and your hormones are just beginning to flood your body with urges you've never had before. But I'll bet you thought you knew what to expect."

"Dad–"

"It's okay, Son. It's no wonder these feelings confused you. Every day you watch television, and you see stories about young men and their interest in young women. You thought you were going to be just like them, and you're not. But I promise you, there is nothing wrong with a young man who develops an interest in other young men. It's less common, but you are *normal*."

His eyes searched mine. He was trying so hard to give me comfort, offering so much understanding. The irony is that he was right. I'd known for years that I was gay, but I was so obsessed with figuring out the shadow and its effect on me that I never even thought about the fact that being gay was unusual, or that my parents might be concerned about it. I wasn't *hiding* it from them. I was hiding something else, which was so huge that I forgot to worry about the normal stuff.

"Thanks, Dad," I said, trying to look... relieved, maybe? He gave me a hug.

"Son, I love you. And I'm proud that you came to me with this. I want you to know that I will always support you, and if you ever have any problems you can always ask for my help."

And that's how I sort of came out to my father. The good thing was that, as far as my parents were concerned, it explained my last two years of increasingly strange behavior. They were wrong, but they only wanted to help me.

Skullkick's parents separated him from the rest of his family once they knew what he could do, and that's just what I was afraid of. But later, as a super villain, I conducted myself like my folks were watching, and I wanted to make them proud. I realize now that my family never would have betrayed me, but if you aren't so lucky, turn to page 146 right away. Skullkick has indispensable advice about the trials that may await you.

To my adolescent mind, the conversation with my father was all the proof I needed that no book or trusted adult could help me. I was going to have to solve this problem on my own. That Saturday after breakfast, I entered the forest for the first time since I was eleven years old.

All of my old trails had grown over, but I pushed through by habit along the same paths I had always taken. The farther in I went, trampling the new ferns and huckleberries, the larger the knot in my stomach became. But I pressed on, because it made sense to return to the place where it all started: the old log across the creek became my research station. That Saturday I sat on the log, closed my eyes, and tried to remember exactly how I felt the first time it happened. I thought about that sensation of something gripping the inside of my chest. Of darkness crowding in from the edge of my vision. The snap of the rubber band.

For an hour or more I just sat on the log and thought about it, freaking myself out but accomplishing nothing. Something was wrong. Something was missing, something so unbelievably stupid that it hadn't even crossed my mind. Professor Francois Buchard of the Royal Institute. My imaginary nemesis. He had been there the first time, and maybe he needed to be here now.

So I imagined him.

I was a little out of practice, but I remembered the way Professor Buchard had always looked: his thin ginger hair, his wire glasses, that impractical sweater vest he wore even in the jungle. Sitting on the log, holding onto the memory of that tightness in my chest, I could almost see the professor standing there in front of the cave.

As soon as I could see him, the sky went dark. My breath grew shallow, but I knew what was coming. This time I didn't fall, I did not stop breathing, and I kept my eyes open.

It was a sideways means of getting there, but it worked. This was the first time that I summoned the shadow on purpose.

This time, I saw it happen. The darkness came out of me. It slithered out of my chest as though drawn along a string, and I felt it leave my body like a splinter being pulled. Once outside of me it hovered close, confusing my senses. It was a ghostly part of me and I could almost feel it. Like seeing a friend get hurt and experiencing a flicker of sympathetic pain.

I was able to stay calm though, to watch the shadow... and it did nothing. The shadow just was. So I did the only other thing that I knew was within my power. I tried to put it away.

I concentrated on the tug, that tension stretching outward from me, toward the darkness. I tried to imagine pulling it back inside. Nothing happened at first, but eventually the rubber band went slack. The shadow funneled back down the line. I felt a jolt when it smashed into my chest, but I was braced for it and I kept my seat on the log. A wave of nausea washed over my body, but I held my breakfast down.

❧

In a way, I started to come out of my shell after that. I still didn't know what any of this meant, and maybe the shadow could still appear involuntarily, but I knew it was possible to turn it off again. I still had to figure out the mental mechanism that controlled it, but I was far less afraid, and waning fear led to an increase in confidence. Not that I became a popular kid or took up sports, but I was no longer afraid to be seen. I walked the halls with my head held high. Nevertheless, most afternoons and all through the summer, I tended to retreat into the woods. I wasn't always summoning the shadow, but I was always thinking about it, and wondering. Wondering if it was alien or mutation, if there were others like me, or if I had a specific purpose that I hadn't figured out yet.

And almost every day, I wished that one of those books in the library had some advice for me. I was lucky my particular ability developed quite gradually, giving me time to cope with each new change. Such good fortune is not very common in this business: take Harshmallow's testimonial from chapter eight as a chilling example. We all know about the terrible effect she can have on human skin. But did you know that she used to be a harmless wall-crawling cat burglar called Scuttlebug before that signature "roasting" power manifested in the middle of a heist?

I kept testing my limits. I learned that I could keep the shadow out as long as I wanted, more or less. It got easier to summon and retract, and while those actions took some effort, it didn't seem to require any significant amount of energy just to maintain its presence. As time went by, the shadow became more defined, and though not yet fully formed, the general human shape was undeniable.

My first real clue, it turned out, was hiding in plain sight. One day, while I was in my mother's sewing room, I noticed that the earliest image of my ultrasound was different from the others. The picture clearly showed two small blobs joined together. It seemed significant, and I couldn't think of a better way to find out what it meant, so I asked my mother.

"You could have been twins," she said, and I could tell from her voice that she had thought about it often. "You started out that way."

"But what happened?"

"Well sometimes, two embryos start to develop, but only one of them survives."

My heart was racing. "Do I have a dead brother?"

"Honey, no, look at the other ultrasounds. This happened very early in my pregnancy. It's actually fairly common. The genetic material just gets reabsorbed by the other embryo."

Not uncommon, and as I eventually learned, it was not even unique as a catalyst for superhuman abilities. But now, young men going through similar circumstances won't have to blunder through these discoveries: they can simply turn to section three for an in-depth study of known origins for both natural and supernatural powers. Pay special attention to the testimonial from Doublemensch, whose story parallels my own in many ways. I wish I had known then, as a young man, that I was not alone.

I was eighteen when the shadow became real enough for me to see its face. Over the past months I had watched its extremities coming into focus, and noted the suggestion of facial features, which I had attributed to a sort of corresponding maturation as I got older. As *we* got older. Now it had my face, but there was something else too. One afternoon in the woods I was wearing this bright green jersey with a white star on the chest when I summoned the shadow. The effect was unmistakable. It stood before me, translucent as always, but plain as day. How had I never seen this before? A man in a red shirt with a black star. Skin so dark it was almost black, a shock of nearly-white hair. Right down to his faded yellow jeans, it was my perfect photographic negative. As I truly recognized the negative for the first time, I got a new shock. Only for a moment. The world spun around, and then I felt it: his feet on the ground, the spring air, not on his skin but blowing *through* him, and through me. For just that moment, I could see myself with *his* eyes. I was standing on the log wearing a look of confusion, and that old familiar panic. Panic I only ever felt around him. I could feel the tug from the other side, from *my* side, and then it was over. I fell off the log. For the first time since I was eleven, I lost control of the connection and threw up in the creek.

Weird, feeling that old sense of trepidation again. My power had become new and scary once more. No longer completely under my control. But it was also a turning point for me—the point where I started to learn what the shadow was. It was only a matter of time before I discovered how to use it.

✹

Over the next few years I learned by degrees, still without guidance. My connection to the negative grew stronger, though I did not experience a recurrence of that sensory overlap for quite some time. What I did have was increasing physical control over the negative. I could move it around, and its distance from me didn't seem to diminish that control. The frustrating thing was that I had a pretty amazing puppet, but it was essentially useless. I could move it around, but I couldn't touch anything. Since it always emerged as my negative, I could change its appearance simply by changing my own. But nothing more. If I had a mentor, some idea of what to look for or how to proceed, I might have unlocked my potential much sooner.

The key to my career came when I was twenty-two. Home for Christmas, I was down in the woods, walking my negative around after a light snowfall. Nothing unusual. We spent a lot of time alone together. I liked to talk to him. That day, I was strolling along the creek with my negative beside me. Like a friend.

"I feel like I've built my whole life around you. I have you instead of friends. I lived alone in college, because I need privacy to spend time with you. But I don't know why I do it, aside from the fact that I can."

I paused, and let the negative take a couple of steps in front of me.

"Lately, I've just been wondering if I'm letting you be my excuse for not having a real life. I don't... I'm not part of the world. And I haven't substituted anything else for living in the world, except for these days with you."

I was surprised at how difficult I was finding this conversation. It's how I imagined it would feel to break up with someone. The negative was still in front of me, and though I didn't quite believe it was a real person, it was hard to look at him right now. I turned around, looked back the way we had come.

"I think maybe it's time..."

Then I saw it. My guilt led me right there. I turned my back on him and I looked at the ground. My own footprints in the snow. And beside them, a faint trail. Not a set of tracks exactly, but scuffs. The snow disturbed as though by gentle puffs of air. It wasn't much, but it meant that my negative was becoming substantial. And if he could touch things, then I could *use* him.

We never finished that conversation.

※

My earliest criminal exploits went virtually unnoticed. My abilities were pretty limited and didn't lend themselves to public display, or the sort of theatrics that would later typify my best work. But I had to try *something* because I had a power, and in this world if you have a power, you do one or the other. You either hurt people, or you save them. I never really got on well with people. To be honest, I never had a particular interest in helping them.

Of course I didn't really want to hurt them, either.

When I think about it now, the appeal of my choice is more apparent. When you choose to be a hero, your entire life becomes about the job. People expect you to be there for them, fixing things that were never your problem, and to be a *good* hero you have to accept that responsibility as if it was yours all along. Call me selfish, but that is not the man I wanted to be. A criminal can have his own life. I would only have to use my power when I needed money, or just wanted to have a good time. It wouldn't have to be a full-time job.

Villainy was a natural career path for me, but I was very conscious of the public's perception of people who make this choice. I wasn't blazing new trails here. Super villains have been around for a long time, dating back at least to early twentieth century America when the Magnificent Stranger terrorized the Midwest with his Traveling House of Illusions. The people he left twisted into funhouse reflections of themselves are the first confirmed victims of supervillainy, and the legacy goes back much farther if you accept the conventional wisdom about Jack the Ripper, Leonardo Da Vinci, and at least two members of the Spanish royal family.

But there is no arguing that the past few decades have seen a dramatic increase in costumed criminals. It has become a bona fide career choice, and like any line of work, the public has certain preconceptions about the kind of folks who decide to take it up. I know I did. After I had committed that first crime I started to imagine myself a criminal, to think about what that actually meant and the sort of company I would be keeping.

Tomorrow's young super villains will be able to refer to the historical perspectives outlined in chapter two, for a better understanding of how they might fit into the constantly-unfolding drama of costumed crime. But what I perceive as the greater value of this book is the opportunity to have criminals like the Delicate Ape, Doublemensch, Skullkick and dozens of others tell their stories in their own words. Talking about the villains who inspired them, why they chose a life of crime or how it chose them, and the rules they live by.

At twenty-two I'd never seen a super villain in real life, but I had seen all the classic footage of people like Smooth Operator, Lariat Joe and Vanishing Boy. Guys who committed crimes with a certain finesse and a minimum of violence; the notoriously conflicting media coverage all agreed that these villains never hurt their victims or any bystanders, and didn't even threaten violence unless provoked. As a young man just starting to find his criminal identity, I felt I could look up to these villains, if not for their specific crimes then at least for an apparent code of ethics. When Tin Soldier and Puppet brainwashed forty thousand people during the Chicago Marathon, news wires were abuzz with dire predictions, but the dastardly duo only forced their victims to play freeze tag. I don't pretend to understand why they did what they did, but I wouldn't be ashamed to be mentioned in the same breath.

But when I say "super villain", are these the people you think of? Maybe, but they aren't the ones you think of *first*. First you think of the monsters, like Captain Meathook or Laser Face. It's not the colorful burglar with the witty banter that the public remembers, it's the freak that set two hundred wild animals loose in a zoo filled with children.

If this was to be my vocation, I knew I didn't want to be like them. I was comfortable with theft. I started small and I liked it that way; I was simply honing my craft, becoming more dexterous at picking locks with the help of my dark, silent partner. And with continual practice came the development I'd been waiting for. I was sending the negative through the door of a walk-in vault when I felt a tingle in my skin. In *his* skin. I couldn't see the negative inside the steel wall, but I could feel him pass through and out the other side. I wondered if I had his sight, too, but the inside of the vault was pitch-black.

The immediate opportunity here was a major improvement on my usual methods. Up until now, to unlock a door from the other side, I needed a simple button or switch mechanism and I needed to know where it was located. But with sensation in my shadow body, I could reach right into the vault door and feel my way through the lock. I could feel the mechanism and trip the tumblers. Which is exactly what I did, and when I had the vault unlocked, I brought the negative back through. He emerged from inside the steel and I saw my own face, smiling, astonished and excited and alive with possibility. I could see through his eyes, and our future was looking very bright.

My debut as a costumed super villain, in which I robbed the Corwin-Brand Savings and Loan, received fairly widespread media coverage and most of the security footage is still available on YouTube. The job went pretty well—the worst thing about it was my costume and that would get better with time. I had myself a white three-piece like a Southern dandy or Colonel Sanders, with a smart-looking derby to match. I hid my identity with a white surgical mask. It looked a bit strange, but it wasn't about me. This was about *us*.

There weren't many people in the S&L when I walked in, unarmed. I reckoned that if I was dramatic enough, and didn't waste any time, I could get away without needing a weapon. So I made a big entrance—the one they used to open that episode of Dateline devoted to me. Nobody thinks about this, but I had to scout several potential locations before I found an S&L with a door that could be thrown open dramatically. It worked like a charm. I flung it open, stepped inside and announced:

"Ladies and gentlemen, you may call me Mr. Positive! If you'll give me just a few minutes of your time, I'll liberate the cash from your vault and then be on my way. I'm sure you won't mind if I invite my friend Mr. Negative to join us?"

As expected, the security guard's natural instinct to apprehend me was curtailed by the sudden appearance of Mr. Negative. My dark double with the black suit, and the skin and mask to match, meant that the rules had changed. These people had never seen me before. If I could generate a negative image of myself and use it to open a vault, who knew what else I was capable of? If the guard had decided to draw his gun, my career might have ended right there. I had no idea what would happen if Mr. Negative took a bullet, but everyone cooperated.

With the money in a bag, Mr. Negative and I retreated to the stolen van I'd parked around the corner. I had him drive while I changed in the back (a maneuver I mastered only after many trial runs). He had to get me two blocks away, where my car was parked in an alley. As we turned a blind corner, I jumped out the side door with a bag of money in one hand and a bag of clothes in the other. I threw them both in the trunk and waited in the car while I drove Mr. Negative and the van through the streets. It took almost a full minute for the police to catch up with the getaway car. I led them another two miles in the wrong direction before I hit the brakes and pulled back Mr. Negative, leaving the police to explain a driverless van with no money in it. I eased my car out of the alley and went home.

So it began. Most of my life after that is more or less a matter of public record. The security footage was on the news by five o'clock that night, and the next day everybody had heard of Mr. Positive and Mr. Negative. I took great care with my public image on those first few jobs. I was loud, amiable, a bit dapper, and always reassuring to my victims. I stole from savings and loans, the odd jewelry shop, and sometimes big multiplexes showing awful movies. Anyplace dealing in large volumes of preferably unmarked cash, and jewels because they were accepted as currency in the criminal underground. Robbing the multiplexes was my attempt at a bit of personal flair. I do object to movies that sacrifice inspiration in a quest for broader appeal. So once in a while, I would rob a multiplex and pontificate loudly, about how the American studio system is devolving the art form, by promoting filmmakers who demand nothing of an audience, which cultivates an audience that neither expects nor desires to be challenged.

The soundbite-friendly speeches were replayed often, adding a charming idiosyncrasy to my already positive media profile. I miss those early days. Each job a new adventure, more about the planning and the outfits, and the adrenaline, than the money. I loved the thrill. I loved the attention. And I think I was rather good at it. Obviously the media agreed, since I got all sorts of good press, and successfully distanced myself from the really scary super villains. My star was rising at the same time that Ghost Medusa held her Christmas slave auction in the bloody wake of the Macy's tragedy, and sharing airtime with her was all the proof anyone needed. Some super villains live only to sow chaos and fear, and Mr. Positive was *not* one of those. My thefts were flashy but entertaining, and when I had more money than I needed I always found a way to do something beneficial with it. Maybe I was just trying to balance the scales, but for a bad guy, I was definitely one of the good guys. My victims weren't too keen on me of course, but the AP and Reuters ensured that news of my exploits reached millions of readers who were not directly affected by my crimes. To viewers around the nation, and eventually the world, I was maybe even a bit heroic. A romantic criminal, like David Niven. Well-dressed. Classy. I tried to bring a bit of John Steed to an industry full of artless thuggery. I was a shy boy with a childhood full of lonely secrets, and I grew up to be America's favorite villain. This truly is a land of opportunity.

All it took to unravel my career was one security guard called Clayton. My destruction boiled down to a ubiquitous 14-second clip played over and over again on CNN, Entertainment Tonight, and of course the Dateline special. Before writing this introduction, I've never had the chance to explain what happened. I was so accustomed to people being cooperative when I robbed them that I was taken quite by surprise when that guard saw Mr. Negative and charged forward. As Clayton came at me, I had two competing instincts: to defend myself the way a man would, or to make Mr. Negative disappear. I wish I had chosen differently. Or *chosen* at all. But I just acted. I threw up the shadow's arms as though to block him, and the guard passed through me. But not cleanly.

When my arms went through his head, Clayton's brains were scrambled against the back of his skull… and the whole thing was on camera. That was the day I stopped being a romantic criminal. Now I was a murderer. Never mind that it was all a horrible accident. None of the pundits ever suggested that it might have been a mistake. Nobody mentioned that what happened to Clayton was proof that Mr. Positive was far more powerful than he let on. That I had deliberately chosen to abstain from violent crimes in the past and maybe I hadn't intended to commit one now. I could have been an unstoppable assassin, walking through walls, immune to bullets, but I had only ever acted as a thief. I could have had Mr. Negative step into the body of another person, then turn him solid and pilot them around for a while before shedding them like an empty husk. But none of the nightmares I *didn't* bring to bear could make up for the life I stole.

I retreated from the limelight. I had no soapbox from which to apologize, no way to make things right. I drove out to my parents' house, empty since they died, and returned to the woods where I had spent so much of my youth. Where I could let the shadow out safely. Where there was nobody to hurt.

I stayed on the property for weeks, spending most days in the woods, contemplating Mr. Negative. Moving him. Moving through him. Testing and retesting how solid or vaporous he could be. Playing patty-cake. Under controlled circumstances, everything seemed to be going fine, but the stress was starting to get to me. I was tired, and that rubber band in my chest was getting heavy. I could maintain Mr. Negative ably enough, but the effort of reeling him back in was growing more difficult.

It was during my time in solitude at the old family home that I decided to make this book a reality. Most young men with superhuman abilities are going to use them on one side of the law, or the other. What I want is for those who decide to commit crimes to have the chance to do so, to the best of their abilities, even if I don't personally approve of their actions. That way criminals like me, who want to do their work without hurting anyone, have the best possible chance of success. There will always be bad guys who want to kill people, but most super villain homicides are the result of collateral damage and plans gone awry, and those are manageable problems. I had been wishing for this book since I was a teenager. Too many angry, lonely boys with more power than they can handle turn to super villainy to get even with the world. This book is designed to get these young men to think about the ways their powers will transform their lives and create opportunities for the future. Super villains with accurate control of their powers and some basic instruction on criminal activity are far less likely to take a life that they don't have to take. With Appendix B, Offshore Accounts and Other Long-Term Strategies, they can even plan ahead for retirement, and I hope that with this book making their lives safer, more of them will live to enjoy it.

As Mr. Positive, I never operated as part of a team, and even without a life of crime I'm sure that my all-consuming preoccupation with the shadow would have precluded me finding someone to share my life. I have remained, for the most part, alone, and I have always contended that super villainy is solo work. You can't start putting criminal personalities into groups and expect things to stay professional. Add super abilities into the mix and sooner or later the games of one-upmanship that normally arise among bonding males escalate into callously (even gleefully) destructive displays of power. That men almost inevitably succumb to such spectacle is shameful enough; that they should end with a body count is obscene. My solitude was part of my determination to be a superior villain, but I would have interrogated the entire criminal underworld to create *Your Changing Body*.

With this project came a renewed sense of purpose, and for a brief time I even imagined that one day I could return to my life of crime. Now I know that isn't in the cards. I buried myself in this book, keeping strange hours, pushing myself hard. One morning I passed out, somewhere around sunup, lying on the couch in my parents' living room. I was exhausted. I don't know how long I slept, but when I woke, I was not alone. Mr. Negative was sitting on the arm of the couch, watching me.

Instantly, by instinct, I put him away, but the significance of this development was not lost on me. Finally, I realized what I probably should have figured out years ago. I wasn't simply gaining greater control over Mr. Negative. Mr. Negative was getting stronger. Every time I let him out, he emerged a little more powerful. More substantial. And, I was starting to believe, more autonomous. The trouble I'd been having lately with the rubber band could surely be explained by Mr. Negative resisting my efforts. What if my control over him was just an illusion, something he allowed? How could I be sure?

I thought perhaps I was still the stronger one, and if he came back I could just stick him underground until he became corporeal enough to suffocate. I also believe it is far more likely that I will awake some morning and he will be waiting for me, only this time Mr. Negative gets to stay out and I will be the one who goes back in. Which raises a lot of questions for me. What kind of man will he be? If he truly is a man, and I have let him out into the world only to force him to steal, then what kind of brother have I been? When I put him away does he disappear or has he been my mute prisoner for decades? When he puts me away, will he ever let me out again, or will I just disappear?

I don't know what my legacy will be once I hand over the reins of the rest of my life. Before that happens, I am determined to see *Your Changing Body: A Guidebook for Boy Super Villains* become a new standard in developmental education. This book will help generations of evil, angry, and just plain lonely boys answer the most important question an adolescent criminal can ask: What kind of man do you want to be?

THE ORIGIN OF THE FIEND
Hal Duncan

Hal Duncan's first novel, *Vellum*, was published in 2005 to some acclaim, garnering several award nominations (Crawford, Locus, BFS, World Fantasy Award,) with US, French and Finnish editions subsequently winning the Gaylactic Spectrum, Kurd Lasswitz and Tähtivaeltaja awards respectively. Along with the sequel, *Ink*, he's also published a standalone novella, "Escape from Hell!", various short stories in magazines and anthologies, and most recently a full poetry collection, *Songs For The Devil And Death*. A member of the Glasgow SF Writer's Circle and a regular online columnist at Boomtron, he also wrote the lyrics for Aereogramme's "If You Love Me, You'd Destroy Me," on the *Ballads of the Book* album, and the musical, *Nowhere Town*, which premiered last year in Chicago. Homophobic hatemail once dubbed him "The... Sodomite Hal Duncan!!" (sic). He's getting a t-shirt made up.

That Accumulated Potential

A five-and-dime store on Lincoln Street, just round the corner from Sam's Malt Café. You stand at the comic rack, captivated by Overman on the cover of Adventure Comics. Circus strong man's leotard in white, blue trunks, boots and cape, he's knocking seven bells out of a robot army straight from the Flash Gordon strips. You guess they're part of some criminal scheme of Overman's arch-enemy, the mad scientist, Rex Roman, but you know you're not supposed to read the comics in the shop, so you beg your big brother for the ten cents. Only ten cents.

We all know Overman's origin story. Sent back in his timepod from the 51st century, a newborn babe arrives in 1920s California where he's discovered by spinster sisters, raised on their orange orchard. On a visit to San Angelo at age 16, he dives in front of a runaway tramcar to throw a child to safety, little suspecting the impact will activate his "hyper-evolved cells." Able to absorb the kinetic energy of any blow, he's invulnerable to bullet or blade. Focusing that power in fists or feet, he has "a punch like a piston, a pounce like a panther."

You wish you had that famous red "O" sigil in your chest, wish it would project a hologram of your father. He'd tell you you'd been sent back to escape the destruction of the Earth itself. Later, in issue #5, you'd discover you can use this Omicron-beam as a weapon, unleash the kinetic energy built up within your body. And where at first your creators simply had you "leaping leagues in a single spring," so many would read those bounds across the sky as flight that soon the misreading would become mythos, that accumulated potential, as ever, the rationale.

You're just like Overman in his cover identity of Grant Cooper, a young law student and intern at the DA's office, investigating cover-ups and thwarting diabolical plans. Not that you investigate cover-ups and thwart diabolical plans—that's not you on the cover of Adventure Comics #19, punching a fighter plane from the sky. You're only ten. But you might study law when you grow up. And you're shy and quiet like Grant Cooper is, bespectacled too. You once yearned to be The Shadow, as you sat by the radio on Sunday evenings, in your pyjamas, but not now.

❧

The Paradox Protocol

The character's popularity (and power) grew like your scrawny limbs, his nemesis's reach scaling up too, Roman gradually recast as war profiteer selling weapons to both sides. Then came the "big turning point," (according to Donald Black's *Overman: The Century of a Saviour*) in Overman issues #23-24, "The Paradox Protocol," where Roman has a minor villain with mesmeric powers, the Fiend, hypnotise the Saviour of the Century and suggest he kill Hitler to end WW2, issue #23 finishing with Overman in flight over the Atlantic.

Your big brother was in France then. If only Overman was real, you thought.

At the last minute, as Overman's about to raze Berlin, his hologram activates—Wait! No! An evil ploy is afoot: if he kills Hitler he'll change history such that he'll never be born; worse, Rex Roman himself will become President. The issue ends with Overman instead saving a crashed fighter pilot (whose features bear a remarkable resemblance to Overman's: "Like a long-lost brother, or even… ancestor!") then returning home with a solemn vow to fight wherever he can because "the smallest battle may win the greatest victory."

You read it in your treehouse, one hot summer day.

July 13th.

According to Jeff Steinman, writer and co-creater with artist Jim Schweitzer, "the whole paradox thing was largely an excuse, a convenience. See, we kept getting letters from kids asking if Overman could stop the war so their dad could come home. And we thought, what are we going to do here? How do we answer this? Then we hit on the idea that this all-powerful character *couldn't* do just anything, because if he did the wrong thing, well, it'd mean he was never born."

You read that interview… when? In college, in the '70s, wasn't it? Or '90s?

As Black writes, "From the Paradox was born a true Paraclete. Expedience or not, in this sacrifice of all-conquering omnipotence on the altar of contingency, the Overman became Everyman, the messiah became mortal, a salvator with strings attached, bound to his terrible cross of consequences. That he fought the smallest battles, on our soil, in our skies, in the streets of our cities, by day or night—this made his struggle ours, the struggle of the human spirit against history itself."

But if his struggle was ours, *your* struggle was never *his*, was it? He didn't have your secret.

⚡

Red Shift, Blue Shift

Polio-stricken cub reporter Gary Gordon may walk with a cane, but when he shouts the magic word three times in a second—"Thunderbolt! Thunderbolt! Thunderbolt!" (try it, kids!)—it activates the powers given him by a mysterious wizard masquerading as a doctor, and Gordon transforms into the fastest man on the planet: the Human Blur, the Blue Streak… the Thunderbolt!

Well, of course, that's the Golden Age origin. The Thunderbolt who heralded the Silver Age with his 1956 revival had his particles accelerated to the speed of light by blue omicron rays… but that's another story.

You remember both.

Caught in the blast of a meteorite, its exotic alien minerals vaporised on impact, permeating every cell in his body, Jake Walker wakes up in the crater, apparently unharmed but for a weird golden glow to his skin, fading even as his head clears. With his thrill-seeking nature though, it's not long before a practice run in an abandoned Speedway track reveals the truth… that when excitement sparks in his heart, that spark ignites his very molecules, transforming him into Flameboy—Flameboy, the Comet Kid, shooting fireballs from his fingers, blasting through the sky like a human rocket. You…

You love them both. You *desire* them both. Thunderbolt can run rings round the super villain, save the planet, and get the copy in before the Globe's star reporter, "Slick" Jackson has even finished his coffee. Often with some friendly banter aimed at fellow Legion member Flameboy along the way. Fighting villains for the fun of it, ribbing the other Legion members, (only to wind up doused by an irate Water Woman or blown out by the Thunderbolt,) Flameboy's rogueish charm is… hot.

"You're light on your feet for a hoofer, Twinkletoes," he joshes. "But me? I'm just plain smokin'!"

"Yeah? Well, light me up a Lucky, hotshot," says Thunderbolt in Legion of American Watchers #18. "I'll try not to snuff you with my slipstream."

That friendly banter between "the Blunderdolt" and "Ginger, the Dancing Zippo" (a reference to Ginger Rogers as much as Flameboy's red hair,) was condemned by Dr Werther Fredericks in The Corruption of the Young (1954) as "blatant homoerotic flirtation, rife with innuendo." Still, it's the most popular pairing in comics, the limited series "Flameboy and Thunderbolt: Red Shift, Blue Shift" one of AC's all-time bestsellers.

At thirteen you drew fan art of them kissing.

※

In Cold Pointed Steel

Fredericks didn't know shit, you think. Overman and Hookman at AC Comics, Monkeyboy at Wonder—none of the Big Three could possibly be "inverts," as one of the least vicious terms had it back then. The Golden Age was an era free of faggots, devoid of deviants… in the surface text, anyways. Captain Steadfast wasn't no queer. The Secret ain't some homo. The Quantum's kinda gay, but not in that sense—in the sense that he's lame. He doesn't kick ass like the Green Blade or Warhound. Warhound *rocks*; he's the only modern superhero even *close* to those classics.

The Hookman does sort of resonate with you though. His origin is dark— mother dead in childbirth, father shot before his very eyes, for gambling debts. That image, the reflection in the young boy's eye, the man hanging by his cuffed wrists from an abbatoir meathook… if you were that kid you'd have his nightmares. Little wonder young John Flynn grew up on the streets, his only break being sent to juvie, where a gruff boxing coach steered him right, put the punk on the straight and narrow.

"Work on that hook, kid," growls Coach. "It's the hook'll floor 'em."

Coach gets Flynn a job on the docks, a stevedore hauling cargo, hook in hand. By night he trains for his first pro bout, fixes up an old Indian Scout motorbike, or reads.

"Brains *and* brawn," says Coach.

Goons in the dressing room, threats—throw the fight or else.

Smack! Crack!

"Tell *that* to the Shark! Tell him to find another patsy."

But the next day Flynn is down on the docks and there's something in the water, a body. Hauled out with a boathook, Coach's limp form lies on the jetty. And that night, the barbed beast is born.

In his steel blue skin-tights with midnight blue trappings—trunks, boots and gauntlets, cape furled around him, he carves a cool silhouette. It's the hooks that are his trademark though, glinting in the shadows. Part welded helmet, part sewn-together mask, his cowl sports the scariest—a metal mohawk, a centurion's crest in cold pointed steel. Spring-loaded hooks built into his gloves slash out for combat or for climbing, fire into the air as grappling irons. He has no superpower but his will—to bring a reckoning down upon all racketeers.

He has his sidekick too, Kid Swift.

✻

Who You Might Be

There have, of course, been a number of Kid Swifts over the years, with various origins. Your favourite was the second, Todd Jonas, an orphaned street kid like Hookman himself (by then, the "the" in the character's name had largely been dropped,) he survived by his wits, "hustling and grifting" until the Hookman took him in.

You'll never forgive the fan-voted outcome of the controversial late-80s storyline, "The Costume in the Closet." You'll never forgive the fact that the world's first homo superhero is no sooner out than he's suffering and dying. You'll never forgive, never forget, never...

You dressed up as Kid Swift one Halloween—red t-shirt and pants, yellow trunks and cape, green mask and belt. That was the year Derek Mason dressed up as Water Woman and all the kids made fun of him from then on, called him queer. Shit, you were all so young, did you even know what it meant? Well, maybe. When Kid Swift on TV said, "Golly gosh gumdrops, Hookman! I don't think it's just the Jester's laughing gas that's making me feel so gay!" you got the word's... other meaning.

Didn't stop you taunting Derek though, scorning him.

Him being a sissy took the heat off you, of course, and with a name like Animus Thrawn you needed a scapegoat. Annie-Mouse, they called you, Annie-Mouse Prawn. Even your friends called you Mouse, the nickname sticking long past the point when anyone but you even remembered it was a taunt. You didn't mind so much after you found this old Gollancz Classic in the library, a science fiction book with a cool street-thief character called Mouse. He sort of merged with Kid Swift in your daydream doodles of who you might be if you weren't you.

But, no. They couldn't let you have that. As if AIDS and Mutual Assured Destruction weren't enough, they had to put a bullet in your very fantasies of a future. Cold steel in Todd Jonas's gut. The Jester's laughter echoed like some creepy carnival automaton as he stood there watching; Hookman kneeling over the dying youth; the Fiend standing over him, behind him, the pure malevolence that had played the City's Sentinel like a puppet, shrouding his mind with illusions to tear.

"What'll you say when they ask how Kid Swift died?" mocks the Jester. "By crook... *or by hook*?"

Hide Your Sins in Silence

A villain wakes from a nightmare, heart pounding, hands grasping the bedsheets in panic. What was that noise? A whisper? An echo? A moan of the soul, a groan of terror in a guilty heart? A fedora shadows a featureless face, a longcoat billows and, in the dark, a grey shape slips away, for the Secret's work is done. Dream on, you wrongdoers who think your soul is safe! Imagine that no one knows your foul deeds! But there is one who walks among the sleeping, one who can damn you with a single word whispered softly into your dreams.

His origin unknown, none can say from whence his powers came, whether his terrible torments are magic, mechanics or mesmerism. But of this you can be sure: you can cover up your crimes, hush up and hide your sins in silence, but the Secret will haunt you to the grave!

"An iron cage?" he scoffs in Awesome Comics, #40. "Hah! There are some secrets that cannot be kept, my friend. Whatever you do, they will… slip out."

And in a little trick of the pen, perspectives shift from one panel to the next: the Secret's free and the villain caged!

You used to love listening to The Shadow serials, but for all that the Secret is homage standing a hair's-breadth from plagiarism, something about the Master of Mysteries has always soured you to him. Vengeful to the point of vicious, shaping the dreams of criminals to drive them to insanity, he exploits hidden shames to enforce his merciless morality. With that callousness and the similar powers, you could easily believe the rumour: that the Fiend was introduced not just to kill Kid Swift, but with a shocking revelation planned—that the Fiend was what The Secret would eventually become.

"It does too work," you argue with Keith Johnstone. "See, in Catastrophe For Universes, Project Moonchild only *think* they've brought a demon from another dimension. Really they've brought the Fiend from the *future*, and that's why he knows everyone's secret identities just like the Secret does, because he *is* the Secret."

You're in your room, comics strewn around you on your brother's bed— vacant since he was called up for Iraq.

"So how come the Fiend can move in time?" says Keith. "The Secret can't move in time."

"Because Project Moonchild doesn't bind him properly. They make him like that."

✺

The Fabric of Spacetime

Of course, later writers were to use the Paradox Protocol as the basis for numerous retcons of AC's continuity. The earliest and still most controversial example came in the wake of Steinman's blacklisting, at the height of the McCarthy era, with "The Red Menace" story arc, where new writer Edgar Franklin had Overman discover that—shock! horror!—Rex Roman has secretly been in league with Stalin all along. To prevent a Communist takeover of the US, Overman has no choice but to sacrifice himself, punching the A-Bomb Roman tries to drop on Washington, exploding it high in the atmosphere.

A nuclear blast was the one thing that could kill Overman, you knew. It was thrilling, that final panel of Overman's shadow burned across Capitol Hill and the question, "Is this the end?" It was *excruciating.*

In the next issue though, "The Paradox Punch," Overman's origin is retold, updated. His hologram father reveals a wild twist: from the temporal shock waves of Overman's death a whole new future-history erupts; now it's a *communist* takeover of the US that'll lead to the Earth's destruction.

You remember the hot July 13th you read that comic, in your treehouse, in another world.

It all hinges on a hint that Overman is one of his own ancestors. By sacrificing himself before he's passed on his genes, he's created a future in which he was never born; but that means he *never went back in time*, meaning he *didn't die*! "Reality warping in a great loop back to the very beginning of it all," a new 51st century is forged. And luckily Overman's father is able to detect echoes of the original history left in the fabric of spacetime by Overman's Omicron-beams, able to warn his son.

Nobody warned your brother, did they?

You'd read the recap of Overman's adventures in this remade continuity, all condensed to a montage of panels. You'd read the thrilling climax, where he again confronts his arch-enemy on the plane above Washington; only this time, with his Omicron-beam, Overman blasts a portal to the Fourth Dimension, hurls the A-Bomb through it just in time.

The whole world rewritten! You had to tell someone. You scrambled down the rope-ladder, ran into the kitchen, the living room.

Soldiers stood, hats in hand.

Your mother sat on the sofa, crying.

The first word you heard was "Korea."

You Can Never Go Home

Shot down in the skies over Pearl Harbour, leaping from his plummeting P-36 Hawk without a parachute, Captain Steve "Steadfast" Sturgeon can only pray for a miracle. And a miracle he gets! Struck by lightning at that exact moment, he finds himself standing before the Archons of the Cosmos, with a choice between Eternity and Earth. But for Steve Sturgeon, no choice needs to be made.

"Send me back," he says. "There's a war to be won!"

There was talk of the movie having him shot down over Afghanistan, like your brother, who isn't ever coming back, not ever.

In the history books, it says there was no third wave to the Japanese attack, but any airman who was there that day will tell you those Nips were turned back by a strange sight in the sky... an angel sent from Heaven, an American Angel. And so began the daring deeds of the hero known as Captain Steadfast.

"We'll finish what you started, No-Joe Tojo!" he says in Captain Steadfast #13. "And that's the truth!"

The truth? you think. Yeah, and Nixon's not a crook.

Home for the holidays, you sit in your old bedroom, hiding from Christmas.

To the people of Atlantis she is Princess Naia, half-mortal daughter of the Oceanid Queen Metis and her long-lost human consort. To the surface-dwellers she is Water Woman, sensual and spritely as Aphrodite, fearless and feisty as Artemis... Water Woman, Mistress of the Seas. When Princess Naia investigates a disturbance among her dolphin subjects, she discovers Ensign Hank

Murray, the sole survivor of a German U-boat attack. "His strange skin… so… pink!" she says. (Top-Notch Comics #8)

And though her people are sworn never to intercede in the affairs of surface-dwellers, she saves him.

Exiled from her beloved Atlantis in punishment, what's a girl to do but… fight Nazis with her electric eel-hide whip!

They say you can never go home again; it's all too true. Two years of college in New York and you've discovered the Village, sex, drugs and shoulder-length hair. It's changed you, is still changing you. It was that drag queen in the Stonewall, dressed as Water Woman—that's when you decided it was time to come clean, to come out. Like you weren't already the beatnik black sheep of the family anyways, the stranger in their midst.

✺

Floating Through Time

Professor Miles Quant is on the verge of replicating the primal state of matter in his physics lab, when he discovers one of his colleagues is a Nazi spy sent to steal the secret for the Germans. Knocked out and left in an overloading photon chamber, exposed to an "uncertainty field" beyond all measure, his atoms are thrown into pure flux. Able to transform himself into any element, to shrink or grow at will, even to teleport by swapping places with something of equal mass, he is no longer Quant, M., Phd., but is now the Quantum, Master of Matter!

You take the joint from him, beautiful hippy farmboy with hair as blond as Captain Steadfast's but long. It brushes across your naked chest as he shifts, tickles. Above you, the sky is a full colour painting in spattered light, Milky Way aglow in acid streamings, wheelings. Ancient gods battle in chariots that whirl apart to mandalas, Celtic knots of weaving dragons. You feel them in your serpent spine.

"Cosmic, man," he says, then laughs. "That sounds like a superhero, right? Cosmicman."

Screw college, you think. Screw Vietnam. It's the Age of Aquarius and everything's changing.

You've got a boyfriend.

"Turn lead into gold?" says Quantum in True-American Comics #3. "No, Dr Von Strann... Into the very stuff both elements are made of!"

It's only later, during AC's Catastrophe For Two Worlds, in an attempt to simplify the morass of rationales for superpowers, that the Prof's "primalised matter" is revealed to be none other than the proteanite toxic to Overman. Fortunately, it's in an omicron-irradiated form harmless to the Man of the Future. Unfortunately, during AC's Ultimate Catastrophe, the Fiend will reverse that omicron-irradiation, turn the Quantum into a doomsday weapon with which to kill Overman himself.

You take the joint from him, beautiful sculpted surfer, hair as blond as Captain Steadfast's but long. It tickles your naked chest as he shifts. Above you, the sky is a myriad of universes exploded to atoms of a cosmic man. Sand under you, surf crashing the beach, its spray aglow in acid glitterings, all is energy disguised as mass, imagination masked as energy, forever shifting, muscles of a horse beneath its skin.

"You know we're floating through time even as we lie here," you say. "Or time is floating through us."

Later, you'll forget why that felt so true.

✺

Vice Will Fall

"You look great," he says. "Dude, you look *hot*."

"I look like a douche," you say.

But you blush as much because the sleeveless wetsuit *does* cut a sleek physique in black and red, lean arms exposed, showing off your shoulder tats like a motherfucking rockstar. You feel so nakedly narcissistic, seeing the strut and stance in the mirror. Shit, however slick you look it's not going to help when you fall off the board. You're so not sure about these lessons. But...

"I'm *so* doing the Fiend in this next Halloween," you grin.

"Mouse, dude. You're such a geek."

Attacked by bandits and left for dead in the Sahara Desert, millionaire playboy Franklin Wallace stumbles on the lost oasis of a mysterious green-robed Moor, Amir Al-Hazred. Bound for centuries by an evil sorcerer's curse, Al-Hazred plays on Wallace's greed and gratitude to trick him into a death-match... where the true conflict is in Wallace's heart.

"Do I fight to win this 'great treasure' he guards? Or to give this poor madman the release he prays for... *in death*? I... I don't know!"

Only as Al-Hazred dies in Wallace's arms does he reveal the truth:

"You were led here, to take my life... and sacred duty. You are the Archon of the Earth now!"

For only a man on the cusp of redemption, a man whose past is vice and his future virtue, can take up the Kamir Husam—a sword that can cut through anything, even spacetime itself.

"When lesser man and greater man, Together with a single hand, Strike out for freedom on command, Then vice will fall and virtue stand!" (The Green Blade #1)

Hypnotised by Project Moonchild, it's the Green Blade who opens the portal, unleashes the Fiend on AC's multiverse.

"You never talk about him," he says, handing the photo back.

"There's not really much to say. And... well, ten years..."

In truth, it feels like more. And less. The scar tissue of teenage grief is smooth, healed to an image, but ever tender. Every July 13th is *that* July 13th for you. But your heart remade, somehow it's almost welcome, a reminder to live your life. To finish your term paper, phone Mom, get your ass to the Prop 8 demo on Saturday and... today...

In the wetsuits, you look like Thunderbolt and Flameboy.

"Come on." you smile. "Surf's up."

The Origin of the Fiend

You were reading "The Paradox Protocol" the day the soldiers brought the news that your brother had been killed in action in France. You were reading "The Paradox Punch" the day the soldiers brought the news that your brother had been killed in action in Korea. Catastrophe For Two Worlds, Catastrophe For Universes, Ultimate Catastrophe. Vietnam, Bosnia, Afghanistan.

You're thirteen years old and you're just finished reading Grant Milligan's new graphic novel, *The Origin of the Fiend*, when the soldiers bring the news that your brother has been killed in action in Iraq.

The Fiend's name has just been revealed.

They stand in the ruins of the Legion of American Watchers' moonbase.

"Animus Thrawn," says the Secret.

"Not any more," says the Fiend.

The story is fucked-up. That's the only way to describe it. The Fiend who killed Kid Swift, the Fiend who killed Overman, the Fiend who turned AC's entire pantheon of superheroes against one another in the Ultimate Catastrophe crossover event… that demon is from the Fifth Dimension, from a universe in which that pantheon is mere fiction.

"From another reality?" says the latest Kid Swift. But the Fiend simply laughs.

"There is no reality," he says.

You're outside the five-and-dime store on Lincoln Street, flicking through a comic, but every page is from a different issue, a different year, a different era. Wait.

You're reading it in your treehouse, every turn of a page a different character, a different story, universe, July 13th. *No.*

But you're running inside, through years of kitchens, to a half dozen living rooms where soldiers of shifting wars stand, and where mothers sit on sofas, here, there, anywhere, crying. *No.*

France, Korea, Vietnam. *No.*

And the story is a kid screaming "NO!" because no superhero saved his brother.

No.

No, that's not the story, you're shouting as galaxies of lives explode around you. In every one of those lives, the story is healing, not hate. It's college and Christmases and coming out; it's bitching about Nixon, Reagan, Bush; laughing with beatniks, hippies, surfers; living; loving.

It's this moment of madness you're denying.

Except you can't deny it, as you stand in the comic store, your boyfriend's hand on your shoulder, as you open *The Origin of the Fiend* to this page, and are torn into infinities of fiction.

And a red rage for vengeance rips out of your lungs.

※

Each Botched and Broken Continuity

A five and dime store on Lincoln Street, but it's a city that doesn't exist in your world, a blend of New York and Los Angeles, San Francisco and Chicago. Passers-by wear fedoras and Walkmans, G.I. uniforms and baseball caps; they come out of cars with running boards, talking on their cell phones. It might be 1910 or 2010, but you know it's both and more besides—your story untold but unfolding across each botched and broken continuity. The Legion of American Watchers fight each other on the street, and you look on, laughing.

It's the Fiend's first appearance.

"Animus Thrawn! Fiend of the Hell Dimension, I bind thee to this world! I bind thee to my will!"

The high priest whirls, his bloody hands raised to the thundering skies. The Green Blade stands behind him, entranced, sword aglow, lighting up the stone circle and the Acolytes of Armageddon, the hooded scientist-priests of Project Moonchild.

"It's too late!" Kid Swift is shouting as the Hookman slams into the high priest.

Crouched in the bloody pentagram, you look into the boy's eyes, remember his death; it's already written. *Rewritten.* The *Elsewhens* one-shot series retold it in Edo Japan.

"What'll you say when they ask how Kid Swift died?" the Jester mocks. "By crook... *or by hook?*"

Another scene. You're looking down upon your handiwork—one dead sidekick, one hero on his knees—and you can *feel* your fucking glee in the destruction. So they wanted a fucking villain? But even as you laugh, you're sobbing, focus freefalling through too many memories of malevolence to bear, to another:

"...by sending his mind back and forth along his own timestream, between his past and future," the Quantum is saying. "It's really quite ingenious."

"That's one word for it," says Flameboy.

Another memory, another, another. No, *memory* isn't the right word; this is raw *experience.* You're blowing up cities, snuffing henchmen, murdering Overman himself, resetting the multiverse in Ultimate Catastrophe. And you can't stop, can't hold to one moment, have no control. But the worst of it is that, as you're shredded in the maelstrom of your future, you realise you will. Eventually.

And you'll be the Fiend. You'll kill Kid Swift, destroy the multiverse itself. Even now you're *becoming* your own demented future, knowing only fury at the brutal secret of your origin: your heart was pure until one day...

※

The Origin of The Fiend

Black with red details, the neoprene skinsuit fits snug to your form, enough stretch to carve your musculature in its shadows but in a hide thick as leather, not some tawdry film of spandex, lightweight and lurid as the 80s. It's snake-skin jeans versus nylon tights, and you look fucking killer in it. Sleeveless, of course, to show off the black sigils graved in the scarlet skin of your arms. In the scar tissue covering your whole body, from being dragged through the searing omicron energy fields between your world and this one.

Black gauntlets, belt and boots.

You're ready.

You flex your fingers, spark up a ball of light in your palm. It's pure illusion, but then so is this whole world, the whole universe, the multiverse. It's not even a true superpower, your trickery, just the science of a few centuries into the future wired into your gauntlets; but that just makes it all the more satisfying, knowing what you're about to do with it. How that tediously earnest paragon of reason, that ponderous fool, Professor Miles Quant aka the Quantum, will bend to your will, reconfigure his proteanite matter to the madness you conjure in his mind.

Then you're there, hand out like Flameboy blasting, fingers twisting, crunching thought; and the Quantum goes boom, Overman swallowed in the blast. You've lived this moment countless times, will live it countless more. You know this, remembering all the pasts and futures you've jumped back to here from. Time travel? No. Time is meaningless.

Reality splits as the Paradox Protocol kicks in, a new multiverse born through the breach, a rebooted continuity in which Overman's timepod will arrive in the early 90s. New to everyone but you, at least. You were still reading after Ultimate Catastrophe. In one life anyway.

You flick through this new timestream to your other favourite moment, the finale of *The Origin of the Fiend*, the Law headquarters in ruins, the Secret crawling over the rubble.

"Animus," he begs. "You *know* this is insane."

You kick him onto his back, crouch to cradle his head, pull the grey mask from his face. Your face.

You were wrong, you know now. That shocking revelation? It wasn't that the Secret would become the Fiend. No, it was that one day the Fiend would reach towards redemption, become the Secret.

"Mouse."

"Not today," you laugh.

And snap his neck.

Check out the whole line
of LGBT graphic novels and
comics collections from
NORTHWEST PRESS

In print and online at
NorthwestPress.com

Teleny and Camille
by Jon Macy

Glamazonia:
The Uncanny Super-Tranny
by Justin Hall

Rainy Day Recess:
The Complete Steven's Comics
by David Kelly

A Waste of Time
by Rick Worley

The Legend of Bold Riley
by Leia Weathington

Transposes
by Dylan Edwards

Al Qaeda's Super Secret Weapon
by Mohammed al-Muhammad
Mohamed and Youssef Fakish

Anything That Loves
edited by Charles "Zan" Christensen